DONE DEAL

Tony Berry is a lifelong career journalist who has worked on national magazines and daily newspapers in his native Britain and in Australia, where he has made his home for several decades. He has written four previous crime fiction books featuring disgraced secret service agent Bromo Perkins, and a family history based on numerous research trips exploring the places where his ancestors once lived. His first two novels, *Done Deal* and *Washed Up*, were short-listed for the New South Wales Genre Fiction Award and *Washed Up* also secured him a mentorship with the Australian Society of Authors. In 2017 he was one of eight writers chosen worldwide for the inaugural crime fiction residency at the Banff Centre for Excellence in Canada.

As an accredited professional editor in Australia and the UK Tony also edits fiction and non-fiction in a wide range of genres. For recreation he battles the curse of ageing as he tries to maintain his status as an elite masters' athlete at national and international level over distances from 3000 metres to the marathon.

Praise for Done Deal

'Richmond is lovingly and accurately rendered'
Nicole Lindsay, *Herald Sun*

'Bromo's dialogue is pretty snappy and he's a man
of action. This was fun and I'm glad I ordered a copy'
Karen, *Australian Crime Fiction* website

Also by Tony Berry

The Bromo Perkins Crime Series:

Washed Up
Death by Diamonds
Twisted Trees
Death Comes By Drone

Memoir:

From Paupers to iPads

A BROMO PERKINS INVESTIGATION

TONY BERRY

DONE DEAL

HIGHSHORE PUBLICATIONS

First published 2011
This edition 2018
©Tony Berry

Highshore Publications
13 Highshore House, New Bridge Street,
Truro, Cornwall, UK, TR12FE

www.yarraboy.com

Richmond is a real place. It is an inner suburb of Melbourne, a city which is regularly nominated in international surveys as the world's most liveable city, although many of its less privileged inhabitants hold a vehemently different view. Richmond's town hall also exists. And so do many of the streets and places where our heroes and villains are to be found. All else, apart from the historical background, is fiction and bears no resemblance to any known persons living or dead.

DEDICATION

To all those family and friends who have provided support and encouragement in my stubborn refusal to forsake this continuing plunge into penury and obscurity.

ONE

THE WOMAN PULLED A slim manila folder from a black leather briefcase. She dropped it on to the café table with a bold flourish. It was a deliberate, attention-seeking action, confronting and demanding. Bromo Perkins lifted his head from his newspaper and glared at her. A brief glimmer of a smile creased the corners of the woman's mouth: she had achieved the desired effect. Bromo winced as she scraped one of the heavy metal chairs across the timber floor and sat down. She waved to attract the attention of a passing waitress.

'Bring me a latte, please,' she said. 'Light, decaf, no sugar.'

Bromo had no idea who the woman was and didn't particularly care. She had already broken the three golden rules in his book of selfish living for single men. No one, but no one, interrupted his first coffee of the day. Second, all talk was to be avoided at least until he had ordered his second cup. Finally, any conversation that did ensue was to be muted and monosyllabic.

Her delivery was staccato, clipped and bossy – all guaranteed to set Bromo's nerves further on edge. Her style of drink added more irritation. It was comic coffee – a concoction for poseurs and those lacking a palate.

'That's not how it works,' said Bromo.

He glared across the table:

'You provide table number, menu item and money. In that order. And up at the counter if you please. Then we can decide if I really am the person you're meant to be sitting with.'

'Dahl, I don't stand up at the bar. I order, they bring,' she snapped back. 'And yes, Mr Perkins, you are the man I'm looking for.'

Despite her abrupt manner, the woman's voice took Bromo by surprise. It was deep and mellow for one so slender; a rich contralto rather than mezzo-soprano. Definitely a seductive toe-curler in other circumstances, he decided.

More disturbing was the revelation the stranger knew his name. Alarm bells began ringing in his head, echoes from a distant past supposed to remain forever secret..

He tried to disguise his unease by pretending she wasn't there, disregarding her presence with down-turned eyes and flicking busily through his newspaper. It told of yet another murder in this supposedly civilised community. Like so many others of recent times, it was conveniently labelled as a gangland killing – the result of so-called wars between the city's drug lords, money men and property moguls. The story sat alongside reports of bashings, road rages and domestic disputes of unbelievable violence. A bright young student had committed suicide in response to some gloomy pop song and the state government was dipping into its enormous budget to fund the teaching of responsible pet ownership. Another typical day in what optimistic civic leaders claimed to be the world's most liveable city.

The woman pushed the folder to one side as the waitress delivered her coffee.

'Run me a tab, please Linda. I'm staying for breakfast,' she informed the waitress. 'This might take a while.'

Her manner said it all: she was a regular customer although not one Bromo had encountered in his frequent early morning sojourns at Dargo's.

Bromo sipped his coffee – a daily heart-starter, ultra-strong, bitter and capped with a crema undisturbed by spoon or sugar. He sighed, drained his glass and voiced his needs.

'Linda, m'dear, I think I need another.'

It was worth a try. Even though technology ruled, if this untimely intruder could get away with it, so could he.

The woman glanced up at the waitress.

'Perhaps this time you could bring Mr Perkins his coffee and save him the trouble of walking up to the bar. We can't have him wearing himself out.'

Bromo was impressed, but there was no way he was going to show it. He'd take what was on offer, and make no comment. If a complete stranger thought she could buck the system and wanted to order his coffee, so be it. As long as she didn't expect conversation with the caffeine. His humour matched the morning; indeterminate, not sure where it was going or how it would end up. Such a typical Melbourne day - slow to start and uncertain of its mood.

He turned the pages of the broadsheet as he felt the effects of the coffee start to kick in. The news brought him little cheer. It merely confirmed that the crims, the ferals, the oddballs and the weirdos were out there walking the streets, anonymous, undetected, riding the trains, pushing trolleys down supermarket aisles and standing in line for tickets to the movies and footy. They brushed shoulders with the commuting masses in buses and trams, sat alongside the latte set in cafes and cinemas, walked the same footpaths. Yet no one knew they were there. He needed little reminding that the malevolent existed amid the mundane.

Maybe his table companion was one of them. Bromo flicked his eyes up from his paper, doing a quick stock-take. She was above average height, gym taut, thin-lipped and - true to Melbourne style - black-suited under a long black coat. At a guess, in her mid-thirties. And blonde - although the hair falling just below the shoulders betrayed roots of a darker hue.

Linda arrived with his coffee and a fresh glass of water.

'Wonder of wonders, the system works,' said Bromo. 'Must be my lucky day.'

'Make the most of it,' laughed Linda. 'Back to normal for you tomorrow.'

Bromo took a sip of water and looked over the rim of the glass at the stranger: 'At least I'll be left in peace.' He paused, eyes fixed on the woman opposite, unwavering, yet addressing his words to the waitress. 'Unless, of course, you are going to continue letting your regulars be pestered by complete strangers.'

Linda ignored him and made her way back to the bar. Bromo huffed and made a show of turning the pages of his paper. The woman leaned towards him, palms pushing down on the table.

'Calm down, Mr Perkins. I'm sure we can sort everything out right now.'

'Are we buying or selling?' asked Bromo.

'We're persuading.'

'And who are we persuading?'

'You. We have a job for you.'

He breathed in deeply. This was more than a man could stand when all he wanted was half an hour of quiet and solitude to help him cope with the start of another day. He made a second appraisal of the woman. There was a brittle edginess to her, nervy and anxious. Her eyes kept flicking around the room, alert and on guard. She was making him uneasy. He'd had enough. Edgy people were not good to be around. Too often he had witnessed the havoc they could cause. He folded his paper and stood up.

'Sorry, m'dear. You've got the wrong man. Must be another Mr Perkins. Try your sales pitch on someone else.'

'There is no one else, and I'm not selling.'

She slid a sheet of paper from the manila folder and flipped it over as if it was the winning card in a big stakes poker game.

'This is you, isn't it?'

It was a glossy, full colour photograph of two people. They were close together, sprawled side by side on a bed, facing the camera. Neither wore a stitch of clothing.

The woman looked up at him with just a hint of a smile: 'That is you, isn't it Mr Perkins?' She smirked. 'Perhaps you recognise the penis?'

He looked briefly at the picture and sighed.

'Seen one, seen 'em all, as the actress said to the bishop. Much of a muchness, really. Can't vouch for ownership of the appendage. But it does look extremely like my face up above,' he said.

'Probably some joker playing silly buggers,' he suggested. 'They tell me it's amazing what you can do with Photoshop.'

It was a lame denial, and he knew it. But it was the best spur of the moment response he could produce. Stall and find out what she wanted: a basic technique, drilled into him years ago and never forgotten.

He sat down and watched as the woman turned the picture over and slid it back into the folder. Bromo noticed there was no inscription on the back. It must be a copy. He knew all too well the words scrawled on the original. They flashed up on a screen somewhere in his head: 'No secrets. Baring all for each other and nothing to hide.'

It had been a moment of drunken madness. Well, more than a moment. More like twenty-four hours. Or was it forty-eight? A whole weekend that had passed in a blur. Aurelia Nuyen was the name of his naked companion. A curvaceous and flirtatious Greek Australian married to a second generation Vietnamese migrant who seemed to have an interest in half the city's restaurants.

The voice from across the table broke into his attempt to piece together all that had happened that weekend. Or how it had happened. And why.

'Does it bring back happy memories, Mr Perkins?'

'There's a simple explanation.' What the hell: a grudging admission.

'There usually is. I'd like to hear it.'

'Some other time.'

'Stop auditioning for Grumpy Old Men and listen.'

'Less of the old, if you please. The pension is still years away.'

Bromo felt a surge of irritation. Basically he couldn't give a damn who knew about his weekend with Aurelia Nuyen. The booze-fuelled interlude might even make an amusing late night tale if he ever got around to organising one of those dinner parties he kept promising to throw. His guests would at least enjoy confirmation that even in middle age he had failed to tone down the philandering ways they believed were his norm.

But this intrusive stranger was a horse of a different donkey, as one of his ex-fathers-in-law had an annoying habit of saying. He sensed there were forces at work more sinister than he had previously encountered since settling into this reclusive stage of his life. Someone was trying to rattle his cage.

'I'm waiting, Mr Perkins.' There was a pause. 'And so is Gerry Nuyen.'

There was an underlying force and menace to her voice. The words were delivered slowly and clearly, giving emphasis to every syllable.

Bromo looked around the room. The annoying plasma TV stuck to the wall flickered away unwatched and unwanted by most customers. There were conversations everywhere. Lots of chatter. No signs of others being shown sneaky pictures of weekends away. More likely they were discussing the latest round of footy results. The two real estate agents over in the corner were doubtless adding up their exorbitant commissions from the weekend's auctions and mapping out strategies for the week ahead. Rich pickings were there for the taking as the property market soared ever upward. Expectations quoted before auctions were turned into conservative fantasies by desperate bidders pushing prices beyond vendors' wildest dreams. Pokey little cottages that sold for a few thousand ten years ago were now topping the million dollar mark. Fuelling the flames was the shady little developer frowning at his laptop two tables away and probably working out how many apartments he could squeeze on to a block once occupied by a single workman's cottage.

Bromo replayed the woman's words, assessing their weight. They were ordinary, everyday phrases yet the underlying threat was clear. How could this be in such a mundane middle-class setting of designer jeans and business suits? He began to wonder whether the two women at the next table were planning a bridal shower or a robbery. Did they have their tips blonded in the salon of a drug lord's mistress or was it the work of a socialite barber rumoured to own a chain of sweatshop brothels?

The huddle of suits over at the corner table could be sealing a massive drug deal or debating their picks for their office footy tipping competition. Who could tell? No one wore labels. Dress codes, such as they were, didn't distinguish wrongdoers from the law-abiding. Nowhere were there pictures of naked couplings.

Bromo took a sip of water.

'So, what's this all about? Whatever it is you're selling, I'm not buying. Try someone else.'

'Obviously there is no one else – just you and Mrs Nuyen. And, as I told you, I'm not selling,' she said. 'We've agreed there's only one man in the picture. Our research shows you are definitely the one we need.'

He made a show of opening his newspaper. The woman's hand flicked at it and turned down the page.

'No time for reading, Mr Perkins. You listen or this picture finds its way on to Gerry Nuyen's desk. And just in case he doesn't know where to find you we'll attach name, address and phone number. Get it?'

He sighed once more. It must be a morning for sighs, he thought. That was the sort of day it was turning into. Like the litter in the street outside, he was being blown by an uncertain breeze, unsure of its direction.

The woman was wasting her breath. Gerry Nuyen already knew where to find him. And Nuyen knew his wife played around. He had even confided as much to Bromo when their paths had crossed briefly during a viewing at Aurelia's gallery. Two glasses of cask wine into the evening and they were almost bosom buddies. Nuyen's passing show of friendship that evening had been accompanied by a strong squeeze on Bromo's arm and a whispered warning. Make no mistake, Nuyen hinted, he could get a lot of pleasure from letting his hoons loose on any of Aurelia's playboys he took a dislike to. To Bromo it sounded like terribly one-sided sort of fun. The hoons would do all the laughing.

Bromo refocused on his unwanted companion.

'Okay, shoot,' he said. 'Or is that a bad choice of words?'

The corners of her mouth twitched upwards. The skin around her eyes creased slightly. The early start of crows' feet was showing. It was the closest she had come to a smile. Bromo felt it wasn't going to get any friendlier.

'Let's not get too dramatic, Mr Perkins. We're serious, and we mean business. But we do try to avoid what I believe is called the heavy stuff.'

She paused: 'Unless, of course, it's really necessary.'

The blue-grey eyes were unblinking and he felt his stomach churn. This was no community service penance or work-for-the-dole scheme whereby he could leisurely repay a perceived debt to society. The heavy people had sent in their advanced guard, perfumed and personable. She was firing the first warning shots.

The woman leaned forward. His nostrils twitched in response to the strength of her scent. She confirmed his fears: 'We know an awful lot about you, Mr Perkins. Your dossier makes fascinating reading. It's an interesting history.'

Years of minor misdemeanours and transgressions gathered side him, swelling into an immense sense of wrongdoing. They still nagged at him so many years on, even though most occurred in the line of duty. He felt his misdeeds were coming home to roost. This must be pay-off time for that other life, the one he'd endured long before he'd settled into the comfortable and almost anonymous rut he now enjoyed.

The tide of guilt surged within. It never fully left him, no matter how hard he tried. Hell, if he was pulled over for a drink-drive test and hadn't had a drink for days he still felt guilty. Little wonder he was suffering deep unease over the insinuations now being fired at him over coffee and toast.

'Okay, so there've been a few indiscretions along the way. So what? How clean is your cupboard?'

He noted a slight shake of the blonde head. That fixed stare. She wasn't buying. Not giving an inch.

'We're not talking about me, Mr Perkins. We're talking about you. So ......'

He raised a hand, palm flat towards her.

'Hang on. You keep saying "we". Who's this 'we' and how many of you are there?'

'All in good time, Mr Perkins.'

With an almost inconspicuous nod of her head she got Linda's attention and the waitress came quickly with order pad in hand.

'Eggs, scrambled, toast on the side and a small serve of grilled tomatoes. Carrot juice first and a latte later. Thanks.'

Bromo shook his head in admiration. To a man who could be the only customer and still be ignored, it was a shining example of efficiency and presence. Maybe she'd give lessons. On the other hand ....

'As I was saying, Mr Perkins, my clients have decided you are the right person to undertake certain delicate activities on their behalf. A quick one-off job. If successful, you will be recompensed. If not ... well I think I have already indicated the likely outcome. Mr Nuyen will be provided with information unlikely to make him regard you with any great pleasure.'

Conveniently the carrot juice arrived, followed quickly by the eggs. She attacked them with a precision that Bromo regarded with intense dread. So much aggression towards a plate of eggs. A display of character that brought him little comfort. She probably came from a large family where every meal was a bun fight and she took no prisoners. A scary display.

Bravado was the answer. 'I think you've huffed and puffed enough,' he said. 'Lots of hints and innuendos, but nothing specific. I think it's time I got on with my day.'

He gathered his paper, knocked back the dregs of his coffee and stood.

'Sit,' she insisted. The tone of voice left little room for argument.

To his surprise, he did as commanded, sinking meekly back into his chair. He recalled a dog he once lived with, which was just as compliant when commands were uttered so precisely. Not a good start to the day. Didn't know what came over him. Taking orders so obediently belonged to that distant past he preferred to forget. Someone said jump, you jumped. No question. These days, he prided himself on having to answer to no one.

'Take these keys,' the woman said.

She slid a cluster of metal and medallions across the table.

'One's to a flat, the other is to a car. You'll find the address and the rego number on the tags. Go to the flat, remove the rubbish in the lounge room and use the car to dispose of it. We don't care where and don't need to know. Just be discrete and be tidy.'

He fumbled with the keys and noted the address on the tag. It was an easy walk away. Down a side street off the main drag.

'When you've done, leave the car outside the flat and put the keys under the passenger seat.'

'Do I ring or just walk in?' he asked.

The woman put her knife and fork together, rested elbows on the table, rested her chin in her hands and leaned towards him. For a moment Bromo let his thoughts wander. Her gaze was unblinking and fixed; but there was a seductive depth there, too, in those deep blue-grey eyes. At another time and another place he wouldn't mind testing the waters. Now was definitely not the time; she made that abruptly clear.

'Walk in, pick up, walk out and do as you're told,' she said with hardly a blink.

'And maybe, if you're a good boy, you might find out if what you're thinking is true.'

TWO

Oᴎ ᴛʜᴀᴛ I sʜᴏᴜʟᴅ be so lucky, mused Bromo, attaching some wishful and fairly lascivious thoughts to his blonde persuader's closing remark as he sauntered off down the street. Maybe she wasn't as hard and power-driven as her attitude suggested. At least he'd scored a free coffee out of their encounter.

He side-stepped a bent and frail woman shuffling forward with a Zimmer frame and let his mind stray into contemplating the possibility of a more intimate, less abrasive session. Perhaps something up close and physical involving beds and doonas and minus the aggro they'd just shared. Maybe his reward was to be in kind, not cash. No payment had been mentioned for the task she'd set him and he was sure he had seen a hint of something else in that final look she had flashed at him.

Ah, dream on, Bromo. More likely she had assumed he would happily settle for the return of the photo and escape from the attentions of Gerry Nuyen's standover men. Not a bad guess: he wasn't into pain these days – his own or anyone else's.

Even so, the sharp Miss ....

Hey, I don't even have a name. Conned again. The mystery woman had not only barged in on his coffee session and applied some low-level blackmail, but she hadn't even offered him a name or phone number.

He backtracked to Dargo's and pushed through the double swing doors. The pack of early customers had moved on. Staff were chatting behind the bar, enjoying the lull before the mid-morning coffee break rush began. There was no black-suited woman to be seen. The table where they'd been sitting was totally empty. Not a skerrick of cups, breakfast plates or cutlery remained.

He ambled over to the Gaggia where Linda was pushing through more orders.

'Another coffee?'

'No thanks. Just a bit of information.'

'I know nothing.' said Linda in a grating mock eastern European voice.

'Not even the name of the woman who dumped herself on my table? She looked like a regular to me.'

'Oh, that's Fiona. Yeah, she's in here quite often. Usually later in the day. You know, the ladies who lunch. One of those. And other things.'

Bromo noted the coda. Something to note. Support for his suspicion about the steely Fiona's connections and extra-mural activities. But for now he persisted with what he came for: 'Thanks for that, but where do we find the fiery Fiona when she's not lunching? And what does she do to earn a crust?'

Linda hunched her shoulders as she frothed a cappuccino.

'Sorry, luv. Can't help you there. I think she's reasonably local but seems to do all her business on her mobile. I vaguely recall she mentioned something about being a consultant.'

That figures, thought Bromo. Everyone's a consultant these days. Walk around with a laptop, chattering into your mobile, wheeling and dealing but without anything approaching what used to be considered a real job. An office in their briefcase. Footloose and fickle. Always on the move.

He stumbled back into the street, still clutching the cluster of keys. Two trams rattled by – one towards the city, the other trailing out into distant suburbs he had hardly heard of and which he had no wish to visit. A parking inspector checked his watch and began marking car tyres. The town hall clock chimed 10. By now Bromo was usually back home brewing one more cup of coffee and singeing a couple of slices of bread in the toaster.

The queues of commuter traffic had thinned. The first shoppers of the day were plotting their forays into Bridge Road's long strip of stores dealing in discount clothing and household wares. The street was the haunt of outer suburban housewives and glassy-eyed tourists who invaded in their thousands in search of bargains, clogging the footpaths as they drifted in and out of shops that bragged permanently, and falsely, of special deals, closing-down sales and today-only discounts. Lines of parked coaches, belching fumes, added to the traffic chaos that choked the narrow streets. They disgorged shapeless women, a tracksuit their dress of choice, labelled with name tags and toting oversized bags for their purchases.

It was a scene Bromo did his best to avoid. Tackling his unwanted assignment now rather than later seemed the best option. Do it before the shuffling masses descended. On the other hand ... no deadline had been given for his task. The forceful Fiona merely wanted some mysterious rubbish removed. She hadn't said when or how soon.

He jiggled the key rings in his hand, weighing his options. He took another look at the address. It could wait. It was a short stroll that he could easily slot in later. Coffee and toast were calling.

He slowed, stopped and reversed his direction. He turned left and into the cul-de-sac leading to the block of apartments he called home. A weedy unkempt man in a torn tweed jacket was sitting slumped against the wall, knees drawn up into his chest. The neck of a bottle poked out of a brown paper bag gripped in one grimy hand. Their eyes met. Bromo nodded an uneasy acknowledgment of the man's presence. He was becoming a fixture – here he began his daily trip into alcoholic oblivion. The man stared back, unblinking and unseeing, eyes glazed.

Bromo walked on, discomfited at knowing there was nothing he could do to help. The man was simply one among many desperates on the city's streets.

A long low black sports car screeched to a halt alongside him, failing to shorten his feet by a matter of centimetres. The window slid down.

'What a surprise. And we've only just said goodbye,' said Bromo to the top of the blonde head which leaned across the passenger seat towards him

His flippancy bounced off her.

'Mr Perkins, you have work to do,' she said. 'Make no mistake, we want it done now. Not when you feel like it.'

The woman tore a slip of paper off a pad clipped to the dashboard and scribbled a line of numbers. She thrust it at Bromo: 'Ring me when you've finished.'

He glanced at it and scrunched it into his pocket. Goodbye coffee. Hallo whatever. Bromo shrugged and turned back the way he'd come. Anything to avoid trouble, especially of the sort Gerry Nuyen was reputed to hand out.

The sports car burnt more rubber as it reversed into the mainstream of traffic then raced off up Bridge Road towards the city, ignoring the 40km/h signs.

THREE

THE HOUSE FIONA HAD directed him to was a slim glass and concrete three-storey newcomer squeezed in between a couple of old single-level villas. Developers had razed a Victorian-era timber cottage with an iron roof to make way for this modern replacement. Bromo labelled it as anorexic architecture. The black mirror-glass windows were like gun slits in a bunker. A high front wall with security gate and buzzer shouted a message to stay clear. Unknown or unseen visitors weren't welcome.

Bromo viewed it from the other side of the street, looking for signs of life; sneaking a look for prying eyes from houses nearby, for some old fogey who'd want to do their bit for Neighbourhood Watch. Places like this rarely gave a clue to what was going on within. They were closed and barred to the outside world, giving nothing away. This was the shuttered society where kids no longer played in the streets and the only access was by pressing buttons on an electronic gizmo. A generation ago, doors would have been left unlocked and neighbours shared their troubles over the fence.

He tried the keys in the gate. One of them clicked home and no alarms screeched.

He crossed the few metres of paved courtyard to the front door. Tried two more keys. The second did the trick. Still no alarm as he gingerly made his way inside. A slate-paved vestibule offered a choice of three doors, one in each wall. Like the old three-card trick. Spot the lady. Place your bets.

He opened the one on the right. Another wager lost. He stepped into a small bathroom with hand-basin, toilet and a large cupboard with doors wide open to display coats, boots and umbrellas. Among them hung a long knitted footy follower's scarf in black and yellow, the colours of the local team. So, he was in a Tiger's lair. At least he had something in common with whoever's home he was invading. If caught in the act, instead of being handed over to the cops, maybe they could weep on each other's shoulders and have a deep and meaningful debate about last week's thumping by the Crows and whether Richo would ever play two good games on the trot.

On the other hand, he knew Tiger supporters could be a pretty mean lot. Their passion bordered on aggression. Their intimidating 'Eat 'em alive Tigers' war-cry of the 1920s was no longer roared from the stands, but the attitude lived on. Fans were combatants in an endless suburban warfare that had been waged in the city's sports arenas ever since the first game was fought out in 1858 on the land where the Tigers' headquarters now stood. Many underworld fringe-dwellers were known to inhabit their ranks - hard cases who tended to regard the police as a distant second option when strangers trod where they were not wanted. Bromo sensed he was definitely venturing into dangerous territory.

He turned to step back into the vestibule when a glint of metal caught his eye. Pinned near the end of the scarf was a circular brooch, about the size of a beer coaster. An outer edge of golden stones framed a tiger's head. Two more stones

- darker, striped - formed its eyes. Oddly, a long-stemmed red flower, a rose or maybe a poppy, was clenched in its jaws.

He'd seen nothing like it in the members' shop at Tiger headquarters down on Punt Road. It could be a bit of junk jewellery or a pricey one-off. Bromo had no idea. In jewellery, as in art, he belonged firmly to the I-know-what-I-like school of assessment.

He opened the left-hand door. It led into a garage. He guessed he was looking at the car Fiona had ordered him to drive. It was a slate-grey nondescript saloon. Hundreds of its clones clogged the city's streets every day. He had no idea of its make or engine size. Another no-go area of knowledge, and interest. It was a car - four wheels, four doors, four seats, shiny, new-looking and presumably with an engine beneath its hood.

One door remained. He turned the handle and pushed it open. Christ!. He retched, gagged on his bile and turned away from the scene confronting him.

The man sprawled out across what had once been a shiny wooden floor had met with a very nasty accident. Someone or something had hit him extremely hard. Mostly around the head and face. The face stared up at Bromo, eyes pooled with blood. More blood, now congealed and dark, had seeped from a lengthy gash above one ear. The man's feet were bare, his shirt unbuttoned to the waist, exposing an expanse of pallid blubber.

Bromo took a deep breath, in the way he'd been taught during his transcendental meditation phase, which had lasted just long enough for him to decide it wasn't going to make the earth stand still for him, or for anyone else. But the deep breathing was good. And, boy, did he need it now. Draw it in slowly, deeply. Hold. Now release, let it out evenly, gently.

Two more breaths and he felt ready to take a closer look at the bloody scene.

Like the man on the floor, the room had been severely trashed. Books were off two shelves. The contents of a file drawer were scattered beneath the desk. Computer disks littered the desk's surface. Pictures were off their hooks as if someone believed that behind every print there was a secret safe – someone who'd been watching too many cop shows and late night B movies.

Bromo often counted himself fortunate that his experience of bloodied bodies was minimal - the most recent being quick sideways glances at a horror smash on the freeway some months ago. Harm minimization was the bureaucratic catch-phrase he'd always been told to follow. Get in, get out and leave the dirty work to the specialists. But he knew enough to be certain whoever was lying there on the floor was not going to be doing anything active for some time.

He knelt slowly beside the body and reached out a tentative hand for the man's wrist, feeling for a pulse. He had to make sure but it wasn't easy to find. The flesh felt cool, stiff and clammy. All life had seemingly been beaten out of him. Maybe there was a very faint pulse. Maybe not. He couldn't be sure. It seemed unlikely.

So, this was what Fiona saw as a mess needing to be cleaned up. A new slant on housekeeping, indeed. Two squirts of Pine-O-Clean and a quick run over with the squeegee mop weren't going to make much of an impression here. His coercer may regard him as a Mr Fixit but this was above and beyond the call of duty.

He pulled his mobile off his belt and unfolded the scrap of paper he'd grudgingly accepted less than an hour ago.

She answered immediately.

'I thought you said it was just a bit of a mess,' said Bromo.

For the first time he detected uncertainty in her voice. 'What do you mean?'

'You said nothing about a body.'

A single expletive exploded down the line. Followed by silence.

'Well?' queried Bromo.

A tremor underscored her response. At another time and in another place he would have chuckled at her loss of composure. All he wanted now was an answer. And to get the hell out of here.

She recovered, the voice strong and forthright'

'Someone's stuffed up. Do your best. Remember those pictures. I wouldn't want to upset your peaceful life but Mr Nuyen can get very violent.'

She'd rung off. The message was clear: he was on his own. The untroubled existence he'd so carefully crafted was looking dangerously feeble. His striving for a laid-back and casual approach was proving as useless as a Wettex in a flood. The fragile façade of non-involvement was being rapidly shattered.

He pressed the speed dial: 'Jase, I need your help.'

He paused to listen to the quibbles coming down the line then cut in: 'No. Now. Quick. No questions asked. And bring the ute.' He gave the address. 'And don't stop outside. Park around the corner and give yourself some exercise.'

He snapped the phone shut and looked at the papers on the floor.

Nothing jumped out for attention; nothing indicated anything out of the ordinary. The way papers were strewn all over the place suggested whoever had been here before him had similar thoughts. A quick run-through, a rapid flicking over of pages, knowing what they were looking for and discarding anything else.

He looked at the desk. More chaos. There the paper mayhem on the floor had been replaced by hi-tech havoc. Computer disks were everywhere. All were clearly labelled, many of them mundane – rates, household, motor vehicle, utilities, fees and so on. The orderly records of an orderly, even anal, mind. A great help. It made a burglar's job so much easier. Read and reject, then move on. Obviously nothing had appealed to the intruders among what was scattered over the desk.

A manila folder lay beneath the scattering of disks. Big black capital letters spelled out the word RAID on its cover. There was little inside. Rough edges of paper clinging to the fasteners showed where several pages had been ripped out. All that remained were scraps of punch-holed documents preserved in defiance of the so-called paperless society.

Bromo noticed a disk bearing the same label as the folder. RAID. He picked it up. Why stop there? It was an instantaneous thought. He had no idea what was on those disks. The labels meant something only to their author. But if Fiona was going to start throwing her weight around it might help to have information to act as some sort of counter-balance to that picture of him and Aurelia.

He scooped up the disks. And added a diary and a notebook to the pile. Then nearly dropped the lot in fright as the ringing of the doorbell sounded through the house.

Bromo saw the massive shape of Jason Conquest looming on the other side of the glass front door. He was a welcome and comforting sight. Jason had been known to keep rough and unlawful company in his younger days but had somehow maintained a clean record so far as the authorities were concerned.

He was wearing his plumber's overalls, the bib braces parted enough to show the trade union's defiant white Eureka flag on his dark blue sweat shirt.

Bromo wrenched the door open.

'Thanks mate. I owe you one.'

'Bit of aggro?' boomed Jason as he barged his way through to the living room and viewed the debris.

Bromo decided explanations could wait. Jason was a man who took things at face value without asking too many questions. What else could be expected of a front-row forward who had packed down for the Old Palladians ever since he'd been booted out of sixth form two decades ago? He had also been known to undertake a bit of heavy work for some of the local night-clubs and the shady characters who frequented them. If this was what Jason considered as a bit of aggro, so be it.

'Got a blanket or two? A doona. Something to wrap him up in?' Already Jason was swinging into action.

Bromo scuttled up and down stairs as if he'd lived there all his life. He tore blankets and doonas off beds, brought sheets to be ripped into strips and watched in awe as his mate rolled and loosely trussed the body into a neat sausage-shaped bundle.

'Okay, where to?' bellowed the still unfazed Jason.

Bromo pointed to the door into the garage.

'Through there. That's the idea.'

'Whose idea?'

'Not mine.'

'That's the best news I've heard all day,' said Jason, hefting the shrouded body on to his shoulders. 'Cheers me up no end to know this isn't your doing. Doesn't seem right for travel agents to go bumping off their clients.'

Bromo raised the boot of the car. Jason rolled the doona-wrapped body inside. They stood back from the car. Two tradesmen admiring their handiwork.

'Your call,' said Jason.

'The tip,' said Bromo. 'Dump it and run. No questions asked, no answers given. Just a bit more rubbish to come.'

'And they'll want to see your rates notice, take your rego number and ask if it's recyclable or for the hard rubbish section. That's fine if you don't mind everyone knowing you've become a one-man body disposal business.'

Good advice, but not what he wanted to hear. Nights spent watching TV crime shows came to his rescue.

'Okay then. The river,' said Bromo 'Drive it in and run. The car's got to disappear as well.'

He dashed back into the apartment, returning quickly with an armful of files, disks and papers clutched to his chest. Jason's great paw of a hand landed on his shoulder. It squeezed the muscle more painfully than anything he'd endured at the hands of his masochistic myotherapist. He looked up into his mate's steely grey-green eyes. And shuddered. Now he knew what it was like to be an opposing forward facing off against this mass of muscle.

'Well done, mate,' said Jason. 'Good thinking. The river it is. I'm too well known at the tip. I'll lead the way in the ute. You follow. A quick dip in the Yarra seems about right. Coupla minutes and it's all over.'

That was the beauty of tradesmen, thought Bromo. So practical. So basic and so simple. No messing about. No complicated schemes having to spin stories to gatekeepers and garbage men. It wouldn't be the first vehicle to finish its days in the river. Many a distraught owner had been told by the police that their stolen and stripped-down car rested beneath its muddy surface.

Jason and his ute led the way through narrow back streets before they came out on to Bridge Road a few metres before its end at the river crossing that gave it its name.

He threw a sharp right across the tram tracks and on to the Boulevard, heading towards Burnley, feet coming off the throttle as they eased past the girls' high school and kept strictly to the 40km/h limit. This was no time to be pulled over by zealous police. They cruised down the curving slope at the Swan Street intersection and under the rail bridge emblazoned with a banner proclaiming *Bracks Buggers Burnley*. Local residents were fighting a losing battle to stop the government cutting down some ancient trees to make way for more office blocks. The alliterated banner was their final defiant outburst as the courts and the State Premier ruled against them.

The two vehicles crawled alongside the horticultural college grounds and past the footy ovals. Jason slowed his ute as it approached a wide right-hand bend beneath the freeway overpass. He pulled into the kerb a few metres before one of the private school boatsheds and signalled Bromo to overtake and park.

Bromo sat and waited for Jason to join him. His palms were sweaty on the steering wheel as his mate slid into the passenger seat. Gripping tight. He unclenched his fingers, stretching and flexing them. This was how it used to be in the old days.

They waited for a posse of brightly-garbed bike riders to pedal past, muscles bulging against skin-tight Lycra. A family of lorikeets scuttled about in the grass. The birds were almost tame enough to touch, but darted just out of reach each time a human footstep neared

A pair of joggers staggered along the footpath, eyes focused on some distant goal only they could see. No one else was around.

'All clear,' Jason yelled.

Bromo fumbled with his door handle and eased it open as he bumped the car up across the footpath and into the scrub. He gave the engine a final revving up and jumped clear as the vehicle surged forward through a few saplings topping the high river bank. Jason was already out and rolling on the tussocks of turf.

They scampered into the ute and Jason gunned the engine, doors swinging shut as they roared off.

'Let's get the hell out of here,' he said.

Neither gave a backward glance.

FOUR

It was as the slogan on one of his tattered old T-shirts proclaimed: *Shit Happens.* Too true, he thought. It was an undeniable fact of life. However, these days, when it did happen, Bromo usually decided the best course was to ignore it. Pretend it hadn't happened. Even if deep in the pit of his consciousness he knew something was going on up on the surface, he could impose a total lock-out. The brain was placed on bypass.

He believed the buzz word for this line of thinking was 'denial'. Bromo decided he liked denial. It was hassle free; a problem solver. If something didn't happen, there was nothing to disturb you. If it did happen but you refused to acknowledge its occurrence, then you remained undisturbed.

He therefore paid scant attention to reports on the evening television news of a car being abandoned on the banks of the river. Maybe it was something about which he needed to be concerned but he refused to process it. Another beat-up of a minor incident. It happened all the time. If they had pictures, it became news. Without pictures, it didn't rate. Tonight, they had vision from the scene.

According to the smooth tones of the TV reporter, the vehicle had been found stuck among saplings on the river bank, its engine still revving and its boot containing the body of a prominent, but unnamed, local businessman.

Another day in the life of a big cosmopolitan city, mused Bromo. Let the spin doctors insist it was the world's most liveable city, but its residents knew it wasn't always so. Far from it: shit happens. There was nothing there on the TV to concern him until someone decided otherwise.

The phone rang and he let the answering machine do its job – his gatekeeper against the nightly flood of calls from barely intelligible young people in India enquiring about his welfare before trying to sell him a mobile phone contract or a subscription to a charity.

'Hey, mate.' It was Jason. 'You seen the news? Bloody car didn't roll. You going to be okay?'

Bromo sipped his malt. Of course he was going to be okay. Good of Jason to ask, but it was nothing to do with him. A minor blip on the radar that would soon fade.

The phone trilled again. Five rings and the answering machine clicked in.

'You bloody dipstick. Ring me.'

No name was given. Or needed. The fury of a Fiona on the rampage was already unmistakable.

Such assumption. To think someone could shout invective down a phone line and not only expect the recipient to know who was calling but also to presume they might feel disposed to respond to such a call.

It seemed everyone was at home and watching the news. Whatever happened to having a session down the pub after work and then grogging on and perhaps having a pizza to soak it up before staggering home and into the cot?

Bromo suspected the answer was that routines had

changed since his roistering days. Now the bright young things would be drifting out far later in the night into slick bars which served fancy cocktails and had *Sex in the City*, *Desperate Housewives* and even *Big Brother* playing on plasma screens that filled a whole wall.

He let the rest of the news wash over him and poured another malt. He settled back into an armchair salvaged from the wreck of one of his marriages. It had seen much better days but remained irreplaceable for comfort and the way it was possible to sink deep down into its spongy embrace. The intercom from the ground floor entrance buzzed. To ignore or not to ignore, that was the question. It buzzed again, longer and then in a series of staccato bursts. Someone was losing patience.

Bruno sipped his malt, put down the glass and slid open the door to his balcony. He peered over the chest-high wall. At least it wasn't the police.

He sauntered over to the intercom and picked up the phone. 'If it's a pizza, it's for downstairs. And if it's Jehovah's bloody Witnesses we're beyond redemption.'

'Let me in.'

'Give me ten good reasons.'

'We've got to talk.'

'I don't do talk.'

'Screw you.'

'Now you're talking.'

'How about doing time? For murder?'

'Sounds like a good conversation starter,' he responded. Fiona was a persuasive woman. 'You'd better come up.'

Bromo pushed the button to open the foyer security door. He listened to the click of her heels on the stairs and settled back into his armchair. He decided a disinterested and placid demeanour would be tonight's theme.

There were a couple of sharp raps on the door.

'Turn the handle,' he yelled. 'It's not locked.'

Fiona came in, and disinterested and placid conceded immediate defeat. Bromo felt interest and arousal rapidly taking their place. What else to do when confronted by a woman who had shed her girl power executive shell for the look of a pleasure princess set for an all-night rave around the clubs?

The long black overcoat was still there, its hem almost sweeping the floor. It was unbuttoned and swinging open. There was not much underneath. A very short mini skirt revealed the slender length of her legs. A halter top valiantly tried to cover her breasts but left her gym-taut midriff completely bare.

'Planning a night on the town or were you in too much of a hurry to get dressed?'

'Stop being a smart-arse and get your brain into gear. We're in deep shit.'

Her attitude riled him. Bromo contrived a world-weary sigh: 'Correction, forget the we. You may have your problems because of today's little stuff-up but that's got nothing to do with me. I ran an errand on your behalf, and at your request. Cleaned up a house. Dumped some rubbish, as you called it. End of story.'

He shrugged and let out another sigh. He hoped he sounded calm and unflustered because that was far from how he was feeling. He wished she'd stop standing over him in a pose he was finding increasingly provocative. Her hands firm on hips, her legs rigid on their stilettos, a view of beautifully symmetrical twin peaks.

'The rubbish, as you call it and which you failed to dump, goes by the name of Peter Rasheed,' she said. 'Does that ring a bell in that thick head of yours?'

Not just a bell, thought Bromo, but a whole bloody carillon. He jerked up out of his armchair, a slurp of whisky spilling over the rim of his glass. There was a whole Big Bob Major peal clanging in his head. It was getting louder by the second as his memory dug up what it could recall of the apparently recently deceased Peter Rasheed - property developer, night club owner, A-list socialite, footy club board member and general wheeler-dealer.

Rasheed was renowned as a man of power and persuasion, both of which were used mostly for his own advancement and profit. Such a reputation made it unlikely he would be greatly mourned and missed in local society's more genteel quarters.

'I think I've heard the name,' said Bromo, almost blushing at his monumentally offhand understatement. 'Was he a friend of yours?'

'I knew him.'

'In the Biblical sense or just socially?'

'We had business connections.'

'So? Is there more to tell?'

Suddenly the brittle armour cracked. Her whole body seemed to shrink inside that long black coat. Hard edges softened. The power pussy had become a kitten without claws.

'Can I sit?'

'Be my guest.'

He gathered half-read newspapers off the lounge and she sank down between the cushions. For a brief moment Bromo was aware of feeling a glow of warmth towards her, even a touch of sympathy. Then other inner voices began making themselves heard, urging caution and speaking reminders of the events that had brought them to this stage.

He waved the bottle of Lagavulin in her direction.

'Would this help?'

'Got any red?'

Well, that was a relief. At least she wasn't going to hoe into his fifteen-year-old malts and adulterate them with Coke or soda or even an overdose of water. Willingly he eased a bottle of quaffing wine from the rack and got busy with his waiter's friend. He mentally chalked up a few points to her credit; a woman who drank red wine definitely had it over her chardonnay-sipping sisters.

He handed her the glass of wine: 'So?'

'I work for Peter Rasheed.'

Her voice dropped to a whisper.

'He wasn't the one you were meant to dump in the river. Something's gone terribly wrong.'

Bromo almost let the bottle slip from his hand as he went to replace it on the bench. This woman was just one surprise after another.

'So why send me to tidy the mess in that house?'

'Fair question.'

She took a sip of red. 'I thought Peter was doing the beating up, not being beaten up himself. He messaged me. Said he was in a hurry and he'd left the place in a mess as there'd been a bit of a fight.'

She looked down into her glass as she twirled it between her fingers.

'Some fight,' said Bromo. 'Or was there another one he didn't get time to tell you about? And why me?'

'God only knows what happened. You could be right in that he messaged me after one fight and then maybe there was another one after he'd rung me.'

Fiona shrugged. She looked defeated; the warrior woman had turned into little girl lost.

'So, it was some other poor bugger who was meant to be dumped. Lucky for Rasheed we stuffed up and the car didn't hit the river. At least you and his mates can give him a proper send-off. Perhaps you should thank me for being so bloody useless.'

She took a tissue from the sleeve of her coat. Dabbed at her eyes and nose. She looked up, rueful and tearful: 'I suppose so.'

Not very contrite, Bromo decided. He watched her take another dab at her face. He wriggled in his seat, uncomfortable, uneasy. He never knew what to do when women turned on the water tap. Taking a sip of whisky helped. It gave him something to do. A chance to reflect.

She played with her glass, swirling the wine, head bowed and concentrating. Or avoiding the issue more likely. He'd seen it all before. Why tread easy? She knew more than she was revealing.

Bromo's mind flicked back to the TV newscast. A link was missing. No name had been mentioned. A 'prominent businessman' was all the reporter had said. It was a catch-all label that could be attached to dozens, perhaps hundreds, of locals.

He tossed this thought into the ring: 'How can you be so sure it was Rasheed who was in the boot?'

Fiona looked up. She sat back in the chair. Bromo saw it as a fresh surge of confidence, bordering on arrogance. The coat sliding off her shoulder, baring still more flesh, was a distraction he could do without

'Contacts, of course,' she said. Then she spelled it out, letting him know, showing her hand: 'The cops.'

Bromo stilled any reaction with a sip of his malt. Say no more. Why was he not surprised? As more and more privacy laws and restrictions were imposed, the breach of them became increasing flagrant. Everything leaked. Not even the police database was secure, as had been shown by several well-publicised breaches, including one by a criminal's girlfriend. Private and confidential was a meaningless term; just something to type at the top of a letter and then forget.

'So who did you think was going to be ditched in that car?' he asked.

She sniffed again and pulled out another tissue. She dabbed gently at her eyes, careful not to smudge the mascara. 'One of Gerry Nuyen's people. That's one of Nuyen's houses. Peter was taking a look around.'

Bromo read between the lines.

'You mean he'd gone there to steal something and they jumped him.'

Fiona ignored him. She stayed on track, 'He thought it was empty. There were some papers he needed.'

'Needed or stole?'

Again, she let his question go unanswered. She slowly crossed one long leg over the other. Flesh showed. Bromo recognised the tease. He held himself tight, showing no reaction.

'You still haven't explained why me,' he said.

'You've a reputation around town as a fixer from way back,' she said. 'People talk. They pass on names.'

'Next time, keep passing,' said Bromo.

He'd done a favour or two for a mate and he'd had some good references for his freelance travel consultancy work. But Fiona's demands were well above and beyond the call of duty. To have people talking of him as a fixer was way out of line unless someone had done some very deep digging into his distant past on the other side of the world. That was another time, another place. A very different Bromo Perkins. A flurry of concern rippled through him. Those days were well behind him, not to be resurrected. His mid-40s body wouldn't cope; the mental drive was no longer there. The danger and disgrace were part of history. She broke into his reverie.

'Don't forget I'm the one who's holding those pictures.'

Whoops! Bromo fired off an internal memo: never underestimate the opposition. Just when he thought she was all meek and malleable the pressure was being reapplied. She uncrossed her legs and leaned forward, presenting a distracting view down the valley of her cleavage. That unblinking stare focused on him.

'We're deadly serious, Mr Perkins. What has happened to Pete is absolutely terrible. But it won't stop us. If anything, it has made us even more determined. And we've decided you're the one to help us. Nice and neutral; the man in the middle.'

She rose from her chair with a swirl of coat and a waft of perfume that Bromo instantly labelled as heady and expensive. The scent was far less pungent than the daytime dabs he'd sensed at Dargo's. This was the nectar of the night. She edged forward, her breasts almost falling from their minimal restraints. One hand reached down to his crutch and squeezed. His eyes closed with the pain. His whole body clenched. Oh, the agony. And the ecstasy.

'You can use them or lose them,' she said, continuing to apply pressure. 'The choice is yours.'

Her hand opened and the pain eased. Bromo wasn't sure whether he had been pleasured or tortured.

When he opened his eyes, she had gone. A manila folder at his feet and two aching balls were the only evidence of her visit.

FIVE

Bromo sipped his malt and closed his eyes, imagining the peat and kelp of the islands. There was no point in rushing. Inertia had much to recommend it, especially when all the signs pointed to his cosy routine having the bejesus knocked out of it. These days, he tended to reckon inaction worked better than deeds. Anything for a trouble-free life after all that had gone before.

He contemplated the folder at his feet, still where Fiona had let it fall. There was something familiar about it apart from a size and colour like thousands of others. Down its outer edge was a single word in bold capitals: RAGE.

Through his haze of scotch and lethargy, he recalled seeing something very much like it not all that long ago. Somewhere, he'd dumped those disks. He eased himself up out of his chair and stumbled through to the back room. The table was covered in weekend magazines, unread newspapers, a bike helmet, two jackets due for the dry cleaners and bottles to be taken down to the garbage bins. Among a pile of unread papers, magazine clippings and accounts to be paid he found a plastic bag, thrown down when he'd rushed home after dumping the car in the river. Or not dumping it, as it now seemed. He rifled through the bag and unearthed what he was looking for — another folder, this one bearing the single word RAID.

Back in his armchair he placed the folders side by side - one with remnants showing where many of its contents had been ripped from the retaining clip. Maybe these were the papers Fiona said Rasheed had been looking for but someone else had got there first. The other folder still contained paperwork which, even now, he was reluctant to look at.

He felt he was dipping his toes into dangerous waters. RAID and RAGE looked back at him, almost mocking his indecision, daring him to look inside.

The sudden trilling of *La Donna e Mobile* trampled on his indecision. He picked his mobile up off the floor.

'Yep?'

'You okay? I called earlier but got the machine.'

'Fine, Jase. Got your message. Never been better.'

'Sure?'

'Sure. Just enjoying a nightcap.'

'Had any callers?'

'No,' he lied. He wanted to keep his mate at arm's length from whatever was whirling around him. The fearsome Fiona was not something he felt like foisting on anyone considered a friend.

'Sure there's nothing I can do?'

Bromo paused, a slight hesitation: 'Feel like answering a question?'

'Sure, fire away.'

'What do the words raid and rage mean to you when they're written in capital letters?'

Bromo noticed the intake of breath. Not your normal heavy breathing.

'Shit, mate. Where've you been? I thought you were in touch with local affairs.'

'Obviously I've missed something.'

Bromo reached for the Lagavulin and poured another slug. He felt an anaesthetic was going to be needed.

'They're not good news.'

'I've gathered that. How bad?'

'Bad bad. You don't want to go there.'

'Too late, mate. I'm on the tram already.'

'Then you'd better jump off right now.'

'Don't think I can do that. The doors are shut and Fiona won't let me out.'

'Fiona? Who the hell's Fiona?'

'It's a long story.'

'Cut it. I'll take the *Reader's Digest* version. I'm coming round.'

The phone went dead. Bromo took another sip from his glass and waited for Jason's ring at the door.

*

They sat nursing their drinks. Bromo with a topped-up tumbler, more ice than scotch and Jason with a green-glassed bottle of Cascade. Intuition said this was no time for heavy imbibing but for calm and contemplation.

Bromo rolled his glass slowly between his hands as he digested the summary of local politics Jason had walked him through over the past half-hour. It was messier and more involved than anything he had imagined. Nothing so obvious as drug pushers lurking around the housing commission high rises or kids overdosing on smack in the laneways off Victoria Street. No insight into teen gangs rampaging through the streets, spraying walls with their tags, mugging the aged and infirm for a few dollars. That was all too bleeding obvious, the stuff of frequent tabloid headlines fed to a blasé public to whom such events were fodder as regular as the footy results.

Bromo lifted an index finger off his tumbler and pointed at the files: 'So what you're saying is that we've got a turf war going on here and things have gotten a bit ugly.'

'A nice summing up,' said Jason. 'But it's a bit more than turf. It's bloody bricks and mortar and cement sheets. Serious money, too. And probably a concrete pour or two you wouldn't want to know too much about.'

He picked up the folder marked RAID.

'Residents Against Indiscriminate Development,' he enlarged. 'A bunch of well-meaning souls who probably live a bit too much in the past and want everything to stay the way it used to be. The impossible dream.'

He swapped it for the other folder.

'And in the other corner we have RAGE - the Rally Against Green Excess, which is a front for a bunch of money men who don't see why they can't knock down all the old cottages and replace them with glitzy modern apartments. Progress and profit.'

'And we're in the bloody middle,' said Bromo.

'I'm not too sure about the 'we' big boy. You seem to be the one attracting all the attention. I'm just the bunny who comes along and cleans up the mess.'

Bromo shrugged and took a sip.

'Sorry mate,' he said. 'I didn't mean to get you into this. It didn't seem that complicated to start with.'

'It never is.'

Bromo flicked through the RAID folder - copies of seemingly innocuous letters, a couple of receipts for office supplies, real estate flyers, an invoice for photocopying. He gave the RAGE folder the same quick perusal, finding a similar assortment of boringly normal documents. Whatever had been ripped from its retaining clips was the only thing that mattered. By now, that was probably crumpled up in Rasheed's pockets if, as Fiona claimed, that was the reason for his visit to Nuyen's house.

'This ain't the real thing.' he said. 'It's a bloody furphy. Or only part of the story. If this mob is all they're cracked up to be there'd be a file as thick as two house bricks. Seems to me Miss Fiona isn't telling the whole story.'

'Or it's been doctored.'

Bromo accepted his mate's verdict. It increased his growing feeling of being on a journey for which he'd never bought a ticket. He had never envisaged his fling with the willing Aurelia Nuyen would have him heaving bodies into stolen cars and becoming enmeshed in the intrigues of desperate developers. On reflection, there seemed little point in Fiona making a big show of delivering a seemingly important folder when it contained nothing more exciting than would be found in any family filing cabinet.

'Seems like a calling card more than anything else,' he said, gazing down into the bottom of his glass. 'I guess we wait and see. Why go looking for trouble?'

'You could try running those disks through your computer.'

Disks? Disks?

Recent events had erased much of what had happened earlier in the day. A good malt made a wonderful anaesthetic. He had completely forgotten about the computer disks he had scooped up along with the battered Rasheed.

'Good idea.'

He shuffled through into the back room. The intercom buzzed as he began another fossick through the room's jumble, seeking the computer disks.

Jason called out from the other room: 'Expecting anyone?'

'Only if she's slim, blonde and decadent. And that's a wish, not an expectation.'

The intercom buzzed again, insistent. Bromo returned from his search, empty-handed. They looked at each other. Bromo shrugged. Jason picked up the intercom phone.

'Yeah?'

Silence.

'No one there, mate.'

'Often happens,' said Bromo. 'Survey people. Idiots. Wrong flat.'

No sooner had Jason put the phone back in its cradle than it buzzed again, long and demanding. Once more he picked it up. Silence.

'Better take a look.'

Together they clumped down the stairs to the dimly lit foyer. Through the frosted glass of the entry doors they could see a huddled heap on the cracked flagstones outside.

Bromo was first to reach the motionless bundle. A heavily bandaged head looked up at him. A faint voice croaked from beneath bloodied bindings.

'You bloody idiots. Get me inside, quick.'

They didn't question his demand. No one questioned Peter Rasheed - especially when he'd apparently risen from the dead and escaped from the boot of a car driven into a murky Yarra River.

SIX

Dulled by events and whisky, they somehow managed to carry Rasheed upstairs - Jason at the head, Bromo clutching the legs - and dump him on the settee.

'Take it easy,' groaned the bundle. 'You've done enough bleeding damage.'

'Yeah, sorry about that,' replied Bromo. 'But I'm not the one doing the bleeding. You can talk later.'

Again the bundle made a mumbling noise. Trying to speak. Bromo bent low over him. He was muttering something that sounded like Max. It meant nothing to Bromo. He knew no one of that name. He could only assume Max was some other local schemer Rasheed needed to meet.

Optimist. He wasn't going anywhere.

Jason shuffled over from the corner cupboard. He'd kicked off his runners and was carrying a glass and a bottle of scotch. He splashed a couple of fingers of the golden spirit into the glass and held it to Rasheed's lips.

'Get this into you. It'll help dull the pain while we clean you up.'

'Glad to see you're not using the good stuff,' muttered Bromo, nodding in the direction of the bottle, the cheap blend he bought for visitors who insisted on adding soda or

Coke. Between them they hefted Rasheed off the sofa and on to a doona dragged from Bromo's bed and laid out on the floor.

Where to begin? Bromo wished he'd got around to doing that First Aid course he'd continually resolved to study. Always told himself that one day it would come in useful. Too bloody right, even if it was tending to a petty crook rather than playing an angel of mercy at a crash scene or house fire. Gingerly he started unwrapping the thick black overcoat enfolding the hardly conscious Rasheed.

Shit! He was wearing PJs. And his bandages had a fresh 'my mum's got a Whirlpool' look about them. Someone had been taking care of him. And professionally. He'd been cleaned up and wrapped by people who knew their job. People who maybe actually cared.

So why did these caring folk decide to handball him to me, pondered Bromo. Again. Twice in one day. Not their problem. Why not? No spare bed for an invalid? Too hot to handle? The world was losing all its compassion.

La Donna e Mobile began ringing out from his mobile. He unhooked it from his belt. No caller ID.

'Yeh?'

'You received the package?' It was Fiona.

'Which package? You referring to Lazarus?'

'How is he?'

'Not bad for someone who's supposed to have carked it. How'd he manage it?'

'Ever heard of the mum in the boot?'

Who hadn't? The headline had run for weeks. Strangled by her husband's lover, the poor woman had survived three days trussed up and locked in the boot of her abandoned car.

She had never regained consciousness and many weeks later her life support system was turned off.

'Okay. Miracles happen. But what's with the cops saying he was dead?'

'Spin doctors. Dangling the bait. They didn't actually say he was dead. Only that a body had been found. Lucky for you the car stopped where it did.'

Bromo looked at the comatose bundle on the floor. The shot of scotch seemed to have knocked Rasheed out.

The ethicists said all life was worth saving. Debatable. The jury was surely still out on this one. A world without Rasheed might have been a better place once the fuss had died down. His survival only added fuel to inflame dying embers. Fiona's voice was still rasping away at the other end of the phone.

'Cool it,' said Bromo. 'We're doing you a favour.'

'Don't forget those photos. They won't make Gerry Nuyen very happy.'

That option was beginning to look like the lesser of two evils. Bromo still didn't know what mess Fiona had embroiled him in. Or even who and what she represented, other than some vague loyalty to Peter Rasheed.

'Okay, you win. For now. What do you want done with Miracle Man? I'm not running a hospice for battered crims.'

Her voice softened. Almost tender and caring.

'Take care of him. He's had a rough time. Checking himself out of hospital didn't help. Once word gets out there'll be people looking for him. Let him rest. Give him a bed for the night.'

'What's wrong with his own bed? Take him home.'

'He doesn't really have one at the moment. He's been squatting. On the move. Keeping out of sight. Too many people know where to find us. I'll fix something. Call you tomorrow.'

She gave him no time to argue. She'd cut the call. Bromo snapped his phone shut.

Jason tucked a blanket around Peter Rasheed's sleeping form.

'Sounds as if you've won yourself a house guest,' he said. 'Better make him comfortable.'

'Yeah,' said Bromo. 'Let sleeping dogs lie.'

SEVEN

ANOTHER DAY, ANOTHER HALF-AWAKE shuffle down Bridge Road with a refuelling stop for caffeine at Dargo's, one eye wary for any signs of a lurking Fiona.

Slightly refreshed, Bromo went on down the street, dodging kiddie cyclists and skateboarders using the footpath as their expressway to school. He waved at Rose behind her dry-cleaner's counter and returned a 'G'day mate' to the stooped old fellow making his way to the bench in the plaza where he'd chew the fat with other senior citizens until it was time for a counter lunch at The Vine.

Bromo stopped outside a door squeezed between a discount bedding shop and a pharmacy. It was a scuffed, nondescript, no-name door. Totally anonymous. Exactly as Bromo liked it. He turned a key in the lock. Ahead was a narrow flight of stairs. On the landing at the top was another door, another lock to unkey.

Inside was sanctuary. A secret place he'd cherished since a couple of artists had told him it was for rent, and going cheap compared with most of the suburb's real estate. He'd been buying one of the painter's pictures at the time and these days viewed her seascape as a marker of a high point in his finances rather than for any artistic merits. Thanks to her he had a haven he cherished. The two rooms were freezer cold in winter and he had to rely on the moods of temperamental old air conditioner to beat the summer heat. But to him they were his hermit's cave.

A huge old oak desk filled a third of the room. Behind it, leaned an equally old wrap-around office chair. Both had been rescued from the offices of an old-style hardware shop forced into liquidation by an invasion of chain store operators.

Bromo took a deep relieving breath. For the first time in many hours he relaxed. Rasheed was still deep asleep when he'd eased his way out of his apartment. No one would find their way in to cause him further harm and if Rasheed wanted to get up and go, so be it.

Bromo fired up his computer. While he waited for the screen to blink into life he tipped the contents of a plastic bag on to the desk. The two manila folders labelled RAGE and RAID lay there along with the documents swept up from the floor of the house where they had found Rasheed. There were also several computer disks, none of them with labelling that made any immediate sense..

Nothing bore any reference to someone called Max. Maybe it was not a person but a place, maybe a bar or cafe that Rasheed had been burbling on about. Bromo could recall no such place locally. He reckoned he'd got to know most of them as he sought somewhere to sit quietly with a long black and tackle the daily cryptic.

After a cursory shuffle through the bag's contents Bromo decided they could wait. He gathered them up and put them back. Normalcy was called for. A dose of routine wouldn't go astray after the events of the past few hours. There were emails to check and a couple of clients had itineraries that needed rejigging. It was the clients, not Rasheed or sidekick Fiona, who helped pay the rent and finance his few pleasures.

The clients were a select group - two or three small but prosperous businesses and a number of well-heeled individuals who paid well for personalized attention. They had all latched on to Bromo in his short-lived travel agency days and some he had come to know even earlier during the time when his former employers had conveniently found a job for him in an international airline's VIP reservations section.

All had supported him when he chose to slow down and branch out on his own after Monique had found religion and left him with a mortgage and a cupboard full of discarded and little-worn designer shoes. What was it with women and shoes?

Two phone calls later he'd confirmed hotel bookings in Budapest and Vienna for Gerry Baskin, who ran a thriving food importing business that helped satisfy the taste buds of many a migrant yearning for their homeland delicacies.

Another call and a couple of emails had him well on the way to ensuring Liz Shapcott would have a hire car waiting for her in Dublin as well as A-reserve tickets to two performances at the Abbey Theatre. Just a little detour on a culture junkie's regular jaunt around Europe's galleries, theatres and concert halls.

As he pulled out the Shapcott file to make notes of these latest confirmations his somewhat sleepy brain clicked up a gear. Liz might have some answers.

She answered on the second ring.

'Liz? Dublin is confirmed. Including the Abbey.'

'You wonderful man. I don't know how you do it.'

Bromo grinned. 'Sheer skill. And knowing the right people. Speaking of which ... what are your contacts on council like these days?'

'Depends. Planning department's twitchy. Finance thinks it's Fort Knox and a couple of the independents are playing hard to get and not turning up to meetings. Plus there's the usual battle over who'll be the next mayor. Fortunately there's always someone willing to talk to a friendly architect who sticks vaguely within the rules. What's on your mind?'

'A shitload.'

'Smelly.'

'Stinks. And it's violent, too.'

He thumbed the edges of the manila folders. Did he really want to involve others in this murky business? Even calling on them for their knowledge might prove risky.

'Tell me, Liz, do Rage and Raid mean anything to you?'

The quick intake of breath was unmissable. There was a long pause.

'In what way, mean anything to me? Important? Significant? That sort of thing?'

Bromo waited through the silence that followed, sensing there was more to come. There was.

'You want to know if I'm involved?' She gave a snappy answer to her own question. 'Not at all. They're just words.'

Yeah, thought Bromo, very convincing. Pull the other one. Seems I've struck a nerve.

'Write them in capital letters and add the name of Peter Rasheed,' he said.

'I think you'd better come round. You know the address. I'll switch the coffee machine on.'

*

It was only a short walk along narrow back streets built not much more than a century ago for horse and dray but now cluttered by the cars of residents who had neither driveways nor garages. Their homes had been built on such tiny blocks of a former shanty town of tents and humpies that they could only expand upwards, which was most of them were doing – raising the roofline, adding entire floors. Most of the houses had already grown ground level extensions that encroached on the rear alleys where, until fairly recently, night-carts clanked along to do their smelly task, emptying the cesspits and backyard dunnies, many of which still existed – if not actually in use – in the 1980s.

A strong warm northerly blew dust in his eyes and scattered discarded junk mail along the footpaths. He passed the corner pub where every day was different - parma day, pasta day, curry day and, inevitably, fish and chips day; and all for ten bucks a serve.

Next door, some poor bastard had had his once pristine white garden wall daubed by protesters. 'Hot chips not woodchips,' ran the slogan. Another example of Greenies trying to make their point by degrading the environment they sought to preserve.

Liz Shapcott lived in one of the suburb's many short streets, and a particularly quirky one at that: it had No Entry signs at both ends that applied only as far as a halfway junction from where One Way Only signs pointed traffic in the other direction. Residents considered it the most bizarre of the council's many efforts at traffic management as both signs tended to be more ignored than honoured by motorists seeking short cuts through the suburb's warren of back streets.

Her house had once been one of the area's many small factories and showed little outward sign of modernization.

To passers-by it was just another solid single-storey redbrick block with three small heavily barred street-side windows and a battered old double-size roller door, once the access for trucks, but now firmly bolted down.

Well-weathered horizontal planks of red gum extended from the wall's end well above head height to form a fenced barricade to a courtyard. A recess chiselled out of one plank held a security intercom. She buzzed him in and called him across the courtyard to an industrial size doorway.

'I thought the panel beaters were in Swan Street,' he said, nodding at the factory facade.

'It used to be an ironworks,' she said. 'Fancy stuff. Metal fences, wrought iron lacework for verandas, candelabra for the gentry's homes across the river.'

'Seems the gentry's moved in,' said Bromo as they went inside.

He took a quick look around the massive space. 'Sure you've got enough room?'

She ignored him and walked over to an espresso machine plumbed into a stainless steel bench taking up the entire length of one wall. Commercial type fridges and freezers supported the bench.

'How do you take it?'

'Black and strong.'

'I should have remembered. Where d'you want to sit - bar, table, lounge?'

Bromo looked around the ex-factory, its bare brick walls still exposed except for the many artworks hanging from tracks bolted in at ceiling height. A bit hard to imagine the lathes, rollers, presses and red hot forges that not all that long ago occupied this same space.

'Seems we're spoilt for choice,' he said taking in areas arranged for cooking, dining, lounge and office, each clearly defined by distinctive and expensive furnishings yet flowing easily one into the other.

The word cavernous came to mind. But he rejected it. No cavern was ever this sumptuous. Cave dwellers didn't sink their haunches into plush Italian leather armchairs. And Liz Shapcott had very long haunches indeed, which she let hang over an arm of her chair, the folds of a full-length skirt gathered loosely around them. Nonchalant, relaxed.

A good act, thought Bromo. But it couldn't compete with the tension he sensed around her.

'So, all the bookings for Ireland have been confirmed?'

'Set in concrete.'

It was a polite, almost formal, conversational opening gambit. Bromo expected nothing less. He'd seen it so many times. Two people coming together to discuss things, ostensibly as friends or colleagues. Yet each had an agenda, something they sought or something they had to give. Or hide. And they sniffed around each other like dogs in the park, waiting for the moment to pounce.

She was fencing. Avoiding the issue.

'Odd name you've got,' she said 'It's always intrigued me.'

Bromo wriggled in his seat. Getting impatient. Knowing he had to play the game. Thrust and counter-thrust. Weigh up your opposition. Until now he hadn't considered they were on opposing sides. Another revelation.

He responded to her query: 'Mum had a weird sense of humour.'

Liz gave a slight enquiring tilt of her head; a raising of one pencil thin, almost plucked to oblivion, eyebrow.

'Where's the joke?'

'There's a military myth that the army puts bromide in the tea of their troops to curb their sexual urges. Mum reckons the old man poured his down the sink. One night of passion and she's got me. Unexpected and unwanted. The no-bromide babe. Hence Bromo.

'She stuck around for a while then decided she'd get back to being a career woman. Bit of a power pussy, it seems. Walked out. So dad did the parenting bit with lots of help from his folks.'

'Ever made contact with her?'

'A couple of phone calls in my teens and we started meeting for a coffee or drink. She's still around – back in the old country.'

He took a hefty gulp of his coffee. They were treading on hurtful ground. Time to change course.

'Enough of me,' he said. 'What were you going to tell me about. RAID and RAGE that you couldn't say over the phone? Are you involved? What's your connection? Why your interest?'

'Too many questions.'

'And not enough answers. Tell me.'

'It's just that I don't want to see you get out of your depth. Getting hurt. I've been a pretty demanding client but you've always done what I asked and never let me down. Stick to what you know and do best.'

'That sounds like a warning to me.'

She unwound herself from her chair and clicked across the tiled floor on four-inch heels.

'Take it how you will. But from what I hear some people are playing a very rough game. And it's likely to get rougher. It always does when big money's involved.'

'How big?'
'Big big. Millions.'
'And Peter Rasheed?'
'Lose him. Tidy up your apartment.'

He tried to show no reaction, digging his fingers hard into the soft cushiony arms of the chair. He took two very deep breaths. Everyone seemed to be taking an interest in Mr Rasheed. Keeping track of his movements yet dumping him anywhere but on their own doorsteps.

'You know?'
'I'd heard. Bush telegraph.'
'We're a long way from the bush.'
'Same thing. Bush or city. People talk.'

Bromo scratched his left ear. A sign of stress. The piercing where he'd rashly hung a gold ring in the Monique era to cover up an old wound still gave him the yips, refusing to fully heal. As Monique had so forthrightly said, it was stupid to try hiding one wound with another. Maybe the itching was a message. Give her a ring, so to speak. Even though she'd got religion she was always willing to listen to his problems. All that bible-bashing and those latter-day sing-alongs seemed to have made her more understanding. And to think a mellow Monique once seemed a most unlikely progression.

Liz walked over to the far corner of the room where an Apple Mac glowed on a streamlined workstation. She picked up a sheaf of papers. Foolscap size, various colours. 'This is what it's all about.'

Bromo reached out an arm. Wanting a look.
'Sorry. Confidential.'

He glimpsed the cover. An architectural drawing. It showed a large building surrounded by an artist's rough depiction of clumps of trees and shrubs. A sketch of what might be. Or not be. A planner's dream or a conservationist's nightmare.

'Looks like just another yuppie development,' said Bromo.

'Tell that to Peter Rasheed. And the rabble from RAID.'

'Sounds like you don't approve.'

'No comment.'

'Conflict of interests?'

'No comment.'

He felt he was swimming upstream with training weights strapped to his ankles. Getting nowhere. Even going backwards. And all because of a decadent dalliance with the luscious Aurelia Nuyen.

There'd been many such previous diversions with a variety of women and some had brought minor complications. Irate husbands, a push for something more permanent, even declarations of love - whatever that might mean. But none had steeped him in such hot water as this one with Aurelia. Perhaps it was time to think twice, even thrice, before yielding to this lifelong weakness. Others succumbed to alcohol, smokes, gambling. They had their cures and treatments - AA, Quit, Gamblers Anonymous. So where was the help for the poor bastard addicted to the opposite sex? Feeling the urge? Call Libido Lifeline!

He appraised Liz Shapcott as she stood over him with the sheaf of papers. Tall, slim, elegant. Forget it. He was in enough trouble.

Her hair was tumbling mass of chestnut ringlets.

'Must be a bugger to comb,' said Bromo.

'No need.' She was on his wavelength. 'Wet it, shake it. It just falls into place.'

If only everything was that simple, thought Bromo. Nice to have things fall into place. He shrugged.

'You haven't been much help.'

'Really? Sorry about that. I thought the message was clear enough.'

He looked at her.

'Butt out, Bromo.'

'That it?'

'Sure is.'

She put the sheaf of papers on the table. The cover page looked back at him. It pictured a long, two-storey brick building, almost window-less with all its doors and loading bays boarded up. Graffiti over the walls. Windows on the upper storey cracked and broken. Abandoned, wrecked and ripe for development. A local eyesore. And on the roofline the name of the company that once lived there: Mack's.

Mack's? He silently, mentally, tested the word. And another he'd been hearing: Mack's and Max. An obvious conclusion. No prizes for assuming this was the Max that Rasheed seemed so anxious about.

He moved towards the door. 'Time to go. I've got all I need.'

She leaned into him. Her arms reached out and held him gently at the shoulders, drawing him to her. Her lips brushed him lightly on both cheeks. It was a soft, lingering kiss.

'Stay safe. Stay friends.'

She pulled back. Gently.

He turned to the door and brushed against a wall rack where coats were hanging. Among them a long black woollen wrap and scarf, brightened only by a circular brooch, its outer edge of golden stones framing a tiger's head with eyes formed by two more stones, darker and striped. In the tiger's jaws, a long-stemmed red flower.

'Classy brooch.'

'You like it? A gift from a friend.'

He stepped out into the courtyard, heading to the gate.

'Aurelia Nuyen gave it to me,' she said.

EIGHT

THERE WAS A SIMPLE solution when the going got tough; one way of clearing the fogged mind; of sieving out the dross and getting down to essentials. You walked. Rasheed could wait. So could the files, disks and papers still waiting to be sorted and examined.

Bromo didn't give them a second glance as he picked up a light backpack, stuffed the daily papers inside, checked his water bottle was full, shut his office door and marched away from the trams, traffic and meandering shoppers of the main drag. He headed up the Church Street hill and through the wrought iron gates on to the path that separated St Ignatius from St Stephen's. The Anglos facing off at the Micks. The two churches of opposing faiths occupied the suburb's highest ground - above their flocks and closest to heaven, the Catholics outdoing the Anglicans with a needle thin spire visible far into the distance and which, when erected in 1928, lay claim to being Australia's tallest structure.

Thirty minutes later he was striding up the lawned slopes of the Botanic Gardens, heading for the exit opposite the Shrine of Remembrance. He followed the hilly path past the exotically fringed xanthorrhoea trees, down into the gully where the fruit bats once screeched and up the rise lined by groves of bamboos click-clacking against each other in the breeze.

Already he felt better. There was something cleansing about walking for walking's sake. Not walking to achieve an objective, to go from A to B, deliver a message, call on a mate, browse the shops, and even exercise the dog. Just walking, briskly, not slacking off for any distractions.

He lengthened his stride on the downhill slope of the lawns surrounding the Shrine, aiming for the Domain Road corner. The traffic mayhem of St Kilda Road, and then Kings Way, slowed him briefly. Once across the busy highway, clogged with trucks and semi-trailers, he picked up pace. Within a few more minutes, he was on the edge of Albert Park, offering five kilometres of unfettered walking around its lake.

A small flotilla of yachts was venturing out from the sailing school, a couple of rowing eights were trying to synchronise their rhythms down by the Powerhouse boatsheds and the usual procession of joggers and plodders was pounding its way around the running track. Situation normal.

Or was it? Something was missing.

Suddenly, it dawned: they'd gone. Decamped. The yellow ribbon mob and their tent were no longer there.

Ever since the road around the lake had been resurrected as a Formula One grand prix circuit an intensely dedicated band of earnest locals had maintained a park-side vigil of protest against the car race. Not merely for days, weeks or even months. But for years.

They'd became part of the scenery, along with the import-ed palm trees, the massive new sports and aquatic centre and the rejuvenated cricket and hockey ovals - none of which they could see as enhancing a previously lifeless and depressingly dreary blot on the landscape. How could they? Their tented headquarters faced outwards. They faced away from the sight of their fellow citizens actively enjoying what these members of Save Albert Park - the SAPs, as one newspaper columnist had derisively dismissed them - so persistently opposed.

Bromo recalled their protests as being mostly passive and peaceful. A bit of aggro occurred with the police lines in the early days. And a couple of outbursts of vandalism by fringe dwellers determined to make their point more forcibly. Their right to protest was acknowledged and there was no doubting their passion, even if it paled alongside that of Ferrari fanaticism on race day. A yellow ribbon was no match for a prancing black horse.

The SAPs had vowed to stay until the grand prix was moved elsewhere. But today their campsite was deserted. The banner proclaiming A Park is No Place for a Race had been taken down. The yellow tent had gone. So had its occupants, their deck chairs and card tables. And the race would be returning for several more years with its senseless and polluting blast of high-octane merry-go-round.

So much for protest, thought Bromo. Ignore it for long enough and it eventually goes away. It runs out of puff. Loses its voice. It becomes toothless and lacks any bite. But not, apparently, where Peter Rasheed, Raid and Rage were concerned. And he wasn't even burning rubber in a public park.

Bromo thought of other protests that had blazed with initial fury, burned brightly in spasms and then fizzled. Done the damp squib thing.

Even now there was a fleet of small boats buzzing angrily around the bay trying to stop a deep-water channel being dredged. They'd been vocal. Made their presence felt, their uniform of bright red anoraks making great TV images against the churned-up water. Then a massive dredger had steamed through them, done its job and berthed safely. Protest over.

Yet those twin thorns in his side, Raid and Rage, seemed still to have potency. There was enough gas left in the tank to get someone to do serious damage to Peter Rasheed, and to run rampant through someone's home and possessions.

They also seemed able to put the frighteners on people. Witness how Liz Shapcott had clammed up and shunted him aside. And the way Fiona was obviously running scared.

He plonked his backpack on a chair outside the sailing club kiosk. He pointed a thumb towards the trees. 'Bit of the scenery missing.' A statement that was almost a question.

The tanned and bearded face looking at him from the kiosk window understood.

'Woke up to themselves at last. Realised they'd never win. Bit like the Minardi mob going round here on race day. Lots of noise and screeching, but never going the distance. You eating?'

'You do toasted?'

'On the griller. Got cheese, tomato.'

'Any ham, bacon?'

'I'll take a look. Not usually my job. Kid didn't turn up.'

He shuffled off towards a fridge, muscly and lean. An outdoors type confined to barracks.

'Coupla slices of ham.'

'Sounds good. And a coffee. Black. Strong.'

'Reckon I can manage that.'

He could. And did. And when he brought it he was inclined to linger. Looking for an excuse to be out from behind the confines of his counter. In open space.

'Not your usual job, then,' surmised Bromo.

'Nah. Mostly out here. Doing the Wind in the Willows thing, mucking about in boats. Maintenance, painting, safety patrol, teaching the kids, getting them out there on the water. Done any sailing?'

'Crewed a lot. Years ago.'

The memory was still strong, and often filled with regrets that he hadn't continued. Nothing so exhilarating as leaning out full stretch, back bending, arms straining, bum wet in the water, spray stinging the face. Skimming downwind then suddenly going about, ducking under the boom, letting out one sheet, grabbing frantically for the other, desperate not to stuff up, lose any leeway.

'Should give it another go.'

'One day,' said Bromo. 'Got a bit on my plate at the moment. Talking of which ...' He pulled out his mobile and flipped it open.

'Leave you to it.'

The kiosk man walked over to the landing stage and helped two schoolgirls haul in a small sailboat. Bromo pressed the call history button, hoping there was a caller ID. Technology was on his side for once. He pressed the number.

She answered. Soft voice. Cautious.

'Can we meet?' he asked.

Silence. At least she hadn't hung up on him. She seemed to be giving it some thought. He held his ear lobe between finger and thumb. Started rubbing at the irritation. Bloody stress.

'When? Where?'

'Sooner the better. Wherever's best for you.'

'I'm in St Kilda. Just finished a kinesthetics session.'

'Whatever.'

More health freak mumbo-jumbo. Whatever happened to a good old-fashioned workout?

'Hope it did some good. I'm in Albert Park. Can you pick me up? I'll finish my coffee and start walking. Probably be in Pit Straight by the time you get here.'

'Twenty minutes.'

'Just make sure you're not being followed.'

He shouldered his backpack and continued striding around the lake's edge, scattering a mob of black swans that had waddled ashore in search of food. Ducks and their offspring paddled in the lake. There was a welcome warmth in the sun but a sharp breeze came off the water, needling his face. Bracing, get-up-and-go weather. Who needed bloody kinesthetics on a day like this?

He marched on to Pit Straight. Rollerbladers were playing their special brand of hockey in front of the vast metal hangar that garaged the teams of the Grand Prix circus when it came to town. Further along, basketballers were ducking, weaving, shooting goals. He saw Aurelia Nuyen's chunky 4WD take the bend into the straight and waved her down. She leaned across and opened the door.

'What's this all about?'

'And nice to see you, too,' he replied. 'Can we go somewhere less conspicuous than the middle of a race track?'

She leaned towards him. A hand on his thigh. A slight smile.

'Well, well. What d'you have in mind?'

Tempting. Too much so.

'Cool it, Aurelia. We're in enough trouble.'

She sat suddenly upright. Smooth tanned legs showed from under a fawn pleated skirt. A thigh-length lightly patterned top clung on to her shoulders by thin lacy straps. It opened well past the swelling of her breasts. He hauled his thoughts back from their lascivious detour. Yep, enough trouble.

*

She took the road out of the park leading into Clarendon Street. Did a left at Park Street and a right at Cecil and found a space on a rooftop car-park. Two floors below, the South Melbourne market was in full mid-week swing. Shoppers arriving and leaving looked too preoccupied with bags and trolleys to take note of others around them.

All the same, Bromo pointed her to a space down the farthest end, next to the railed parapet. No one would go past them. They had only to worry about people in the vehicle on his left. He turned his back to the window, facing her, shielding her from view.

She'd said little on the short drive from the park, asking only if he was well and cursing volubly at a cyclist who had wobbled into her path.

She turned to him and picked up on his comment in the park.

'So? What sort of trouble?'

'Hard to be precise. I'm still finding out. But pictures of you and me in the nuddy don't help.'

A hand went to her face. Covering an open mouth gasp. 'Shit.'

'In a word, yes.'

Now her hands were in her lap. Pressing down, body leaning slightly forward, tense, a frown creasing her face.

'But there's only one print.'

'You sure.'

'Course I'm sure,' she snapped at him. 'I printed it myself. You don't think I went round to Photo Express.'

'Well, I suppose that's the good news. The bad news is that at least one other person has a print.'

He paused.

'And the really bad news is that it could well find its way to Gerry. Which I don't think is such a good outcome. For you, or me.'

He'd expected an outburst. Fury perhaps. At least some weeping. Maybe a bit of wailing. She wasn't the most placid of people and there'd been times when Bromo had watched from the sidelines as all her Greek heritage came to the fore while she put on a stellar performance over some minor incident. Callas in Norma without the music; just the fireworks.

'So, who's this other person,' she asked. 'And how'd they get a copy?'

'Woman by the name of Fiona. No surname. Bit of a mystery.'

'Shit. I might have guessed.'

'You know her?'

'Thirty something, slim, blonde, sports car?'

Bromo nodded. A neat and concise description. But, then, it could apply to every second woman lunching at Dargo's. He reckoned there must be a huge gene pool somewhere cloning them in bulk for the benefit of the city's fashion shops, cafes and bars – and the lads who liked to leer.

'Sounds like her.'

He sensed a storm warning hovering close by. Aurelia was coiled tighter than a sleeping cobra. And just as ready to strike

'Bitch. Bloody bitch.'

The storm warning had been spot on. She was thumping the steering wheel, punctuating each shouted word.

The flimsy shirt began sliding off one shoulder. It signalled tornado time. But fortunately not for long. Bromo gave silent thanks as he watched the storm centre pass almost as suddenly as it had arrived. Aurelia tugged the bra strap back into place. She rested her head on hands still clenched around the wheel and took three deep breaths.

'They tell me it's good for you,' offered Bromo.

'What is?'

'Breathing.'

He paused. Had a rethink.

'Yeah, well, of course breathing's good. Can't very well do without it. I meant the deep stuff. Been trying it myself. Seems to work.'

There was a knock and a bump against the side of the car. They both twitched, almost in unison. Startled, they sat upright and watched as an overweight woman hefted a loaded shopping trolley into the neighbouring vehicle.

'Let's hope she's not shopping for one,' said Bromo. 'She'll never shed those kilos.'

'Maybe she's happy that way.'

He shrugged. Shifted a lever and pushed his seat back, stretching his legs.

'So, fill me in. I'm in those pictures, too. And I'm the one being threatened. How did the lovely Fiona get her hands on them if you were being so bloody secretive?'

She shook her head, frowning, puzzled. He watched as the carefully layered coloured streaks became tousled with the shaking and then fell back precisely into place. A tribute to the hairdresser's art.

'I think I know what happened. The bitch got lucky. She came into the gallery a couple of weeks ago, looked around then asked if she could borrow a camera to take some shots to show a couple of works to possible clients. Which she did - and then downloaded them into her laptop. But ...'

He saw it coming. So bleedingly obvious and such a stupid mistake.

'But ... you hadn't erased those other pictures from the memory card.'

'Correct. It's the only explanation I can think of. She's a schemer, a user. For anyone like that it was a gift.'

He tapped a hand on the dashboard. The other went up to his ear, rubbing. Bloody stress. Stumbling across pictures like that would be money in the bank to anyone on the make. Or even just wanting to twist an arm or two.

'So it wasn't the first time you'd come across this woman.'

'She's been in the gallery occasionally. And our paths had crossed at other times elsewhere.'

Enigmatic. Not giving much away. 'Perhaps I should give her a call. She got another name?'

'Leoncavallo. Fiona Leoncavallo.'

'Very musical. Operatic even.'

The references seemed to faze her. She shrugged. Ignored them. Moved on.

'Australian, but Italian connections on her husband's side,' said Aurelia. 'Although I think she's kicked him out.'

'Probably walked of his own accord. I would.'

And he'd got the record to prove it. Three times, each for a different reason but always running away. Taking the easy way out. He could find all the stress he needed out on the streets without having to handle it at home. On the other hand, the

Leoncavallo woman did have a certain raunchy allure about her. There'd been suggestive undercurrents eddying around their brief encounters. A look, a word, a touch. All the ingredients in the recipe for getting down and dirty.

Aurelia turned to him, a hand reaching out to hold his arm. Comforting. Calm.

'It's okay, I'll fix her. Just give me time. I think I know what this is all about. A few things need straightening out. And Fiona's one of them.'

'And Peter Rasheed?'

He felt her hand tighten on his arm.

'Oh shit, not him as well. You have been busy.'

'Not me. He found me, thanks to Miss Leoncavallo. I didn't have to go looking. Stolen pictures, coercion, blackmail, beaten-up tycoons and lots of paperwork for organisations calling themselves Raid and Rage. And that's all before lunch. How was your day? Nice and relaxed at the health centre, having a massage, tuning up with kinesthetics or whatever?'

Her grip on his arm tightened further.

'I didn't realise,' she said. 'I enjoy our times together. They're fun. You're good for me. I never thought it would lead to this. I really will fix it.'

She twisted her body round towards him. Put a hand on his knee. Another up to his neck, pulling him gently towards her. Face turned up, lips on lips, mouths open, her tongue probing, pushing, bodies taut and firm against each other. That wayward shoulder strap again slipping revealingly down her arm.

He could sense himself reacting, hard and fast, yet reluctant, a cool corner of his mind sending out warnings. Very tempting, but this was neither the time nor place. He pushed her away, gently but firmly.

She pouted, looked hurt. He ignored it.

'Later, Aurelia. Later. We've got things to do.' Rasheed was still cluttering up his lounge floor. There were computer disks and files to trawl through. And it was time he had a chat with Miss Leoncavallo.

He let himself out of the car and made for the central staircase leading down into the market. *La Donna e Mobile* started to trill from his mobile but there was no caller ID.

'Yeah?'

'That was a close call.'

He didn't recognise the voice. It was light, muffled, distorted. Even hard to define whether it was male or female.

'What was?'

'You and her. Just now. Nearly another photo opportunity.'

The line went dead. He looked around. No one nearby had a phone to their mouth.

NINE

Bromo was in no hurry to return home. If he stayed away long enough maybe Rasheed would have decamped by the time he got back to his apartment.

He spun out his time at the market, starting with a slow wander among the stalls open to the footpath along Cecil Street, fussily selecting fruit and vegetables from several different sellers. Then he drifted down the broad aisle of the meat, fish and deli section, joining the keen-eyed last minute bargain hunters. He beat a hesitant young couple to the punch to snare a heavily discounted tray of chump chops. Fodder for the freezer; cheap cuts to be stored for later use.

At the bottom of the aisle's gentle descent, he turned right, into the narrower lanes of hardware, clothing and gift stalls. Still delaying the inevitable. He allowed himself to be distracted by a display of jeans and even stepped into the curtained-off change room to try on a pair, not really caring if they were a fit or not. They weren't. Too long in the leg, too tight at the waist. A waste of time. Deliberately so.

Back outside the market he followed the seductive aroma of a coffee roast at Cottles and stocked up on a kilo of dark maragogype. From there he strolled on to Clarendon Street and took the 112 tram that ran past the gaudy casino, over the river and into the city. Then switched to the 75 along Flinders Street and on to Richmond.

Rasheed was still there. He was sleeping, but somehow looking more comfortable, on one side and curled up in a position of his own choosing.

Jason emerged from the back room, stretching, rubbing his eyes.

'Been having a zizz. Had an early start. Been on the go since 5.30. Thought I'd drop by and see how the invalid was doing. He woke up about an hour ago, still hurting. So I gave him a coupla Panadol.'

'Should've fed him the whole bloody bottle. I've had enough of this. It's time to get him out of here.'

Bromo flipped open his phone, thumbed down the record of received calls, checking names and numbers. She was there.

'I'm returning your package. Damaged goods. What address shall I use?'

She swore, and shouted. He held the earpiece at arm's length, shrugging.

Jason grinned: 'Not happy?'

'Immense displeasure. She'll get over it.'

The doona-wrapped roll on the floor stirred at the sound of their voices. Rasheed opened an eye and looked up at them. Bromo brought the phone back to his ear. Fiona was still talking, but quieter, slower, determined.

He broke in. He'd had enough of this.

'Forget the threats. Think about Rasheed. He's your baby. Find someone who cares enough about him to give him the attention he needs. Perhaps the local vet.'

'Bastard.'

'Very likely. But irrelevant. Just get him out of here. He's making the place look untidy.'

There were burbled sounds coming up from the floor. Mostly indistinct, muffled by bandages and bedding. Jason bent down and listened.

'Same story,' he translated. 'Seems pretty keen to contact this Max guy.'

Bromo thought back to his meeting with Liz Shapcott, her guarded manner, her veiled warnings and the portfolio of architectural drawings. And then what he'd learned from Aurelia.

He decided to test the waters.

'Miss Leoncavallo ....' He detected the intake of breath.

'Yeah, been doing a bit of snooping myself. People been talking, filling me in. Discovering your name was just the start. It seems you're not the flavour of the month in some quarters. Somehow I don't think that picture you've been waving around is going be quite such hot property. Maybe you should just destroy it. Now, about your battered friend....'

'Okay, I need to make a couple of calls. I'll arrange something.'

The voice had softened, sounded almost reasonable. She promised to ring back in five minutes.

Bromo looked at Jason and nodded towards Rasheed.

'Better make him comfortable,' he said. 'He's going on a journey. One-way ticket out of here.'

They eased Rasheed into a sitting position and held a bottle of water to his lips. He sucked in thirstily; smiled and grunted his thanks and laid back on to a heap of cushions Jason put under his shoulders.

Fiona kept her promise. She rang back: 'Okay, we'll pick him up. But we'll need a hand.'

'Anything to help.'

'We're on our way.'

Not only were they on their way, Bromo realised, but they'd also be going on to somewhere else, depositing Rasheed.

'Got your wheels, Jase?'

'Yeah. Got lucky. Manage to find a park around the corner.'

'Get down there. Quick. Do a bit of sleuthing for me. When Fiona and crew leave, try tailing them. See where they go. But don't do anything stupid. Keep your distance.'

'No worries. My middle name's Caution. I'll ring you on the mobile.'

The door closed behind him. They'd cut it fine. Within minutes the security phone rang, long and insistent, signalling impatience. Bromo buzzed them in. They clumped up the stairs: two slabs of sub-humanity, shaven heads, no necks, walking like apes, no small talk - just grunts.

They motioned for Bromo to lend a hand in lifting the co-matose Rasheed. Somehow they got him down the stairs and into the back compartment of a wagon with tinted windows, engine running. Fiona was behind the wheel. She turned round, shades up on her forehead.

'Thank you, Mr Perkins. We'll be in touch.'

She pursed lightly lipsticked lips into the beginnings of a smile: 'We have some unfinished business, I think.'

Bromo jerked his head up. What was that - a hint, an invitation, a threat? He looked at her, seeking interpretation. But the shades were back down. Black impenetrable lenses stared back at him. Like a head of section he once worked under, always behind dark glasses, never showing her eyes, knowing they could reveal far too much.

The van screeched off. Rubber burned. A consignment of damaged goods about to be delivered.

Bromo watched as Jason eased out of his parking space, following in light traffic. Down Bridge Road, shops closing, no spare seats at footpath cafe tables, both vehicles taking a sharp left. Out of sight.

Already he was having second thoughts about involving his mate. It wasn't Jason's problem. Car chases, tracking other vehicles, trailing people were best left to the experts. It was tricky, risky stuff he once knew too much about. Dangerous business. It belonged in a distant world to which he had long closed his mind. One he was reluctantly beginning to revisit.

He opened his phone. He had to tell Jason to come back.

It rang before he could push a button.

'Shit, that was short.'

'Yeah. Motor didn't even get a sweat up. They pulled up a few blocks away. Outside some bloody great brick building. Quiet street. No one else around. Couldn't stop. Would've been too bloody obvious.'

Thank God his middle name was Caution, thought Bromo.

'Parked around the corner and walked back. Took a sticky.'

'What happened to Mr Caution?'

'He's fine.' There was a chuckle in his voice. 'Didn't get too close. It looks like some sort of factory, all boarded up. Not my usual part of town. All a bit dark and industrial.'

Bromo didn't want a commentary on the back streets of Richmond. He tried to keep the impatience out of his voice.

'Cut the tour guide stuff, Jase. What about our friends? Where'd they go?'

The sound of failure and disappointment in Jason's voice was all too clear.

'Not too sure, mate. Must've found a way in. One minute they were there, next minute all gone. Car drove off.'

'Anything else?'

'Building's still got a name high up on one wall if that's any help.'

'Go on, surprise me.'

'It says Mack's.'

'No surprise, Jase. No bloody surprise at all. Come back here. I'll shout you a beer.'

TEN

When would he learn that nights were made for sleeping? That no one in their right mind spent the dark hours staring at the inanities of Letterman or wading through the shallows of America's early morning news shows.

Some nights there were videos to watch of programs he'd missed earlier in the evening, or delayed telecasts of footy and rugby. Other times he'd spin the dial of the radio on to one of the FM classical music stations which ventured into works by lesser known, edgier composers once the traditionalists had slumbered off. On many a night he'd been soothed and calmed by the mesmerising ripples of Philip Glass or even the more discordant notes of Ligeti.

He knew he needed more sleep. But old habits die hard. The night was when you had to be on your guard. It was in the middle hours when they came for you, catching you unawares, knowing the body was at its most defenceless. Not the time to relax totally like 9-to-5ers everywhere seemed to do so easily.

He picked up the two manila folders, seeking answers. But they revealed little more than Jason had told him, and what others had hinted at. There were the usual divisions. Those wanting development under the label of progress were at odds with equally vocal opponents determined to preserve the past, even if it meant forgoing modern comforts and conveniences.

The folders contained minutes of meetings, letters to and from council officers, a couple of non-committal legal opinions - as if lawyers ever offered any other sort of view, fence-sitters all. He found it all run-of-the-mill, predictable. Not enough to go rampaging through someone's home over. And certainly no reason for the beating Rasheed had suffered.

Bromo skimmed once more through the folders, checking. Rasheed wasn't even mentioned. There were no answers to be found there. The plans he had glimpsed at Liz Shapcott's indicated she was somehow involved with the Mack's building. However, she was saying nothing. Fiona Leoncavallo knew more than she was letting on. And Aurelia showed all the signs of turning into a loose cannon and taking matters into her own hands, regardless.

The radio station programmers had done the right thing and turned once more to Philip Glass. Tinkling, stream of consciousness music. Dead of night stuff, taking the mind down byways it found too hard to access during daytime distractions.

For a while, Bromo laid back, eyes closed, letting images of recent events flicker across the screen of his mind. It was unlinked, jerky, episodic stuff, making no sense. A flickering old movie with no clear links between the frames.

He picked up his jacket from where he'd slung it over the armchair. It was a cool night outside. A southerly was coming in over Bass Strait, bringing polar chill.

Even at this late hour there was life out on the street. A steady stream of cars commuting from city to suburbs. Shift workers shuffling into the 24-hour supermarket. A mechanical sweeper whirring along the footpath. Late night desperates putting their cents and dollars into the pokies at the all-hours pub while others lined up the balls at its pool tables. He turned a corner and almost bumped into a couple of drunks pissing their night's intake up against the wall.

'Not a good look, lads. Didn't your mums teach you not to do that?'

'Fuck off.'

'In your boot.'

He kept moving, quickened his pace. Shouldn't have done that. No point in inviting aggro.

Jason had been spot-on. Mack's was just a few blocks, a short walk, away. And dark and industrial. No traffic. One old codger, huddled and limping, giving his equally ageing mutt its last toilet break of the day, shuffled past and disappeared into one of a row of low, squat weatherboard cottages.

Looming over everything was the massive three-storey brick pile where Jason reckoned Rasheed had been offloaded. Facing one long side was fenced-off wasteland, probably used as a parking lot during the day.

Bromo looked up, checking. A sign high up verified this was Mack's. Lower down, a real estate agent's board offered the site for sale, for redevelopment. A big 'Sold' sticker was angled across the board, its edges peeling away, flapping in the breeze. It had all the appearance of being far from recent. Sold, maybe, but there were no signs of action by the buyer.

The only windows were ranged high up under the roof line, out of reach, many of them cracked and broken. What must have once been doors for staff were boarded up, covered in heavy wire mesh, padlocked. Big wide entrances for trucks and semi-trailers had their roller doors firmly bolted down.

Attempts had been made to push in one of the roller doors but the gap was covered by thick wooden beams bolted to the brickwork. Another door had been forced inward, but was now covered by steel mesh. It was a factory fortress, barricaded and barred against intruders and squatters.

Bromo walked briskly round the perimeter, seeking an entrance, anywhere that could have been used to get Rasheed inside. He found a door in the only alcove not littered with bottles, plastic bags and old newspapers. It was padlocked. A folded card inserted in the hasp showed it had been checked by a security service. He turned back to the street. Heard a noise, but reacted too slowly, too late.

The two no-necks who had removed Rasheed from his apartment loomed over him, filling the narrow doorway. One dug him in the ribs. He felt a heavy hand on his shoulder from the other. Saw the swinging arm far too late. Coming down to the side of his head. Knocking him down and sidewards.

His head struck the brickwork. The first bruiser caught him as he fell, wrapping arms around him. He enjoyed a brief moment of lucidity, thinking so this is how gorillas embrace. Then darkness.

ELEVEN

The room had been set up as an office, complete with desk, filing cabinet, fax machine, printer and the inevitable computer. It looked like the inside of a Portakabin - one of those multi-purpose prefabs seen on building sites and used as temporary dwellings, offices and classrooms when fire or other disaster struck. Fully plumbed with electricity connected. A reverse cycle air-conditioner, jutting out high on one wall, whirred noisily as it strived to freshen the musty air.

'Welcome to Mack's,' said Fiona. She had a laptop in front of her, lid open. 'Time to talk, I think.'

Bromo sat facing her across the desk. He had little option, the heavy hands of the two no-necks kept him firmly in place. One stood behind him. The other was at his side.

'Any chance of a drink?'

She reached under the desk and brought up a litre bottle of water, splashing a measure into a paper cup.

'Gee, thanks.' At least it wasn't out of a tap with a questionable connection to the nearest standpipe. 'Got anything stronger?'

'Later. Maybe.'

'If I co-operate, isn't that the phrase?'

'Could be.'

He studied her face: a small oval shape, slightly concave with snub nose, thick eyebrows neatly trimmed, their blackness betraying the blondeness of her hair. The lips were two thin lines, subtly outlined and, just occasionally, turning slightly up: a glimmer of a smile, softening the harshness he'd come to associate with her.

'Where's Rasheed?'

A slight nod of her head to one side.

'In there.'

He noticed a door in a side wall.

'How is he?'

'Sleeping. Getting better. He's got all he needs right now. Bed, toilet, water.'

Again she almost smiled, as if to reassure him. Perhaps she did have a soft and caring side. He felt a tightening of the pressure on his shoulders. Solid fingers digging into tender flesh, finding the pressure points. They were getting through to him. It was time to change the subject, move on.

'So, what are we talking about?'

'You, Mr Perkins.'

'Short talk, then.'

Fiona tapped at the laptop's keyboard.

'I don't think so.' She peered at the screen, a slight screwing up of her eyes.

'There's plenty in here.'

Bromo stiffened, rolled his shoulders. It provoked a quick reaction from a no-neck, tightening his grip.

'Ease up, mate. I'm not going anywhere.'

He did another shoulder roll, deliberate, defiant.

'You heard her, we've got things to discuss.'

The pressure on his shoulders eased.

'Leave us,' she ordered. 'Mr Perkins has got the message. He's happy to stay and talk.'

'Not happy. Not talking either. Just listening.'

The heavy pair moved away. Bromo glanced over his shoulder as they went side by side through a door barely wide enough for them to squeeze through.

'You're right,' she said. 'They won't be far away.'

'Never gave it a thought.'

She tapped again at the keyboard, bringing the screen back to life. 'So, what's a former British intelligence agent doing running a part time travel agency in suburban Melbourne?'

Silence.

'And why was that intelligence agent suddenly shunted off to Australia a few years ago?'

Silence.

'Especially when an inquiry was about to begin into the death of an entrepreneur rumoured to have links to foreign activists.'

His hand wandered up to his ear. Started rubbing. They'd promised his cover would never be blown. He would have a new life, a new identity, and no links to the past. And now some two-bit blonde hustler seemed to have access to his complete file.

'It's all history.' Shrug it off. Bluff.

Her thin lips turned slightly upwards. A knowing smile. A downward tilt of her head towards him.

'History lives, Mr Perkins. You can't dismiss it that easily.'

'Henry Ford did. He thought it was bunk.'

'He was entitled to his opinion. Tycoons generally are. However ...'

Bromo noted a slow intake of breath, a lifting of the shoulders, showing her impatience.

'You're no Henry Ford and it's you we're talking about,' she said.

Bromo's head still ached from the thumping he'd received outside. His shoulders felt bruised, the whisky and fatigue were kicking in. He saw no reason he should be sitting in a deserted factory being bailed up by some slick sheila and her hoons just because she had somehow laid her hands on a couple of happy snaps and gained access to his security file. He'd had enough.

The metal feet of the chair grated as he pushed it back. He stood and grasped the edge of the table, bending forward and lowering into her. She leaned back, away, startled. For the first time he saw a lack of confidence, alarm even, in her eyes.

'I don't know who you are or what you're after,' he said. 'You threatened me with a couple of pictures which I'd rather didn't go any further and I did what you asked. You've made your charge. I've paid the bill. End of story.'

The door crashed open as he ended his outburst. A pair of massive hands clamped down on each shoulder, forcing him back into the chair, body pressed hard into the seat. The no-necks had come running as soon as the chair leg had scraped out its message.

He shrugged, resigned. This was beginning to look like old times; the past revisited. He recalled a hint somewhere in the manual suggesting it was sometimes best to take the line of least resistance. Right now it seemed like good advice.

'Okay, I'll listen.'

Her steely composure had returned. With an upward wave of her hand she dismissed the two heavies.

'I'll be fine. Mr Perkins has had his say. Now we're going to have a friendly chat.'

As they loosened their grip Bromo felt the shorter of the two give an extra squeeze on his upper arm. Their eyes met. The man winked.

'Take care, buddy. You'll be right.'

They went as quickly as they'd come – out into the empty factory.

TWELVE

Fiona reached sideways and downwards, pulling out the lower drawer of the desk and coming back up with a bottle in one hand and two glasses in the other.

'I believe your preferred drink is scotch, Mr Perkins. Mind if I join you?'

'It's your party.'

She poured. Generous shots, a cheap blend, no water.

'Okay. Here's the deal. You help us solve a few problems and you'll get the pictures back. Gerry Nuyen will know nothing of his wife's activities and you can go back to pretending to be a travel agent.'

'What's your role in all this?'

'I'm a consultant.'

He shrugged and let a grin crease his face.

'That much I know. And it means bugger all. Everyone who can't get a real job becomes a consultant. The government's full of them. Who's your boss?'

'I don't have bosses. I have clients and allegiances. As I said, I'm a consultant.'

'The highest bidder wins, eh?'

'If they pay as well as bid.'

She stared back at him. Unblinking. Deeply dark eyes giving nothing away.

'Enough of me, Mr Perkins. We're here to talk about you. You have a most interesting CV. There are aspects of it which attract us. I suppose you could say you have been head-hunted.'

'No comment.'

It was a slight deviation from what he'd been taught. Stay silent. Give them nothing. Old habits die hard and their training had been unforgiving, relentless. At least it had ensured his survival in many places where the presence of strangers was questioned. He'd practised it for years, but rarely had to use it. More often it had been a matter of making conversation, edging his way in, embroidering the character he was using as a mask. Blending in, becoming part of the local scene. A slim but stocky build and average height helped. So did a slightly swarthy non-English complexion. In so many countries where he'd operated tall people were regarded almost as freaks and fair hair was a beacon.

He still fumed at the ineptitude of his masters who had assigned him to a Latin American country in the company of a six-foot-six basketballing blond beanpole who attracted a chattering trail of amazed five-foot-nothing swarthy locals wherever they went. But he'd survived. And he was still doing it.

Fiona took a sip from her glass, a heavy silver band on her middle finger clinking as it knocked the side.

'So, once again, what's a Pommie intelligence operative doing working as a travel agent in an Australian suburb?'

'Wrong. I'm an Australian. I've gone through all the ceremonies. Fully naturalised, neutralised, cauterised.'

She sniffed. Almost derision.

'Once a Pom, always a Pom. The great colonisers, still believing they've a divine right to rule the world. Their way's the only way.'

'Be careful or I'll start singing Jerusalem.'

'I'd rather you didn't.' She cracked a smile. 'We had a bellyful of that during the Ashes. Could be your last hurrah, too. Seems they're going to ban it for fear of upsetting your Moslem compatriots.'

Her smile faded. Her palms pushed down on the desk as she stretched her spine, firm breasts pointing almost aggressively at him. Enticing, seductive.

'No comment is not really good enough, Mr Perkins,' she said. 'We know too much. It's all in here.'

Bromo nodded towards the laptop.

'In that case, there's probably nothing more I can add. Seems like you've got me all wrapped up.'

He shrugged, turned his palms upwards.

'Stalemate.'

He felt the silence between them. It was fragile and tense. Moments stretching into seconds, both leaning back in their chairs, each staring down the other. He gave thought to walking out. Then remembered the two thugs waiting in the wings. He thought, too, of the photograph and the damage it could do, not so much to himself but to Aurelia. He might survive but he feared for her.

Bromo was the first to hear the groan from beyond the door at the end of the room. He twisted his head in the direction of the sound. Eyebrows raised. Then she heard it, too.

'Seems like your patient needs you,' said Bromo.

She turned to him as she headed for the door: 'I think you'd better come too. He might want to talk.'

Bromo picked up the bottle of scotch.

'Maybe he'd just like to have what we're having,' he suggested.

There was a foldaway bed halfway along the room, pushed against the wall. Rasheed was trying to ease himself up into a sitting position, levering his body on the arm not swathed in bandages. What they could see of his face was creased in pain. Fiona put an arm around his shoulders, helping him up. Bromo edged the bottle against his lips.

'Painkiller medicine,' he said.

One corner of Rasheed's mouth turned slightly upward. A smile? A grimace? A thank you? No way of knowing.

Bromo sneaked a look around the room. Sink, small electric two-ring stove atop a cupboard, a curved plastic cubicle in the far corner presumably housing toilet and shower, one shabby armchair, even a TV set in a cabinet.

'Good set-up.'

'It does what it's supposed to do,' she replied, her skirt tight around haunches and buttocks as she fussed over the battered Rasheed.

'And what's that?'

She straightened: 'It's his home. For now.'

Bromo feigned interest. 'How is he?'

'It'll take a while. We've had him checked out. He's got a broken arm, two cracked ribs, lots of cuts here and there, plenty of bruises. A bloody mess, in fact.'

'Who did it? Why?'

The questions seem to light a fuse, sparking Rasheed into life and using his good arm to call Bromo to his bedside. His voice added a couple of decibels and became more coherent, no longer groaning.

'They're all bloody bastards,' he ranted. 'All of them.'

Bromo leaned over him: 'Who are they?'

He felt Fiona's hand on his arm, firm and restraining. But he persisted. 'Who, Rasheed? Who?'

'Council peoples, cops, Nuyen, newspapers.'

He was almost shouting.

'Peoples, peoples everywhere.'

Fiona pushed Rasheed gently back into the pillows, soothing, calming.

'Not now, Pete. Rest. We're taking care of things. Mr Perkins is going to help us.'

She turned and glared at Bromo: 'Aren't you, Mr Perkins?'

Now was not the time to disagree. He almost felt sympathy for Rasheed. And why argue with a Fiona reverting to her steely best?

Rasheed burbled on: 'I just try to run a business, make money for my family, my children.'

His voice was less strident, softer, and the words were running into each other, a verbal collision, his burst of energy spent, eyes closing. Fiona rested a calming hand on his forehead.

'Try to get some sleep, Pete.'

'The consultant as nursemaid,' muttered Bromo.

She glared: 'Smart arse.'

Bromo fell in line behind her, holding the whisky bottle, as she made for the door, heels clicking on the bare boarding. The two hoons were nowhere to be seen. Bromo assumed they were lurking elsewhere in the building and doubtless well within earshot. He didn't imagine they'd be far away.

'Another night's sleep and he'll be much better,' she said, turning off the light in Rasheed's room and marching back across the office area.

Two masked figures barred her way. One was a gross caricature of George W Bush; the other, much taller and broader, a rough imitation of Tony Blair, the mask's creased papier-mâché grin giving no clue to the person it hid. They moved quickly, silently. The George Bush look-alike clasped one hand over Fiona's mouth, the other round her waist, pinning her arms to her side. The person in the Tony Blair mask shirt-fronted Bromo as he stepped through the doorway.

'Say nothing, do nothing,' said a voice that sounded deliberately deepened and distorted. However, it left no doubt as to his gender. Or to his ability to wreak grievous bodily harm if disobeyed.

'Wait two minutes, then go home,' the would-be Tony Blair growled. 'Don't argue. We'll leave the lock open. Just phone a friend to let you out.'

Silently, swiftly they bundled a kicking, struggling Fiona out through the door, closing it gently behind them.

Bromo's first instinct was to follow. He took a step towards the door. Then he realised, he was alone with a sleeping Rasheed in the other room and a laptop with its lid raised open and its screen still glowing. To hell with Fiona and two minutes. She could fight her own battles and he'd take all the time he needed.

For a while Bromo stood stock still, recovering from the suddenness of his captor's own abduction, but also listening, trying to detect movements beyond the exit. There was nothing, except for muted traffic noise. He thought of waking Rasheed to tell him what had happened. But the man needed his sleep.

He took a fresh look around the room. It was a toss-up between the laptop and the filing cabinet. The cabinet won, the computer to be saved to last. Hopefully something to savour and spend time with - like the woman he dreamed of but had yet to find. Two tugs on the cabinet's metal handles told him what he'd really expected but had hoped would not be so. A man in denial. The cabinet was locked.

Bromo moved behind the desk - a cheap and basic two-drawer structure, matching its surrounds. He was just looking, not touching. Not really expecting to find much of use. A notepad lay open, but hadn't been used. A coffee mug, empty but unwashed, stood on a beer coaster. A cluster of ballpoint pens contained in an old honey jar. A small porcelain dish with a few coins in it. Loose change for parking meters.

Two phone books and a street directory sat atop each other on the desk's far edge. They were dog-eared and two years out of date. As a modern business miss, Fiona obviously phoned Enquiries rather than obey the adverts' urging and let her fingers do the walking through a book. Costlier, but presumably better for the image among her contemporaries.

Bromo gently eased open the deeper bottom drawer. Hardly a treasure trove of corporate secrets. An electric jug, a jar of instant coffee, four coffee mugs, a chunky pocket umbrella and a pair of runners, each with a sock tucked inside.

So, he concluded, she offers visitors a cuppa, kicks off her high heels for comfort and is prepared for bad weather. And she keeps her secrets somewhere else.

He pulled open the shallow top drawer. More odds and sods of office life. Paper clips, pens, pencils, old receipts, glue sticks, a stapler, two lipsticks and a partly used book of daily tram tickets, although he couldn't imagine the sleek Fiona strap-hanging on the Number 75 into the city. Also mingled in the mess was a compact disk envelope containing a CD of the type used for copying data or downloading music from the net.

It told him nothing. It could be the warbling of Britney Spears, Beethoven's Ninth, Fiona's housekeeping budget, a hundred things to do with mushrooms or the inside gen on Peter Rasheed and his business empire. All of which seemed unlikely, Bromo decided, as an indelible pen had been used to write LLL on the disk's surface - three letters which not even his ability as a cryptic crossword addict could link to anything he'd so far encountered. Unless some Shakespeare freak was studying *Love's Labours Lost*.

All the same, he decided, it was worth holding on to. That left the laptop, with its lid still raised but now with the blank screen of Windows at rest. Somewhere inside that little box Fiona was keeping the secrets of his former life. Until tonight Bromo believed they were just that - secret. Not destroyed as he would have wished, but at least safely retained deep in the archives of supposedly secure agencies.

He touched the mouse pad. The laptop's screen glimmered into life. The news was all bad. What he should have expected. Windows welcomed him to Fiona Leoncavallo's computer – and for a password to be typed in. She must have logged off before going in to tend to Rasheed. Savvy girl.

With faint hope he tapped out Fiona. Zilch. No response. Which is what he expected. She wouldn't make it that simple. He tried Leoncavallo, expecting nothing. Spot on. Zero.

The silence was becoming oppressive. He felt entombed. This was not where he wanted to be, now or at any other time. Briefly he thought of checking on Rasheed. And just as briefly thought better of it. Bugger him; he's why I'm in this mess.

Bromo moved to the door through which Fiona had been bundled. Cautiously he turned the handle, pushing outwards, wary and guarded. He stepped out into a vast walled-in space, soaring up more than two storeys to steel rafters and a pitched corrugated iron roof. Sections of metal tracks remained embedded in the floor.

Bromo stood still, gaining a sense of size and space. He discovered the portable that Fiona had made into an office for herself and lodgings for Rasheed was wedged into the far corner, looking lost and tiny, a mere toy box in such vastness.

This was serious factory space that once housed a rolling mill for steel fabricators, turning the stuff out in sheets, rods and pipes. He could almost feel the rumble of gigantic machines pounding away, sense the heat and dust endured by factory hands whose skin was permanently embedded with grease and grime. Yet they'd all long gone. Like so many of the suburb's factories, the place had been stripped back to its brick walls and pitted concrete floor. Not a skerrick of its former life remained.

He felt dwarfed by the immensity. You could hold a couple of footy games in here and still leave room for spectators. Or lose two or three semi-trailers.

The walls were covered by a massive display of graffiti - huge tags, painstakingly drawn and coloured. They went well above head height, bright slashes of cobalt blue, huge condensed white lettering outlined in black. Patches of red and yellow ensured the mural's continuity, obliterating the original brickwork.

Bromo appraised it. Considering it as art. Standing back in typical gallery-goer's pose, one arm supporting the elbow of the other, a hand gently caressing his chin in earnest contemplation. He judged it colourful, vibrant, and skilfully executed and a definite improvement on forlorn bare brick factory walls. He marked the artists down for their house-keeping habits. They showed an unhealthy disregard for their surrounds.

Cans, fast food wrappers, pizza boxes, plastic bags and bottles littered the floor. Despite all the external signs of forbidden entry, it was obvious someone other than Rasheed and his cronies had made their way in. Bromo picked up a McDonald's hamburger flip-top container. It was almost clean. A recent occupant's. One of the pizza cartons provided further proof. It was as good as new, pristine, untouched by the factory's grime. Bromo raised the lid and found the remains of a capriccioso – someone didn't like olives. It was stale but not yet on the nose. Two or three days old at most.

He'd grown accustomed to the gloom, relieved by the diffused glow from street lights sifted through the mesh-covered windows at the roof line. He noticed what looked like benches lined up against the far wall. He picked his way carefully through the litter and debris. There were not only benches, but an assortment of cupboards and broken down trestle tables. On their last legs, he punned to himself. Spray cans and tins of paint sat on the benches. A tall easel like structure stood waiting for some modern Rembrandt. A couple of long ladders leaned against the wall. A graffiti artist's workshop.

Bromo opened the one cupboard door not already hanging off its hinges. Inside were two rolled-up sleeping bags, a torch and a bong. He guessed it to be a street kid's refuge. He walked the length of the wall until it ended at a floor-to-ceiling opening, wide enough to drive a truck through. It led into another deserted space. More rail tracks on the floor, a couple of rusted chains hanging from roof-high pulleys and one lonely tubular frame chair, its canvas seat intact but the fabric for its back support hanging torn and useless through the frame.

The graffitists had yet to make their mark here except for one small panel where a rectangle of brickwork had been given an undercoat of white. In the centre was a perfect replica of a tiger's head framed in gold stones and clenching a long-stemmed red flower in its jaws. It was almost identical to the brooch he'd seen at the house where Rasheed was bashed, and again on Liz Shapcott's coat. This time there was the addition of two words. Underneath, in a bold cursive script, the graffitist had painted Tiger POPPies. He walked over to take a closer look.

'Hey. You. Stop right there.'

The voice echoed off the factory walls. Bromo froze. His mind went into flashback mode. He was back in familiar territory, on risky ground he had no wish to revisit. Slowly he turned. In the gap he'd just walked through stood a tall scrawny youth, hands clasped around what even in the dim light looked very much like some sort of firearm. A shotgun, most likely. Did it really matter? Firearms are firearms.

Bromo recognised the signs. The youth was edgy, caught unawares, probably sleeping rough in some corner of the factory. Dangerous, he assessed. Play it cool. Keep calm.

'Just looking,' he said. 'I like your work.'

'Not mine,' grunted the youth.

He had a blanket around his shoulders, a woolly beanie clamped over matted long black hair. Baggy cargo pants covered skinny legs standing in a pair of dirty runners.

'You're off limits,' said the youth. 'You know the rules. You come, you go, and you stick to your space.'

A case of mistaken identity, guessed Bromo. Some agreement seemed to have been struck between Rasheed's people and the graffiti artists. The two sides had assumed the roles of landlords and tenants and neither were legal occupiers. He spread his arms wide. A supplicant. Never upset a man toting a gun.

'I'm new here,' he offered.

'Thought I'd take a look around.'

The gun jerked sideways.

'You heard. No looking. On your way.'

Bromo gave a shrug. You'll get no argument from me it said as he moved towards the exit. He pointed towards the tiger's head.

'That your work?' he asked. 'Pretty snazzy.'

The youth hesitated, uncertain how to respond to this conversational gambit.

'Maybe,' he grunted.

He focused the gun again on Bromo, reinforcing his role as armed guard.

'What's it to you?' he asked..

The conversation continued. Bromo seized his chance.

'Interesting work. What's it all about?'

He could almost hear the cogs grinding away in the youth's head, assessing the situation, afraid of losing the upper hand, weighing up the risks of talking.

'A special job. The women asked me to do it.'

'What women?'

Bromo saw him tense. He recognised the signs. The youth had said too much, was losing his grip on his role and was about to compensate.

'Shut up. Time to go. On yer bike.'

Bromo moved cautiously to unflip his phone: 'Jase? Sorry mate. Come and let me out.'

99

THIRTEEN

JASON TOOK A WHILE to get to Mack's, but had little trouble in finding the door in the factory wall that Bromo's phone calls guided him to.

'It's locked. It's got a security guard's ticket in it.'

'Window dressing,' said Bromo. 'Give it a pull.'

He did, and the door squeaked open. Bromo squeezed out into the street. They replaced the lock and the security company's calling card.

'Great security,' grunted Jason. 'Someone must be on the take.'

'And that's only part of the story. Where's the ute?'

Jason pointed, but said nothing. Bromo was slow to pick up on the message. He'd been pushing the boundaries of friendship and Jason's silence on the drive home let him know it. Bridges needed to be repaired.

They pulled up outside Bromo's apartment. As usual, he'd left the lights on. It provided a comforting welcome.

'Thanks mate. I owe you one.'

'Make that one dozen. With ring pulls.'

Bromo opened the car door.

'Come up. You can open the account now.'

Jason kept his hands on the steering wheel, shoulders slumped forward.

'Another time. I've got more urgent business. If she's still there.'

It was said with feeling and several layers of meaning. Bromo turned back into the car, reaching out a hand and clasping Jason's arm.

'Sorry, pal. I didn't realise. Quite forgot. Give her my apologies. Do I know her?'

Jason shrugged. He said nothing. Bromo let go his grip and got out of the car. Once again he'd forgotten other people didn't live solo, celibate lives. They had order, routine, friends they met regularly, women they shared a bed with, even socialised with, and created a template for their lives.

He trudged up the stairs, remorseful at the expectations he'd imposed on his friend. No man should be called upon to leave a warm bed and a warm woman at the whim of a mate. But Jason had responded. No questions asked.

Bromo keyed open his front door, thankful to be back in his cocoon but unable to stop his mind whirring over the puzzle presented by the tiger's head. There seemed to be a link between Rasheed, Liz Shapcott and Aurelia Nuyen. But what was the women's connection to street kids and graffiti artists?

'The women asked him to do it,' the youthful guardian of the logo on the factory wall had said.

And what the hell was a tiger - the aggressive symbol of the local footy team - doing chewing on a flower? A poppy, no less: Tiger POPPies, as the wall writing specifically declared.

It was all too much for Bromo's weary mind. Bed beckoned but, as he began undressing, he felt the CD in his jacket pocket. Curiosity scored a victory over sleep.

As the disk whirred in the computer slot, he poured a jigger of scotch. Maybe not a good idea in the eyes of the health police, but a man needed some quiet pleasures.

The screen came up in a blaze of psychedelic colours and rapidly changing patterns. After a few seconds, this visual assault settled into a single page bordered by pictures of an array of busty young women. In the centre ran the bold words Locality Love Links. And, underneath, to leave the viewer in no doubt: Linking Local Lovers: Where Real Men Meet Real Women.

Bromo sipped and sniffed. So that was LLL. Yet another online dating service. One of the dozens, probably hundreds, littering the internet as the world's dateless and desperate searched for their perfect partner.

He put the cursor on an arrow pointing to the next page and clicked. More girlie pictures. Not an ugly one among them. How strange that only the good-lookers, the ones least likely to be hard up for a date, were used by the site builders to lure the lovelorn. When would the poor suckers wake up to themselves?

Then it dawned: this was a one-way street. It was directed completely at men trawling the net for women. No pictures of beefcake males, with polished pecs. Not a muscly male to be seen. This was no genuine dating site, not even close to one, despite its promises.

He noted the usual warning about needing to be over 18 before delving further into the site. It was a waste of words and screen space. Simply more window dressing, suggesting responsibility but, in reality, working less as a warning and more as an inducement to proceed.

He clicked to turn the page. And there was the sales pitch:

Why go searching the world for romance when the love of your life is probably living almost on your doorstep? Too many sites bring heartbreak when they should bring love. You find that ideal woman, the dream girl, only to get a response from the far side of the world.

Locality Love Links removes the heartache. It removes the disappointment. Our advanced search engines make sure you contact only those women in places where you want them to be. Our local lovelies are looking for love. And they're waiting for you. Your fair lady's on the street where you live.

'Oh my gawd,' Bromo cussed aloud as he read the conclusion's clichéd come-on. 'Oh my bloody gawd.'

Were there really men sitting gazing into computer screens responding to this lurid language? Silly question; of course there were, but that didn't make it any easier to understand. Less obvious was the reason for the LLL disk being in Fiona Leoncavallo's desk drawer. She was clearly no sad sack frustrated male.

Bromo sipped from his glass. He thought of his encounters with Fiona. Maybe she was somehow using the information to do some more of that so-called gentle persuading Bromo had experienced with that picture of him and Aurelia Nuyen. Or perhaps the answer lay with Rasheed. Maybe this was how he spent his spare time and she was simply keeping the disk for him to play with once he felt better. Recuperation by perving.

He clicked with the mouse. Another page, another come-on. One improbably curved and barely clothed long-haired blonde siren almost filled the screen, smilingly invitingly at the viewer. 'Tell me where you live and I'll find you love' promised a message ballooning from her puckered and luridly painted lips.

Bromo moved on. The next page was simple and formal. Love awaits, it claimed. I bet it does, thought Bromo. And waits, and waits, and waits. He was asked to type in his post-code and tick his preferred age group. In went 3121. He hesitated over the age groups. Clicked on 30-35. What the hell, everyone lies on the internet.

Another page came up. A banner headline proclaimed, 'We're waiting to meet you'. Ranged in a column down the screen was a gallery of briefly-clad women. His eyes wandered down the names alongside the pictures: Sonia, Delia, Tanya, Natasha, Livia …. There seemed an odd sort of sameness about them; understandably false to cloak their real identities, but also as if fabricated by just one person with a narrow sense of the exotic.

Whatever happened to Jenny, Madge and Annie, wondered Bromo. Were such names deemed too ordinary to be presented as love chicks?

There was a sameness about the women's appearance, too. These were the faces seen wherever sex was used to sell everything from sports cars to soap powders, or where sex itself was being sold.

Already he was bored. He couldn't imagine how anyone could spend time trawling through such an obviously fake site. These weren't the women you saw walking the local footpaths, drifting in and out of the shops, chattering away over coffee or chardonnay or hustling for sales at an estate agent's Open for Inspection.

These were the bodies of airbrushed, waxed, uplifted, Botoxed and totally plastic dolly birds. Not the chic executive types who spent thousands of bucks a year on shoes but also surrounded themselves with all the gadgetry modern technology could offer. Thinking, buzzy, go-getting types who weren't averse to a good lay and going online to seek it – and there were plenty of them out there - would never present themselves like this gallery of inflated airheads.

He tried one more click. It brought up another gallery of make-believe allegedly local lovelies. Only one stood out as what Bromo found himself defining as a real person. And it looked like a face he knew so well. Woozy and tired, he craned forward to make sure.

Halfway down the page, was Aurelia Nuyen. Or her double. The face, hair and eyes were those of the Aurelia he knew far too well. Only here she was called Carla.

And, as he well knew, the excessively bosomy body beneath was not hers but that of some other woman.

FOURTEEN

The ring was unfamiliar. Not the mobile. It took him a while to work out where the noise was coming from. By the time Bromo had thrown off the bedclothes and stumbled through into the living room the answering machine on his landline had taken over.

He ran his fingers through his matted hair, scratching his scalp in a feeble attempt at stimulation. Too bloody early by half. A faint lightening of the sky behind the triple towers of the housing commission high rise flats was pushing the night away. Two hot-air balloons floated over towards the east, the spasmodic flare of their burners clearly visible. It wasn't what he considered a time for telephone calls. Not even those accursed call centres in Mumbai rang at this ungodly hour.

He turned back towards the bedroom, leaving the answering machine to do its job. It had moved into message-taking mode.

Bromo stopped when he heard the voice, high-pitched, sing-song, almost falsetto. It was no one he recognised.

'This is your special invitation to a sensational showing at the Aurelia Nuyen Gallery,' trilled the voice. 'Be there when all is unveiled at 8.30 this morning. It is a show not to be missed.'

The recording stopped and shut off.

Bromo replayed it, listening intently. Someone was playing silly buggers. The voice sounded disguised, put on.

The answering machine's dial told him it was 5.50. Not a time he believed existed in a normal world. That was the dreamtime and the mischief-makers knew it. It was the hour when they came for you, aware that the barriers were down and they'd meet zero resistance. It was no time to be making calls inviting people to gallery openings. And what gallery lifted the shutters on its exhibitions at the Weetabix and coffee hour?

Bromo rolled back into bed, puzzled and weary. Something was definitely out of sync yet he didn't want to give it any more brain time. He'd already had a late and confused night trying to understand Aurelia Nuyen' s presence on the LLL website. He had scrolled through more pages of the dating service and found several other faces of women he thought he recognised. The closer he looked the more certain he was that none belonged to the bodies they were attached to.

Twice he decided to investigate further, clicking on the 'local lovely's' name and finding himself confronted by a page seeking payment by credit card for a subscription of three, six or twelve months. No pay, no view was the obvious message. Briefly he was tempted, if only to discover how Aurelia, otherwise known as Carla, was presenting herself to the lovelorn.

It was all too easy, especially in those dead of night hours when the depressed and rejected, probably loosened by booze, were reaching out for whatever company they could find. Simply type in a few personal details, add a credit card number and they could let their fetid imaginations wander through a galaxy of pseudo available beauties.

Reluctantly, he pushed the alarm button on the bedside clock, setting it for eight o'clock. That would allow just enough time to roll out of bed, scoff a coffee and amble up the street to the gallery. Something told him he had to be there, no matter how much he'd rather still be under the doona at such an ungodly hour. He switched off the bedside lamp, fumbled in the drawer for an eye mask against the encroaching light and gathered the bedding around him. The dreamtime called.

He never had a chance to respond. An explosive crack shattered any hopes of sleep. Bromo sat up shaking and sweating.

'Shit,' he uttered. And then there was silence.

He waited, frozen in the moment, expecting a sequel. There was nothing. He clicked the light back on. The splintering of the window had showered shards of glass over the floor and bed. Half a house brick lay on the floor by his bed, wrapped in a piece of paper held by a rubber band.

'The medium is the message,' muttered Bromo as he leaned over and picked it up. He slipped off the rubber band and unfolded the piece of paper.

The writing was large, black and bold. And illiterate.

'Be their,' it ordered. 'It all hapens at 8.30 this morning. Its a gallery event not to be mist.'

Bromo pondered the imperatives and the bad spellings. Did they point to the identity of the writer or were they a clumsy attempt to mislead? Someone must be out of their mind and completely out of touch to expect any of the arts crowd to be awake enough for an opening before sundown. A chilly breeze from the broken window and eyes he couldn't stop from glazing over persuaded him all questions could wait to be answered, at least until 8.30.

He went back to bed.

FIFTEEN

THE FOOTPATHS WERE STILL wet from a brief early morning shower that had crept in unexpectedly and unpredicted. by the weather bureau. Soggy sheets of paper and fast food wrappers clogged the gutters. The rain had passed as quickly as it had come and a thin layer of grey clouds was breaking up to reveal patches of blue. A fine, cool day seemed sure to follow – something that the bureau had forecast.

Bromo trudged up the hill, huddled into a nylon waterproof jacket and loathing the need for such activity this early in the day. He grudgingly admired the brisk young women in business suits and running shoes, power walking their way into the city at a pace spasmodically faster than the cars inching their way forward behind commuter-crowded trams. At least there were some who cared enough to wage war against the onset of the fat society.

He turned the corner. The Aurelia Nuyen Gallery was a couple of hundred metres further along. No directions, banners or signposts were needed. Just follow the crowd. Fifty or so people were clustered on the footpath outside the gallery. Cars were double-parked.

'You scored an invitation, too?'

It was Rob, regular gallery-goer and local arts freak.

'Yeah,' responded Bromo. 'Special event, it said. Couldn't miss that.'

Rob sidled closer, drooped his head, confiding.

'From what I hear it's extra special. Beyond art, if you know what I mean.'

Bromo didn't. It sounded too much like art-speak.

'Sort of cutting edge, eh?'

'More sort of in your face.'

'Gotcha.'

Bromo eased himself away, towards the police car he'd noticed parked at the kerbside. Its window was down and the arm of Senior Sergeant Grant Mayfield rested on the rim. Bromo leaned in: 'What's this, the culture cops?'

'Too right. Some of us can read as well.'

'Things are looking up. Last I heard it was all done by grunts and signs.'

'Stone Age stuff, man,' replied Mayfield. 'Your era. Things have changed. Anyway, what are you doing here?'

'I could ask the same of you.'

'Invited guest.'

'Me, too.'

'You and the rest of rent-a-crowd.'

'Bet you didn't get a brick through your window,' said Bromo.

'Only a funny phone call,' said Mayfield. 'Boss said we'd better take a look. Anyhow, what's the story? Isn't it a bit early for this sort of shindig? I thought you arty types only came out at night.'

'We can be tempted.'

'Didn't see any mention of free grog in the invitation.'

'Just hoping, I guess. A heart-starter wouldn't go astray.'

Bromo pushed back the cuff of his jacket and looked at his watch.

'Almost show time,' he said.

He nodded in the direction of the gallery. Its tall and solid double doors remained closed. A large canvas blind covered the huge window down to floor level.

'Not much sign of life,' he observed.

'Another bloody hoax if you ask me,' said Mayfield.

No one else seemed to agree. People were still arriving, many nursing takeaway cups of coffee. They clustered in small groups, looking towards the gallery. Bromo noticed Liz Shapcott on the far fringe as he tuned in to snippets of conjecture. A tall, thin woman wrapped in a calf-length black cape wondered aloud: 'What's Aurelia up to now?'

Her squat companion sporting cropped brown hair streaked with red strands acknowledged, 'She's always full of surprises.'

An elf-like man, sprightly but weathered and wizened, once an astute politician but now retired to a life of gallery openings and writers' festivals, suggested it was just another publicity stunt. But he'd stick around, just in case.

From the window of the patrol car came a sourer comment: 'All the usual suspects.'

'Handcuffs at the ready then?' said Bromo.

'You'd better believe it. This isn't a gathering of the innocents.'

'Care to name names?'

Mayfield fixed him with a long hard stare: 'What's it to you? I thought you'd given the game away, Bromo. Turned into an innocent bystander these days. What's your interest?'

Bromo shrugged, resentful at the way Mayfield had delved into the police database to unearth details of his former life yet recognising him as an old mate he perhaps could ask for help over Rasheed and his brush with the bruisers at Mack's. It might help to drop a word or two that there were heavy squads operating on his patch.

The decision was never made. A collective roar from the crowd had him spinning round to face the gallery. The window blind had been triggered swiftly upwards. Floodlights beamed down on to the single exhibit – a stark naked Fiona Leoncavallo strapped to two polished wooden beams in the shape of an X.

As the blinds went up she stared out at the gawpers on the footpath, like a roo caught in the headlights. Then realisation set in and her head slumped forward, her eyes squeezed tight as if by shutting them she'd make her audience disappear. No one was moving. The tableau was mesmerising.

Bromo found himself staring along with the rest of them. All his lurid imaginings had been proved correct. She certainly had a body to be admired - everything in desirable proportions with firm breasts in no need of support, a definite waist, slim hips, and an overall look of fitness and athleticism. She was obviously a good customer of the local tanning salon and was prepared to suffer the tortures of hot wax to achieve a neat Brazilian pubic coiffure.

At the foot of the spread-eagled Fiona was a boldly lettered sign, a title for this living exhibit and a possible explanation. Double Cross, A Study in Betrayal, it said.

As the surprise wore off the sound level picked up and the whispered comments began. Bromo heard a puzzled 'What's it about?'

Someone gave a wolf whistle, and was hushed by the woman in the black cloak. A twenty-something man in a business suit spoke into a mobile phone urging someone to 'Get down here quick.'

Bromo felt a presence. Mayfield had eased his bulk out of the patrol car and moved in alongside him.

'Now, that's my sort of art,' the policeman said. 'Perhaps we need to take a closer look. A charge of obscenity or indecent exposure could be on the cards.'

His colleague, already pushing at the gallery doors, stumbled forward as they yielded unexpectedly to his touch and he collided with a life-size statue of cavorting nymphs blocking the foyer.

'Seems we're in,' said Mayfield. 'I've always wanted to rescue a damsel in distress.'

'Pervert. Treat her gently,' Bromo urged him, sliding into the gallery while the chance was there. 'She's a victim, not an exhibit.'

'You know her?'

'In a business sort of way. Fiona Leoncavallo's the name. There are links to Peter Rasheed.'

'Oh shit. You'd better come with us. But quietly. If anyone asks, I didn't invite you.'

He moved in close behind Bromo and steered him into the gallery. His offsider had run ahead through to the rear of the building. He came back puffing as Bromo and Mayfield reached Fiona.

'No one there. Someone must have pulled up those blinds, but they've scarpered.'

'Speaking of which,' said Bromo, and stepped briskly across to the window, tugging at cords to shut off the view from a noticeably bigger crowd of spectators.

Mayfield pulled gently at the ties around Fiona's wrists and ankles. Despite his macho comments outside, he made efforts to avert his eyes from her nakedness. Bromo had no such qualms. He stood directly in front of her, his gaze fixed on her body.

'So now we're quits. I showed you mine and now you show me yours. Note, however, that I'm not taking pictures.'

She brazened it out, returning his gaze.

'Okay, you've had your look. Now find my clothes. They're probably in the office.'

'Use this for now.' Mayfield held out sheets of cloth that looked as if they were used for cloaking artworks.

Bromo helped her wind the sheets around her, blocking an urge to hold her close for a comforting hug. He'd had his fun, made his point and was almost feeling sorry for her. Playing the sympathy card might help him discover why she had embroiled him in a business that seemed to be getting nastier and nastier.

He put a hand gently under one elbow and helped her towards a corner of the room. It was partitioned off to hide a desk, filing cabinet and two chairs, one of which held a bundle of clothes.

'Care to tell me what happened?'

'Later. I'd like to dress before the fuzz start pestering me.'

She sorted through the garments on the chair and pulled out a flimsy piece of lacework. Letting the sheet fall loose, she dangled it from one hand, tantalising, like a stripper moving towards the finale of her show.

Bromo felt himself tense, stiffening with a sense of sexual excitement. She was playing with him, tempting and teasing. It was game-on if he wanted to play but he sensed she was just as likely to call time-out once he'd made a move. This was neither the time nor the place. He stood his ground, holding her gaze. A brief smile turned up the corners of her mouth.

'Sorry, show's over.'

It was as he'd thought: a tease, dangling a line to see if he'd bite. Bromo shrugged. The temptation was there but now was not the time or place to join in her game. He moved away, nodding towards the gallery and the two policemen.

'I'll go and chat to them. There are things they're going to want to know. I'll get them to go easy if I can.'

'Thanks. There's really no need. No harm done and I won't be laying charges. It was just a practical joke that went too far.'

Some joke, thought Bromo. She's taking it far too lightly. There was little funny about the sign that said Double Cross, A Study in Betrayal. Where was the anger, the fury? Once again she was covering up, protecting someone or something. And she was using him in her scheming.

If he could get the police to go easy on her he might get far enough into her good books to persuade her to confide in him. Call off the dogs and he might be able to worm his way in. If she was going to trample all over his comfort zone he at least deserved to know why.

The police sergeant and his offsider were standing in the centre of the gallery space, hands on hips.

'Well?' asked Mayfield. 'What's the story?'

'There isn't one. As you know, I lead a quiet life these days. The lady tells me she feels the same. No complaints, no charges to be laid, just a practical joke as far as she's concerned.'

'Oh yeah. How about causing a public nuisance? Perhaps a charge of assault. Someone did this.'

Bromo tugged at his earlobe.

'Not her fault. An innocent party. And no harm done.'

'The Rasheed connection?' asked Mayfield.

'He's involved somewhere along the line. Him or his hoons. Probably decided to let people know he's still around after his near death experience down by the river.'

'That was Rasheed?'

'Don't pretend you didn't know. Your boys probably helped rescue him.'

Surprise furrowed Mayfield's brow.

'Truly, that was Rasheed? We were ordered to steer clear. The homicide boys handled it. We were told nothing. The corpse story came from them.'

'Dangling the bait,' said Bromo. 'But it seems no one was biting. It's business as usual.'

'Meaning what?'

Bromo turned away and made pretence of looking at a huge unframed splash of paint hanging on one wall. Now was not the time to invite investigation of his own recent activities. Fortunately he was dealing with uniformed police, the foot soldiers. He'd make their day if they could avoid having to write a lengthy report on something that had ended as little more than a bit of titillating street theatre for commuters.

The click of heels on the polished wooden floor diverted their attention. Fiona was back to street-smart mode. She'd donned a long and flowing dark green and fawn dress with an uneven hemline, held in tightly at the waist by a wide leather and metal belt.

Mayfield showed concern. He offered her a chair.

'You okay, miss? Should we call a doctor?'

She shook her head: 'Nothing a hot shower and a coffee won't fix.'

'Sorry we can't oblige. We do need you to talk us through what happened. We'll let you get away as soon as possible.'

Bromo moved over to the window and eased an edge of the blind back from the glass to sneak a look outside. Traffic was again flowing freely. Liz was no longer there.

Most of the other onlookers had also gone. Little excitement was to be found in looking at a window with its blind pulled down. Only a few persistent stragglers remained, no doubt hoping the show would continue. All were familiar faces to Bromo.

The middle-aged woman in daggy tracksuit would have paused on her way to the gym to continue waging a daily and endless war on her ample waistline. The old woman clinging to her walking frame was from the nursing home a few doors up. Jim the Greek, wizened and stooped, walked the streets punching parking meters in the hope they'd spew out loose change for his chain-smoking habit. He classified them all as innocent bystanders incapable of throwing bricks through his window in the pre-dawn hours.

Bromo worked his mobile. There was a missing link he needed to find.

The response was abrupt: 'Yes?'

'I'm at the gallery. I think you should be, too.'

'So I heard. My wake-up call was a police inspector.'

'What's going on?'

'You tell me. You're the one who's there.'

Bromo hunched in closer to his phone and sneaked a look over his shoulder. Fiona and the two cops were walking towards the exit.

'I was invited,' he said. 'Was that your doing?'

He heard the clink of a glass or crockery at the other end of the line. The sounds of coffee being made. Her words were fuzzy.

'Sorry,' she said. 'Just grabbing some breakfast.'

He was losing patience, wanting to raise his voice but stymied by the police presence. He spat his words down the line.

'Take your time. What's the rush? After all, it's only a break and enter and an assault causing a public nuisance and a traffic jam. Nothing to worry about.'

She cut him off in mid-tirade.

'Look, if that wop tart decides to make an exhibition of herself and flaunt her pussy at passers-by that's hardly my concern. The sight might cause a few palpitations among the old pervs in the street but I can't imagine too much damage being done. Why should I care?'

His anger was rising.

'If you're not worried someone's broken into your premises and stirred the police into taking a closer look at your affairs, then you might at least think where this leaves you and me.'

He paused, drew breath, measured his tone.

'Somehow, Aurelia, I'm getting dragged into something rather dirty and I don't like it. Also I'm beginning to think you know more about this morning's business than you're letting on.'

His voice went up a notch, louder, firmer.

'Forget the coffee and get down here. Now.'

He slammed the phone shut and suddenly realised Mayfield was looming next to him.

'Good call,' said the policeman. 'Saved us the trouble.'

Bromo stared at him, holding out, admitting to nothing.

'Aurelia Nuyen, I assume,' said Mayfield.

Bromo nodded: 'She's on her way.'

SIXTEEN

It was only mid-morning but it felt like a whole day had passed. Bromo looked in the bathroom mirror. A stranger peered back. Someone older, more lined and creased, than himself. Paler and less tanned than he used to be. The eyes seemed recessed, drawn back into the skull, with shadows in the hollows beneath them. Not a good look, he decided, and tried to convince himself it was simply the result of too many early mornings, rather than late nights and long solo conversations with a bottle of malt.

But he knew otherwise and recalled a recent cocktail party chat with one of those painted ladies who sold cosmetics in the mirrored and marbled ground floor of a city department store. Within minutes she'd analysed him as a night person and been one of the few ever to correctly guess his age.

'One hour's sleep before midnight is worth two after,' she had recited like a mantra murmured into the ears of clients as she applied layers of creams and unguents which promised to turn leather into satin and keep them looking forever young.

Yeah, all very well, he thought. Right now he could do with sleep at any time, day or night. Bugger this business of getting up at sparrow's fart. The birds were welcome to those sunrise hours. Dawn choruses were off his musical agenda.

Aurelia padded into the bathroom, put her hands on his shoulders and stood on tiptoe to peer into the mirror alongside him. He felt her nakedness warming his back.

'Not a bad looking couple,' she said.

'One half's okay,' he said. 'The other's looking a bit ragged.'

'Should I ask which half?'

'Not necessary. Take it as a compliment.'

She gave him a gentle squeeze and planted a kiss gently between his shoulder blades.

'Thanks for this morning,' she said. 'It was just what I needed after all that business at the gallery. You've been a great help.' She giggled: 'And a great fuck, too.'

He turned round, hugged her to him, then stepped into the shower.

'We always aim to please. Perhaps I should ask you for a reference.'

He turned the taps to their limit, welcoming the force of the water as much as its warmth.

'Best I get moving,' he said. 'Gerry's probably not too keen on having me as a house guest.'

The water powered over his head and streamed down his body. It was the next best thing to a massage. It got even better when he stopped the flow of hot water and left the cold running. The icy drenching needled his body, stimulating the nerve ends, bringing him alive.

As he stepped from the shower and wrapped a towel around him he felt surprisingly refreshed. His befuddled head seemed to be overcoming the lack of sleep. His mind was functioning enough to do a quick rewind of events of the past few hours.

He drifted through to the kitchen. Aurelia was making coffee, a thick white towelling robe enveloping her.

'So, who spread around those invitations to this morning's little shindig if you didn't?'

She looked startled by his sudden questioning, then busied herself frothing the milk.

'I've no idea,' she snapped. 'I told the police, I told you, I know nothing about it. Someone's simply making trouble for me.'

'And the police believed you?'

He knew the answer. She had played the sympathy card for Mayfield and his offsider, seducing them into seeing her as an innocent pawn in someone else's mischief. She had lodged no official complaint, Fiona had laid no charges, there was no damage done, not even the sign of a break-in. The sisterhood was at work, protecting each other even if they were on opposing sides. Mayfield was happy: the police wanted to go on their way with the minimum of paperwork to complete.

'Of course they believed me. Why wouldn't they?'

Why wouldn't they indeed? As for him, a cold shower and a strong coffee worked wonders. Once again he had been easily led into her bed, the frantic haste for each other's body leaving no time, or inclination, for questioning what had gone before. Just as the police had accepted her simpering explanations and false show of concern for Fiona's plight.

'Didn't they wonder how Fiona got there, who strapped her up, how anyone got into the gallery?'

'Of course they did. But I'm not the one who knows the answers. And I'm told the Leoncavallo woman didn't seem too upset. Probably enjoyed the exposure.'

She sidled past him and patted his towelled backside.

'C'mon, stop fussing and get some clothes on. You don't want Gerry to catch you like that.'

Ah, yes, Gerry. There was a name that had slipped through the loop. Fiona had used him as a threat with her photographs and Peter Rasheed had cursed him during his delirious tirade from his sickbed at his factory hideout.

'So, I suppose Gerry has a spare set of keys to the gallery.'

She caught on right away.

'Of course he does but that doesn't mean he had anything to do with this.'

'Why not? He could have organised the whole thing.'

Bromo finished buttoning his shirt. He pursued his theme.

'Gerry has the access. He has the muscle. And the messages I'm getting tell me he's not exactly in love with Peter Rasheed and anyone connected with him.'

She moved towards him, arms out, the towelling robe untied and revealing more than it was hiding.

'Cool it, Aurelia.'

He had an overpowering feeling of being in the wrong place, and probably at the wrong time, too. Too much was happening that he couldn't control, or couldn't explain. It was like watching a puppet show, seeing the action on stage but knowing someone out of sight was pulling the strings.

'I need to get out of here,' he said. 'Now.'

Bromo put his hands on her shoulders, firmly, fending her off instead of drawing her to him.

He rearranged the robe, pulling it tighter around her, closing the flesh-revealing gaps. There were times for succumbing to temptation and times when it had to be fought. He had always found it easier to succumb than to fight - and usually enjoyed the results. Today, however, pleasure had to defer to survival.

She stiffened in his grasp. Her face formed a pout. Oh God, thought Bromo, not that act again. He had seen it too often in the past not to recognise it for what it was: a lame attempt to play the sympathy card.

'I'm sure Gerry wouldn't do anything like that,' she said. 'He's not really a violent man.'

'Of course not. I'm sure he helps little old ladies across the street, is nice to traffic wardens and does the dishes whenever you ask. Meanwhile, his goons are out on the loose doing his nasty work.'

She turned away, fiddled with a box of tissues on the bedside table.

'I've got no complaints,' she said.

'Oh no? So, what am I doing here? Seems dear Gerry doesn't meet all of your needs.'

Aurelia picked up the box of tissues and hurled it at him. 'Bastard.'

'Maybe, but a loveable one it seems.'

He grinned at her as he picked up the box.

'I guess that's what's called a parting shot. Thanks for not throwing the lamp.'

As he turned towards the door Aurelia's mobile started trilling from somewhere in the pile of bedclothes. She found it, flipped it open and listened. A short one-sided conversation.

'It's Gerry,' she mouthed. 'He's on his way here.'

Any further conversation would be with the walls of her room. Bromo had gone. He knew an exit cue when he heard one.

SEVENTEEN

RICHMOND'S TOWN HALL IS an imposing edifice, lording it over the traffic of Bridge Road. Four massive columns soar up to support an unused porte-cochere and create a grandiose portico totally inappropriate for the times in which it was built. It was in the Depression era, when many of its ratepayers were ekeing out a living on sustenance that the council undertook renovations which included the creation of this monumental facade that historians have since likened to some stolid Stalinist edifice. Councillors of the time won even fewer favours by staging a lavish mayoral ball to celebrate their splurging of ratepayers' monies on an interior which they claimed would be paid for by dances and shows. The flaw in their argument was that the impoverished populace couldn't afford such extravagances. Out of work and out of money, dancing the two-step or laughing at some music-hall act was the last thing on their mind.

The shenanigans of the Depression days were a far cry from the hall's original opening in 1869 when an eight-year-old songstress surprised the large audience with a performance beyond her years – and launched the future Dame Nellie Melba on an international career.

Bromo saw little point in dwelling on the past yet savoured the sense of history the building engendered. Partitions of timber panelling and glass now divided the once spacious interior but the sense of grandeur remained. As he fronted the enquiry counter he imagined the areas beyond and how they once housed rooms pandering to the egos of a wealthy and venous minority.

'Probably not much has changed,' he muttered.

'Sorry. What was that?'

The woman behind the counter was looking at him, puzzled and enquiring. Bromo faltered. He realised he must have been talking to himself. Not a good habit but one you tended to fall into when living alone.

'Nothing. Must've been thinking out loud. Wondering if Melba's ghost haunts the rates office. Any chance I could have a look at a planning submission?'

It was easier than he imagined. The ratepayers' right to know was being honoured. Wheeling and dealing no doubt continued behind closed doors but at least at street level attempts were being made to stay true to the concept of open government.

He unrolled huge sheets of architectural plans brought to him by a clerk from a back room. They showed the site on which Mack's at present stood from every possible perspective. It was an architect's vision, full of artistic embellishments. The surrounds and inner courtyards were dotted with depictions of trees and shrubs in the hope of forestalling any Greenie objectors. There was off-street and underground parking to forestall the traffic worriers. Neatly dressed pedestrians were shown strolling along bush-lined lanes – a far cry from the harried and unkempt masses and littered streets outside. There was even a corner section set out with tables and chairs where stick figures were shown enjoying the café life. A folder held details of planning submissions and approvals.

'That's the latest version,' said the thirty-something woman behind the counter, long strands of multi-coloured hair falling forward over a face decorated with a nose ring. A bolt was pushed through her lower lip.

'One day they'll make up their minds,' she added.

She resumed gazing at a computer screen as if searching for some deep secret of the universe, occasionally scrolling down, no emotion showing from eyes rimmed by thick black lines of mascara, their lids layered in purple eye-liner.

'Councils tend to be a bit like that,' offered Bromo. 'Indecisive.'

Her eyes didn't move from the screen.

'Yeah. Depends who's pissing in your pocket. But it's not the council's fault this time.

'No?'

'No. Bloody protesters and then the developers. None of them know what they want.'

It was all delivered in a monotone. Deadpan. A commentary devoid of any involvement as she maintained her trance-like staring at her screen.

Bromo turned the sheaves of paper and began noting names and dates. Everything was in the name of companies that gave little clue to the people behind them. Meaningless names such as Nominee 123, Plan 54 or simply Options. A detailed company search would be needed to discover the people involved and even then it would likely be secretaries and accountants rather than the real power brokers. Letters and submissions were from legal firms on behalf of clients, again revealing little.

The woman behind the counter stretched, stood up and began moving away from her desk.

Bromo looked up: 'If this is the latest, where's the earlier stuff?'

'Filed away I suppose.'

She spoke in an 'I only work here' voice.

'It won't tell you much,' she added.

Bromo took a punt: 'But you can. You seem to know what's going on.'

The unblinking look focussed on him. He realised he was being assessed on some unknown scale of reliability. Her purple lipsticked lips flattened into the glimmer of a smile. He reckoned he'd scored an A-plus.

'Maybe. But I'm on my break right now.'

'So, a cup of coffee and a bikkie? Across the road?'

Again she gave him that look, drilling into him but still smiling.

'What's your interest? You wouldn't be trying to corrupt or influence a council officer by any chance?'

'Wouldn't dream of it. Mind you, I wouldn't be the first if I did. Look at the history of this place; corruption was the password.'

She made a snap decision.

'I'll see you outside in two.'

She moved away into the vastness of the back rooms and Bromo began rolling up the sheets of drawings. It was only then, as the bottom of the pages rolled into place, that he noticed a small panel in the lowermost corner - Architect: Liz Shapcott.

So the delectable but enigmatic Liz was much more than a mere consultant with good contacts in the planning department. She was the most recent designer of the whole bloody thing.

EIGHTEEN

A sudden squall of driving rain came blowing down Bridge Road as Bromo made his way out into the street through the town hall's high front doors.

He stood waiting for the counter clerk to emerge, sheltering from the chilling onslaught atop the flight of steps leading down beneath the soaring portico. He gazed at the huge fluted columns, recently repainted, and pondered the venality of a bunch of civic fathers who could squander so much public money on such a grandiose edifice yet have it built famously out of alignment with the rest of the street.

Probably par for the course. It was ever thus. There were devious self-serving operators within the council back in those Depression years and clones of varying levels of duplicity had been busily plotting and scheming down the decades. Nepotism and veniality ruled until recent times.

Little wonder Liz Shapcott had been so secretive about the activities of the protesters from RAID and RAGE. She had her own interests to protect and these were entwined with the politics and policies doing their bureaucratic dances along the corridors of the town hall.

Her gentle but firm warnings about his involvement with Peter Rasheed began to make sense. She was far better informed than she'd let on. Her warnings had stemmed not from gossip but from direct knowledge of the people involved. Now he wondered about the type of connections Liz claimed she had within the council.

The rain stopped as suddenly as it had begun. But the chill remained. He pulled his coat tighter round him and looked over his shoulder for his would-be informant.

'Down here.'

She stood at the foot of the steps, wrapped in a calf-length black cloak, its hood pulled up over her head. Clunky, thick-soled black boots were laced up to well above her ankles, encasing black mesh stockings with jagged holes revealing patches of pale white flesh. A Goth down to her bootstraps, it could be said, although Bromo decided such a comment would probably be unwise.

She pointed to the side of the building. 'Tradesmen's entrance,' she explained. 'Helps us avoid cranky ratepayers.'

'You get many of those?'

'Lots. Really nasty types. They get quite aggro, blaming the council for everything.'

Bromo offered the predictable coda: 'And you're just trying to do your job.'

'Yeah.' She gave him that unwavering stare. 'You taking the piss?'

'Not at all.' Or at least he wouldn't admit it.

They weaved their way through the incessant traffic stream, dodging cars, trucks and trams – an artery feeding the city that helped motorists avoid the freeway tolls.

'Where to?' he asked. 'What's your choice?'

She pointed to Dargo's. 'Not there. Too many business wankers at this time of day. The Humming Bird's better.'

Might have guessed, thought Bromo. Horses for courses. The Humming Bird Haven was a large functional space with basic chunky tables, hard wooden seats, bare pastel-painted walls and no attempt at decoration apart from a few plastic flowers. An endless tape of ambient music soothed frazzled nerves. The peace-promoting collective who ran the place took a leisurely approach to everything they did, including the service. Calm was the keynote. Physical and mental health formed their mantra. They'd rewritten the book of vegetarian cuisine with a daily menu of fresh and tasty dishes that even attracted carnivores for lunches and snacks.

'Not too light and airy for a Goth?' teased Bromo. 'Thought you people liked darkness and dungeons.'

She heaved another bored sigh.

'God, why are people so bloody predictable? Too many assumptions. Why don't you ask if I'd like a sip of blood with my muffin? And what's a demonic girl like me doing in a nice place like this?'

By the time they'd placed their orders and sat down there was an uneasy wall of silence between them. Bromo leaned forward, arms on the table and turned his palms upward.

'Can we start again? No glib assumptions. No smart remarks but thanks for coming.'

She allowed a smidgen of a smile. 'Okay. Done deal. What do you want to know?'

'As much as you can tell me about Mack's - without getting yourself into trouble.'

'That'll be the day. Trouble's my middle name so far as that lot's concerned.'

She tilted her head towards the town hall.

'I'm not really one of them.'

It was an admission Bromo would later recall with a wry smile. For now, he wasn't surprised. A darkly clad Goth stalking the corridors among much more formally clad bureaucrats and civic officers seemed sure to cause a certain amount of disapproval, if not outright rejection.

'Wouldn't have anything to do with your outfit, by any chance.'

'Nah. They're cool about that. Some of the girls are much worse than me. Look like they're dressed for a rave rather than work. All tits and thighs, if you know what I mean.'

He grinned. He certainly got the picture. It was one he'd seen on numerous occasions as the office staff trooped to and fro across the road for their coffees and snacks. They seemed so scantily clad, so much flesh showing and often not in any appealing way. More negligee and underwear than business attire. This seemed to be the norm. There were no dress codes these days.

'So, if it's not the dress, what is it?'

Coffees arrived along with a saffron coloured pumpkin scone and a muesli biscuit.

'S'pose I ask too many questions; make too many comments. Some of the things that go on just don't seem right, especially with the councillors. Most of the staff are pretty straight but sometimes they seem afraid to tell the councillors to take a running jump. They tend to do what they're told rather than stand up to them.'

Bromo sipped his coffee and bit into the muesli biscuit, a thick and chunky rough-hewn mix of grains and fruit.

'Surely they've got rules and regulations to follow. Not like in the old days.'

She shrugged and broke off a chunk of the scone.

'It depends on how you follow them. What they call a matter of interpretation. That's where I tend to rock the boat. That's how I get into trouble.'

'Sounds like the old square peg and round hole problem,' suggested Bromo. 'What are you doing there? Why stay?'

She gave him that unnerving stare, boring into him, summing him up and revealing nothing of what she found there.

'Don'tcha see? I'm doing to them what they do to everyone else. I'm using them. I'm also doing my little bit to set things right when I can. Why do I stay? Odd as it may seem to you, I happen to like my job. It suits me. As I said, I'm using them so that I can move on to something else. I won't be there any longer than necessary.'

Bromo stirred his coffee, although it contained neither sugar nor milk. It helped to scrape the caffeine crust off the sides of the cup. It also gave him time to think.

He wanted to turn the talk back to the plans for Mack's but felt it might be best to go with the flow and let her meander towards the point of their meeting. There was edginess about her that he felt could quickly turn against him if he pushed too hard.

He tried another tack.

'And where does a Goth find work when she moves on from city hall?'

'Who knows? But wherever it is I know I'll be the one making the decisions.' She paused. 'There's only so much pushing around a girl can take.'

She was crumbling the scone, putting small pieces almost absent-mindedly into her mouth, looking blankly at the table top. Bromo tensed. He felt he'd lost her. She seemed to have drifted miles away from the cafe and from the town hall.

A paramedic wagon went screaming past, lights flashing and sirens going full blast. The cacophony startled her. She jerked, shook her head and looked up. Again that faint smile.

'Sorry, I wandered off. I guess this isn't what you came to hear. I don't often open up but somehow you pushed all the right buttons. I felt good about you and the questions you asked about Mack's. It's good to have someone else doing a bit of digging. I like that. We need it. There's definitely something funny going on there but I'm not prepared to blow the whistle on my own. Too dangerous. Right now I've got too much to lose.'

'Such as?'

'My future. This is my first real job. It's my big break, the chance to make something of myself. They don't know it over there ...' She glanced again at the town hall... 'but I'm studying urban planning at uni in my spare time. Mature age student. There's no way I'm going to stuff it up. Life's been too shitty up to now.'

'Perhaps you should forget about Mack's,' offered Bromo. 'I'll find someone else to help me.'

'No way. I want to nail those bastards and no one else is going to help you like I can. Think of it as my mission in life, at least for now.'

'Peter Rasheed?'

'He's the least of your worries.'

'You know he's hidden away inside Mack's'

'Squatter's rights. Condoned by the councillors. Or at least by those.in the know. The rest are in the dark.'

'And Liz Shapcott?'

'Tricky. Ethical, lovely lady, but trying to play one side off against the other. A dangerous game.'

'Gerry Nuyen?'

'Snake in the grass. Bit of a porno merchant from what I hear. Grubby and lethal. Lots of muscle behind him. His wife's tricky, too.'

Bromo gulped, tried to show no reaction. He looked at the handwritten bill beneath his cup and put some cash on the table.

'But none of them are councillors,' he said.

She gave him that look again, assessing, weighing him up, making decisions.

'Right. You obviously haven't caught up with Steve Delgado, chairman of the planning committee.'

Bromo had noticed the name in press reports of council decisions and put a mental underline beneath it.

'Tell me more.'

'I'm working on it.'

She looked at her watch, gulped back the last of her coffee and wrapped the remains of her scone in a paper napkin.

'For later,' she explained. 'Gotta get back to the loony bin.'

He spread his arms, palms up, puzzled. 'But ....'

She cut him off: 'Yeah, I know. I haven't really been much help. Yapped on about myself and haven't told you what you really wanted to know. But I will. Promise. Give me a number and I'll call you.'

They stood on the edge of the pavement, waiting for a break in the traffic, Bromo leaning in towards her, his whole body pleading. She, turning away, more concerned with making her way back to the town hall.

He took the newspaper from his jacket pocket, tore off a corner and scribbled his mobile number. She grabbed it, saw a gap between a food delivery truck and a VW Golf whose teenage driver was too busy texting a message to worry about pedestrians, and dashed away from him.

Bromo watched the billowing, hooded figure. All she needs is a broomstick and black cat, he thought, as she'd disappeared down the side of the building as quickly as she'd seemingly manifested herself in front of him a mere half-hour ago. And he didn't even know her name.

'Been trying a bit of black magic?'

Bromo jerked round, surprised. Two men had emerged from Dargo's and were standing on either side of him and uncomfortably close. The shorter, stockier one he recognised from his sessions at the gym, a lunch-time pumper of iron and occasional treadmill user. He wore a black business suit, crisp shirt and conservative tie.

The other, looming over him, was a complete stranger: a muscular six-footer with a flattened nose, a scar above one eye, little neck and a shaven head.

Beneath his black jacket, a black T-shirt was stretched tight over a bulging chest. It was the suit man who had spoken. Bromo turned to him with a slight smile.

'Sorry, just realised where we've met. I didn't recognise you with your clothes on.'

The man grinned back.

'Yeah, it gets a bit like that. Only time you see some people they're in gym gear or coming out of the shower. You never know what they do to earn a crust.'

Too true. The gym was a common meeting ground. No one asked who you were or what you did. Over the years Bromo had found his fellow exercisers included a leading sur-geon, a builder's mate, a couple of architects, retired teachers, a newspaper artist, women from public relations and numerous waiters, waitresses, cooks and bar staff. Among them was the neat-looking businessman standing alongside him, his hand now thrust out in introduction, although Bromo had no idea why.

'Steve's the name.'

'Oh. Hi. Bromo.'

A staccato, hesitant response. He took the offered hand, limp and clammy, and shook it briefly, still puzzled at the contact. The other man had inched closer, almost touching. Bromo felt intimidated, uncomfortable and edged away.

'Got to go,' he said. 'Guess I'll see you later. At the gym.'

'Yeah. Sure.'

The man didn't move, stayed blocking his way.

'Before you go, I was just wondering how well you know Delia.'

'Delia?'

'Yeah, Delia Dunstan. The woman who's just left you. Works at city hall.'

'Oh, that Delia.'

Bromo filed away the information. At least now he knew her name. It seemed to suit her.

'How many Delias do you know?'

'Not that many. Perhaps just her and Delia Smith.'

He gave a nervous laugh. The muscle man was too close. Bromo was on the edge of the footpath and had nowhere to move.

'Learnt how to boil an egg from her.'

'Useful. However, I was more interested in Delia from Planning. A much more interesting person. I was curious about your connections.'

Bromo's composure was returning. He'd had time to think.

'Sorry, mate. How I spend my time and how Delia spends her tea break are between her and me. Let's say we're just good friends.'

It was stretching a point for a relationship less than an hour old and with very few signs of positive results so far as he was concerned. But he'd resisted intimidation in the past and was not about to yield now.

'She doesn't have friends,' said the man in the suit. 'She has contacts. And she's a nutter. A loose cannon. Stay clear.'

'Harsh words. Probably libellous.'

'Truth is our defence.'

This can't be happening, thought Bromo. It's broad daylight, middle of the morning in Bridge Road, coffee and Herald Sun time, the lull between the morning commuter rush and the frenzy of lunch-hour. Men in business suits don't stand on the footpath uttering veiled threats to fellow citizens.

Wrong.

'Let me introduce you to Gus.'

The muscle man moved still closer and looked even bigger, taller.

'This is Gus Thompson. He'll be looking after you.'

'G'day.'

Thompson stuck out a chunky hand. It was at the end of an equally chunky arm, imprinted with the inky blue, red and yellow squirls of a tattooist's artistic imagination.

'Everyone calls me Gunner.'

Bromo decided to play along.

'What's that, army service or for shooting roos?'

'Neither mate. I was gunna be a boxer, I was gunna to be a champion, I was gunna retire rich and famous. Now I'm gunna kick the drink."

He gave a throaty giggle, revealing an incomplete row of stained and cracked teeth. He was pleased with himself. He'd made a joke, his joke, the one he'd used countless times before in gyms and pubs. He had the speech pattern and the smile of the slightly sub-normal. Thompson shrugged.

'All gunna. Did none of them, except me and the drink are boxing about even. Maybe I'm winning on points.'

'What happened?'

'Got taken for a stroll down an alley behind the gym by a bunch of crazies just before the championship. They made a bit of a mess. End of story.'

Bromo almost felt sorry for him. Maybe Gus Thompson was the archetypal gentle giant and any menace was in his own imagination. No such hope.

'Gus gets upset when people step out of line,' said the suit named Steve. 'People seem to have a terrible habit of asking questions and poking their noses into matters that don't concern them. That upsets him, too. Very much so.'

'I can imagine. He'd obviously find me very boring.'

'Possibly. Provided you stay clear of our lovely Delia, let Mr Rasheed get on with his business and forget all about Mack's. See you at the gym.'

He walked away. The mound of muscle remained. Bromo looked up at the impassive face.

'Tell me, Gus, was that a threat?'

Unblinking eyes looked down at him. No warmth but no discernible hostility either. A neutral blankness. He relaxed into a toothy grin.

'Couldn't say, sir. You never quite know with Mr Delgado.'

NINETEEN

THE STEAM ROOM WAS full of the usual suspects. Dicko, Johnno, Davo and Cammo were perched on the benches like a line of pudgy, plucked chooks. Margot, the fifty-something redhead with a tattoo of a long-stemmed rose drawing attention to her left breast, sprawled on the side bench.

Bromo thought of it as the O Club and considered he had more rights than most to belong. His name was ready-made for such company. True to the Australian way with names, the others had seen this as a too-easy means of entry. So, to them, he became the contradictory Fatso. Or, sometimes, the Travelling Man. He felt even more welcome because of these labels.

These were the morning regulars. You could set your watch by when they arrived at the gym, did their routines in the exercise area, shuffled out to the pool, and then went their separate ways. Their conversation was rudimentary, often rough. They kept well abreast of current events and had a ready opinion on politics, sport, the economy and anything else that had made that day's headlines.

Despite their daily workouts, their bodies never firmed up, the flabby waistlines never quite disappeared and the concept of taut, trim and terrific remained a distant dream. Yet they were fitter and livelier by far than most of their pensionable contemporaries.

'Hey, make way for the Travelling Man,' roared Dicko as Bromo slid into the room, taking care to avoid letting in too much cooler air.

'You're a bit late today, mate,' noted Johnno.

'Yeah,' acknowledged Bromo. 'Bit of business.'

Four heads nodded. The body language was clear: they understood such intrusions happened to working people but considered them more nuisance than necessity.

'Hope it was worth it,' voiced Davo, the scrawniest and oldest.

'Depends,' replied Bromo.

He'd come to the gym the long way round, stopping off at Mack's, walking all the way round its bricked-up, shuttered exterior on a whim he couldn't explain. He'd peered through gaps in the shutters trying to see some sign of Rasheed or Fiona but clusters of pigeons provided the only movement. The street kid was nowhere to be seen. He'd tried the padlocks on a couple of doors. Security company calling cards were folded into the hasps and the locks wouldn't yield. Someone was doing their job at last. Or was it window-dressing?

'Sounds like you've found another woman.'

Margot, the eternal flirt, had sat up and was grinning at him with a teasing smile. Bromo played along. It was part of the game.

'Could be.'

He thought of the black-gowned Delia. Couldn't imagine them ever becoming an item. He offered a lie to keep the banter going.

'Found myself a Goth,' he informed her.

'Looking for some black magic with your sex?'

'Magic sex of any colour would do me,' Cammo chimed in as he scratched at the scar on his left buttock - a memento from a bullet he'd unwittingly stopped when a couple of hoods started shooting at each other down near the docks.

The incident had made him a bit of a legend within the O Club, especially as there were whispered doubts about the extent of his professed innocence in the shootout. For years he'd worked on the wharves, notorious for standover men and an employment policy that provided job opportunities for any criminal seeking easy money and anonymity. It seemed too much of a coincidence that the fracas occurred outside a pub frequented by wharfies and a couple of days after the shooting he'd been offering a good deal on stereo outfits that had somehow come his way.

The others nodded in silent agreement at Cammo's plea. Their libidos had long left them but celibacy was only grudgingly accepted as a normal feature of their lives.

'Where'd you find her?' persisted Margot. 'Been trawling the dungeons? I thought you were on with that bird from the gallery.'

Four heads turned in unison towards Bromo.

'Hey, what's this,' chiacked Johnno. 'An art tart?'

Their raucous chuckles echoed around the tiled chamber. They'd been provided with another topic to call up whenever there was a lull in their chatter. Such information was the life-blood of their daily banter.

'That the one who did a strip show in the window this morning?'

'Yeah,' Bromo replied.

Not strictly true, but what the hell. It would be good for a giggle or two when conversation lagged. He was only mildly surprised that word of Fiona's naked display had spread so quickly. You could never accuse this bunch of steam-room gossips of not knowing what was going on around them. Bromo reckoned they beat the bush telegraph hands down every time. But they treated their information for what it was; it had no value beyond being fodder for conversation at the gym or the pub. Unlike the corporates who shared their gym space, they were unlikely to use it for commercial or personal gain. Gossip was not a tradeable commodity.

Cammo was the first to digest this latest grist to their rumour mill.

'Geez, you lucky bugger.'

Johnno wasn't so sure.

'Don't think I'd want any sheila of mine getting her gear off for everyone to see.'

Bromo realised his mistake. His admission had them concluding Aurelia had been the naked showpiece. But it was Margot who beat him to the correction.

'That was another art tart,' she said, flashing him one of the teasing looks which had made her a firm favourite of the O Club.

'Bromo's woman is the one who owns the gallery,' she informed them.

Her eyes were laughing at him as she nudged him with an elbow.

'At least, her husband does.'

'You cheeky bugger,' said Cammo, standing up to ease his stiff leg.

'Anyone we know?'

Bromo looked at Margot. Her smile was still teasing, hard to read. He'd often seen her trawling through the suburb's numerous galleries so it was no surprise she was well aware of Aurelia and Gerry Nuyen. Until now, however, she hadn't let on to Bromo that she knew of his link to Aurelia.

She held his gaze, letting him fathom out how much she knew, and whether she'd reveal it to Cammo and his mates.

'Depends,' she said. 'I don't know what you boys get up to when you leave here. I didn't think you were all that in with the gallery set.'

'Not any more. Rather lost interest,' dead-panned Davo. 'Gave all my Picassos away. Made the place look untidy.'

Dicko nodded in agreement.

'I know how you feel. Did the same with my Nolans. All those bloody Ned Kellys gave people the wrong idea.'

'But you probably know Gerry Nuyen,' said Margot.

The chuckling stopped abruptly. Margot clasped her hands between her knees, bent her head forward and studied the floor. Bromo winced. He felt a chord had been struck. A silent chord. No one spoke as they took their time to digest this revelation.

Johnno slid off the bench, the paunch he perpetually swore he was getting rid of hanging out over his baggy grey shorts. He moved towards the door, one hand against the glass, ready to push it open. He looked at Bromo.

'Mate, are you fucking mad, or what?' He shook his head in disbelief. 'Gerry Nuyen. Gerry bloody Nuyen.'

Johnno's head was still going side to side as he opened the door. A shaft of cold air rushed in. The door closed behind him and they watched him douse himself under the shower outside.

'He's right, y'know,' offered Dicko. 'I don't know about Gerry's arty bizzo but you'd be bloody crazy to mess with anything else he's involved in.'

'Especially his missus,' added Cammo.

'Yeah, especially his missus,' echoed Davo. Margot glanced up, looking contrite. She rested a hand on Bromo's knee and gave it a squeeze.

'Seems it's a bit late to be thinking about that,' she said.

'Nah, that's the least of your worries,' said Dicko. 'It's all the other stuff you've got to worry about. The payola, the migrant stuff, the drugs, the porn, the property deals. And his muscle men. We have corn flakes for breakfast, they have steroids. Makes 'em very nervy. And then they go right off. Very violent. Very dangerous. You just watch it, Bromo old son.'

He scratched at his crotch, adjusting himself inside his bathers.

'Anyhow, I'm done. Sweated more than a jockey on Cup Day.'

He followed Johnno's route to the shower. Cammo and Davo followed.

'Well ....' said Margot, her thoughts trailing off unspoken into the mist.

'Well, indeed,' responded Bromo. 'Seems there's a bit more to Mr Nuyen than I realised. A bit suss, yes. A wheeler-dealer, tricky, devious. All that. But I wasn't aware of the rest.'

He thought of the bloodied body of Peter Rasheed and the hooded men who'd kidnapped and presumably stripped and displayed Fiona Leoncavallo. Were they the Gerry Nuyen muscle men Dicko had referred to? If so, who were the bruisers who had conveyed Rasheed from Bromo's place to Mack's and given Bromo a headache to remember when he'd tried to take a close interest in the building? He had assumed they were Rasheed's men yet they were nowhere to be seen when the kidnapping pair appeared.

He was beginning to think every businessman in town had their own heavy squad running around enforcing their own sense of law and order. And now he'd had his own personal minder thrust upon him by Steve Delgado. He thought of the looming mass of Gunner Thompson and shuddered.

Margot wriggled her backside on the bench. She gave his leg another squeeze.

'Looks like you're in deep shit, m'dear.'

She sauntered towards the door. Bromo went with her.

'Let's hope your Goth can help,' said Margot. 'Seems you need a bit of magic in your life.'

TWENTY

Bromo's phone buzzed. There were words on its screen: 'You have a new message: read now?'

Technology was so polite, something that frequently surprised and impressed him. He welcomed the fact that something as impersonal as a telephone could still display a measure of grace and manners. Perhaps some of the waiters he'd encountered should start texting to replace their abysmal attempts at service. The phone system was programmed and regimented, but at least someone out there in cyberspace was striving to preserve the simple courtesies. He pressed the keys. The message appeared:

'UR OK. 2nite. Pistons @ 8. Delia.'

So much for the simple courtesies. They'd gone overboard with the advent of text messaging. It was a language apart and one he was only slowly grasping. Pop singers that feigned American accents and mumbled incoherently in American slang were bad enough but a sub-language that relied on short-forms and misspellings seemed to be another nail in the coffin of literacy.

He used the system nonetheless. He keyed in 'OK'. He'd find out where, or what, Pistons was later. It was probably one of the many bars that seemed to open almost weekly throughout the suburb and change hands just as frequently. They occupied mall shop fronts, traded under odd names and attracted a clientele that seemed bereft of any dress sense beyond clothes that were scruffy and torn.

Bromo hurried towards his office and the cool of its air-conditioning - if the cranky old unit felt like working. The earlier rain and chill southerly had been pushed aside by a vile north wind that was turning the streets into a furnace. It was close to 40 degrees yet the sun was only spasmodically seen. Once again the city was living up to its reputation for serving up four seasons in one day.

A thick haze was being blown over the city from bushfires ravaging country communities not many kilometres away. Homes had been lost and people killed. The forecast was for worse to come before the promised cool change arrived. Bromo trudged up the stairs, keyed open the door, slumped into his chair and fired up his computer. There was work to be done. Homework. Research. He needed to know more about the Linking Local Lovers website and how Peter Rasheed was involved. All the signs were that he wouldn't be doing it for the good of the community.

Bromo started trawling the internet. The main browsers had tempting links to the sites he was seeking, holding out invitations to find soul-mates by using pictures of laughing beautiful young men and women purportedly eager to make contact with like-minded lonely hearts.

The first site visited seemed fairly innocuous. Most were people looking for friends or companions for outings, the movies, a meal or a show. A high proportion listed themselves as tertiary educated and employed in the professions. Their pictures, mostly simple headshots, showed well-groomed, pleasant High Street, cinema foyer, art gallery faces. Not a tarty look among them. Their pleas were uniformly simple – for caring, companionable males, unattached and with no emotional baggage. Those with higher expectations wanted their knights in shining armour to be tall, good looking, financially secure and with GSOH – a good sense of humour. They said they wanted someone to share a movie, a meal or to go dancing. Oddly, a walk on the beach seemed a recurrent wish. It was a mirror image of the ads which appeared in The Age every Saturday, mostly from mature age women broadcasting their need for male companionship.

As he explored he noted recurring phrases, almost a code. Women described themselves as loving, tactile or sensuous. They suggested cosy nights at home with a bottle of red – not a chardonnay-sipper among them - and hinted at the pleasures of a spa, often adding the coquettish wish to 'let's see what develops.'

He used a Hotmail service and pseudonym to log into other sites and avoid the risk of spam. As he delved deeper he soon found himself exploring a totally new world. He had long been familiar with the concept of sex as a commodity, as something that had a monetary value, with women selling their bodies on the streets and in clubs, brothels and hotel bars. Usually they were making a living or feeding a habit. Many lived dangerously, precariously, even when plying their trade under the protection of pimps and brothel-owners. The common factor was that they all turned their tricks for money.

Now he found himself venturing where seemingly ordinary people were seeking partners simply for the pleasure of sex. No payment was asked or expected. There was no indication of any money changing hands. He had unearthed a pulsating, throbbing host of hot, horny, sex-seeking people living behind the venetian blinds of suburbia and catching the 8.42 to the city every morning. They were blatant in what they offered and in what they sought.

Some preserved their anonymity by keeping pictures of themselves in a private folder, accessible only by those they decided to provide with a password. Many more happily went public in a very big way - not just the modest head shots of the first site he'd accessed but full body pictures, clothed, half clothed and fully buck-naked.

As he worked out the technicalities of the site he found that by clicking on the main pictures he opened up a gallery where even more explicit shots were offered. Bare boobs were just the beginning. There was little pretence at privacy or subtlety. Or glamour. As he flicked through screen after screen Bromo realised many of those who described themselves as cuddly were being loose with the truth. For the majority so labelled cuddly was clearly a synonym for fat, blubbery and grossly overweight. It seemed to matter little. They were offering their bodies, not for sale but for pleasure, and had no shame or modesty in going public with their needs and openly wanton desires.

The ring of the phone interrupted his perusal of a ghostly white woman with huge thighs and a flowing mane of straggly unkempt hair being mounted by an equally large and excessively tattooed man.

'Cliff here, mate. How're the bookings going?'

Cliff Rankin. Another loyal and long-standing client who paid well for the personal touches Bromo provided. He had travelled well and widely on his own for some years, presenting

Bromo with challenging tasks as he ventured well away from the main tourist trails. Now into his 50s he had belatedly found himself a female companion and settled into more traditional routes and a liking for first-class travel and five-star hotels.

'Coming along well,' said Bromo, reaching an arm out for a file. 'Just a couple of flights to confirm. They keep changing schedules on me. Then I can finalise the hotels in Vienna and Prague.'

'Sounds good,' said Rankin, as easy-going as ever. 'I'd just like to get the account settled by the end of the month.'

If only everyone was that prompt with payment, thought Bromo. Most weren't too bad but there were a couple who lived by the 90-day accounting principle, and then some.

He glanced at the coupling duo on his computer screen. And wondered ....

'How's the romance going, Cliff?'

'Bubbling along. Pity we didn't link up years ago.'

'Probably wouldn't have been the same.'

'Yeah, guess so. Timing's everything.'

The mood was easy, relaxed, two mates chatting. Bromo took a breath, flicked the papers in the file.

'You never did say how you two met. Bit of a story there?'

Rankin chuckled. Then seemed to hesitate. Silently Bromo urged him on.

'Bit embarrassing, really,' said Rankin. 'We met on the Net. One of those dating sites. We'd both put ourselves out there. Hoping, not really expecting to find anyone. I met some real weirdos ...'

Bromo broke in. 'Tell me about the weirdos. How weird? In what way weird?'

'They were nothing like what they presented as in their profiles. Using old photos, years out of date. Telling porkies, pretending they were some trendy, go-go type when they were as boring as bat shit. Claiming to be slim or slender when they were balls of blubber. You soon learn cuddly means fat and you watch the non-smokers itching for a fag.'

Bromo laughed: 'I'm getting the picture.'

Again Rankin gave that familiar chuckle: 'And then Lydia came along. We hit it off straight away. The system works.'

Bromo glanced again at the picture on his screen.

'Any sex being offered?' he ventured.

'Not much on the site we used. Not openly. It's pretty much above board. Fairly ordinary people looking for companionship. There are a few hidden messages about cosy evenings cuddling up in front of a fire, or romantic dinners and being the tactile sort of person. Two of the women I met before Lydia came along were pretty desperate. One had her fingers going up and down my thigh while we were having a coffee. The other just came right out with it and suggested we hop into bed.'

'Well?' prompted Bromo.

'Well what?' snapped Rankin. 'Nothing happened. They were both dogs. It's what I was saying, there's a lot of half-truths and false pictures out there. And a lot of desperate people.'

Bromo persisted: 'But no sex?'

'Geez, Bromo, what's got into you? Aren't you getting enough? I thought you were rattling the rafters with that Nuyen woman.'

Bromo grimaced. It seemed everyone knew about their so-called secret affair.

'Of course there's sex,' continued Rankin. 'Oodles of it. The suburbs are full of people asking for it and giving it. And it's not all straight. There are couples, threesomes and foursomes; men on men, women with women, group gropes and even gang bangs. And it's all free. No money, no commitment. I'll give you a few addresses to get you started if you're that keen. Or take a look at late-night TV. It's full of 'em.'

So friend and client Cliff Rankin now had him painted as a desperate sex fiend. At least he had the information he wanted and he'd saved hours of aimless mouse-clicking and screen-gazing. He noted the addresses and promised to give some urgent attention to Rankin's travel plans. Rankin sounded pleased.

'Thanks for that. I thought for a while there you'd be too busy surfing for sex.'

'Not me, mate. Got enough problems. Ever heard of a guy called Peter Rasheed?'

'Shit.'

'I wish you hadn't said that. It makes me uneasy.'

'So it should.'

'Steve Delgado?'

'That bastard at the city council? C'mon Bromo, what are you playing at? Rasheed, Delgado, porno sites, Gerry Nuyen' s missus ... I thought you had your head screwed on.'

'So did I. Seems a screw or two must have got loose. Perhaps you could give me a briefing.'

'Sure, if you've got an hour to spare. Right now, I've got to dash.'

There was a knocking at Bromo's office door.

'Me, too,' he said. 'Seems I'm wanted.'

Bromo ended the call and began easing himself out of his chair. Visitors to the office were rare. Most of his business was done by phone and email, or by calling at his clients' homes and offices.

'Come in,' he called out.

It was a wasted invitation.

Two large men, one slightly Oriental in looks, and one petite woman had already closed the door behind them. For big people the men moved quickly, almost sliding across the room on soft-soled shoes, stepping behind his desk and standing uncomfortably close to him, one on either side.

'Mr Nuyen is expecting you,' said the woman, leaning in towards him across his desk.

From somewhere deep within he summoned up a bravado once used in that life he'd tried hard to erase.

'I only do house calls for my regular clients,' said Bromo. 'Perhaps Mr Nuyen would like to make an appointment.'

He made pretence of turning over the pages of his diary.

'I think I'm free late this afternoon.'

'We think you're free now.'

The words were a growl in his ear from the man on his left. They were accompanied by a prod in the ribs with something hard. Experience told him it wasn't a bony finger, but something more unyielding and explosive. That same experience told him to stay calm, don't antagonise, avoid sudden movements. The last time he'd reacted quickly had been a fatal mistake. Never again.

He turned the diary's page once more.

'Hmm. I must've made a mistake. Looking at the wrong week. Seems I could squeeze Mr Nuyen in right now. Lead on.'

A long low limousine with tinted windows was waiting at the kerbside. Its highly polished duco gleamed in the glare of the sun. A couple of kids on skateboards were eyeing it off. They wheeled away when the two heavies emerged with Bromo between them and steered him firmly into the rear seat. Doors slammed and obesity ruled. He felt squeezed by the sheer bulk of the men either side of him.

'Give us a bit of room.'

'Shove it,' one growled.

'I would if I had some space.'

He tried wriggling his backside on the seat. No good. They were immoveable objects.

'Sit still,' grunted the one on his left.

The woman was sitting alongside the driver - also female with a long ponytail of sleek black hair trailing from beneath a while baseball cap. Neither showed any interest in what was happening on the back seat. They stared implacably ahead, stiff and expressionless like characters in a computer game.

Bromo leaned forward to sneak a look outside. They were cruising through narrow back streets lined by terraces of small weatherboard homes clustered under iron roofs. The high rise towers of the Housing Commission flats loomed nearby as they bounced over speed humps on a route he knew was leading them inevitably into the city's Vietnamese quarter.

TWENTY-ONE

It was broad daylight - a conspicuous time for parking a limousine outside one of the stripped-down and basic restaurants lining both sides of the crowded street. Yet the vehicle failed to score a sideways glance from passersby. The footpath was busy with shoppers and diners – mostly a mix of Vietnamese, Thais and Chinese who tended to shuffle, rather than walk, taking their time, relaxed in mind and body. By contrast, the few taller, brisker Westerners negotiating the footpath had to side-step around them in their impatience.

The situation distracted Bromo from all thoughts of being a captive. There was a brazenness about his captors' actions which intrigued him. It spoke of power and control, of noses being thumbed at authority. Kidnapping and enforcement were part of a normal business day. No need for subterfuge or waiting for the cover of darkness.

The limousine's engine was still running. The woman in the passenger seat stepped out and opened the rear kerbside door. She took a quick walk to a door set back in an alcove between two restaurants. She gestured back at the car.

'Get out. Walk to the door. Fast.'

The man still clutching Bromo's right elbow had spoken. His commands were precise, demanding. There was an underlying menace. Bromo did as he was told.

The bunch of them was hardly through the door than it clanked shut. Bromo heard a lock hit home behind them. He imagined the limo purring off with shuffling shoppers taking no note of its stopover. His guardian placed a hand firmly in the small of his back, pushing him towards a flight of stairs. The woman sprinted up ahead of them, tight track pants straining even tighter and revealing the line of her mini briefs.

At the top, Bromo noted a camera beaming downwards. A door swung open. Again, there was a firm push in his back. He stumbled forward into a cupboard doing duty as an office. A tiny cramped space. Just enough room for a filing cabinet, two foldaway chairs and a basic desk. Behind the desk sat Gerry Nuyen, a squat, broad, unsmiling man in an open neck pastel pink shirt, chin resting on hands clasped in front of him, elbows on the desk top. One hand dropped down and forward, palm upwards, gesturing towards one of the chairs.

'Please, Mr Perkins, have a seat.'

He spoke softly with a slight Asian lisp; clipping the words, courteous but firm. It was an order more than a request, made all the clearer by a firm downward push on Bromo's shoulder from one of the heavies.

'I think it's time we had a talk.'

Bromo stayed silent, his eyes focused on a poster on the wall to the left of Nuyen's head. Pictures of dishes of food encircled the words Hanoi Heaven Restaurant. He fancied the skewered sesame prawns on a bed of bok choy. Nuyen must have read his thoughts. The skewered prawns were not to be.

'The best we can offer is green tea,' he said, reaching under the desk for a large flask.

He pressed the nozzle and filled one of several small floral cups on the desktop.

'It's good for the nerves,' he smiled, pushing the cup towards Bromo.

'Scotch is better.'

'Ah, the Western panacea. In the East we tend to work from within rather than without. Strengthening the mind, not numbing it. Calming it rather than confusing it with alcohol. That way, Mr Perkins, you do not know whether I am angry or pleased that you have decided to visit me or whether ...'

'Did I have a choice?' Bromo interrupted.

'Let's say it was an invitation you found difficult to refuse. And let's also remain calm. Try your tea.'

His hand gestured gently towards the cup. Bromo hesitated, resolving an inner battle where aggression and diplomacy were fighting for the upper hand. He took a sip. For now, diplomacy had won.

'As I was saying, I've asked you here . . .'

'Forced,' Bromo interrupted.

Nuyen sighed, weary of debate.

'Words, words, words, Mr Perkins. Different interpretations. Regardless of our point of view, you are now here and we have matters of mutual interest to discuss.'

Bromo's heart did a couple of backflips. Or were they somersaults? Perhaps two-and-half turns with pike. It seemed his dalliance with Aurelia was on the agenda. And anything Nuyen had to say would be backed up by his trio of enforcers. Nuyen gestured to them.

'Wait outside.'

Again, Bromo had that unnerving feeling his thoughts were being read, assessed and negated. One of the minders hesitated, showing doubt at Nuyen's command, uneasy at leaving him alone with their captive. Nuyen reassured him.

'I'm sure we'll be all right; Mr Perkins is worried I might be upset about his friendship with my wife, but we have more private matters to discuss.'

Bromo heard a flurry of squeaky movement behind him; soft-soled shoes turning on the tiled floor and the door being slowly closed. He relaxed slightly, although it was no use kidding himself they were alone. Outside, three pairs of ears would be keenly tuned for any signs of violence or dissent.

Nuyen's elbows were back on the desk, clasped hands showing perfectly manicured nails with a hint of polish, head leaning forward just enough for Bromo to see the beginnings of a bald patch.

'So, Mr Perkins, what can you tell me about Peter Rasheed?'

At last, Nuyen was getting to the point. This was what this was all about. Aurelia was off the agenda. Bromo took a deep and calming breath. Better to face a dodgy businessman than an angry husband. Another intake of air was needed, another deeper breath, drawing it down, down, down and holding it before slowly releasing. He hovered on the edge of a trance. Nuyen's voice jerked him back.

'I asked you a question, Mr Perkins. About Rasheed.'

Bromo closed his eyes and shook his head, urging himself up from the semi-conscious depths of his meditation. His eyes blinked open.

'Sorry, I can't help you. From what I hear, you probably know much more about him than I do.'

Nuyen smiled and Bromo wondered how such a small movement of the lips could say so much. It spoke of patience, forbearance and determination. As if to confirm Bromo's interpretation, Nuyen gave a spoken translation.

'Come, come, Mr Perkins. I am well aware of your recent activities so you might as well tell me what you've discovered. I am also a patient man and I can come back when you feel like talking. However, if I decide it's taking too long I might have to call on my staff to exercise their various talents.'

The smile remained, but Nuyen now managed to invest it with a change of meaning - sinister and threatening. Bromo rapidly made a new translation: menace. He didn't do menace any more. It was time to comply.

'Okay. What do you want to know? Rasheed doesn't seem to have too many friends around town. Those he does have are probably on the take or have their own shonky deals. It's even been suggested you might be among them.'

'Ah.'

Nuyen's hands parted rapidly and one slapped the desktop in time with his exclamation.

'So that's their game.'

'What game? Whose game?'

Again Nuyen slapped the desktop.

'I'm asking the questions.'

The smiling facade of serenity had cracked. Bromo pushed his back hard against the chair frame, allowing more space between them. The lessons of old remained with him: ease tension by creating neutral territory. It seemed to work. Nuyen was again steepling his hands, and almost smiling.

'My apologies, Mr Perkins. Not your fault. You are merely

reporting what you have been told. There are many people out there who wish to do me harm.'

'But at least you haven't been bashed and left for dead.'

'Ah, yes. That was somewhat excessive.'

'So, that was your doing?'

'Not me, Mr Perkins.' The smile broadened. 'My hands are clean.'

Bromo nodded in the direction of the door.

'And the hands of your staff, as you call them - are they clean?'

A slight shrug from Nuyen, his head tilting slightly forward. The bald patch was larger than Bromo had realised.

'Perhaps sometimes they get over-enthusiastic. I must talk to them.'

'So you were at least indirectly responsible for Rasheed's injuries?'

'History, Mr Perkins. History. I have seen violence and I don't like it. But sometimes it is necessary. I just want you to tell me what you've discovered during your recent adventures. We'd really like to know where we can find Peter Rasheed. Simple questions needing simple answers.'

Bromo studied him, pondering the background of this man who seemed so assured of his power. There was only a hint of Asian antecedents in his facial appearance. His accent, though clipped and precise, showed few traces of a Vietnamese heritage. Outwardly, everything spoke of a gentle, mannered softness. Yet there was little doubt he would have seen horror, violence and deprivation way beyond anything experienced by most of those he now lived among. A hardened man, definitely. But a hard man? Maybe not. The jury was out on that.

'I've discovered nothing and I've no idea where Mr Rasheed might be,' Bromo lied.

'Sonia.'

It was a command more than a name. Bromo hardly had time to register it before he heard the door open behind him. He sniffed a heady perfume, as the women's arms came down either side of him, a leather strap between her hands. The strap encircled his chest, jerking him hard against the frame of the chair as she buckled it tightly. His arms were captured in the strap and pinioned to his sides. Strands of the woman's hair tickled his neck as she bent close to tighten the strap.

'Nice perfume,' said Bromo.

'Poison,' said a soft voice close to his ear.

'Appropriate.'

Nuyen was making circles with his right hand.

'Round here, Sonia. Mr Perkins is taking too long to answer my questions. Perhaps you could hurry things along by showing him some of your tricks.'

She squeezed easily between Bromo and the desk. She was short, compact and he guessed no more than 50 kilos. She'd discarded the jacket of her black suit. A white sleeveless T-shirt fitted like a second skin over a body made almost breast-less by the strictures of a clearly outlined sports bra. Every sinew and muscle in her arms was sharply defined in the way of someone very familiar with the inside of a gym and with lifting and pressing weighty rounds of metal in the name of fitness.

She pushed in between Bromo's knees. She reached for his trouser band, deftly undid the two buttons and began sliding the zip down. Bromo tried to retain his composure.

'You've done this before.'

'Sonia's very efficient, Mr Perkins,' said Nuyen. 'Highly trained in the martial arts. Always goes for the most vulnerable points.'

'Oh, I thought this was her idea of foreplay. She had me quite excited.'

He tensed as her hands pulled open his trouser front and moved down towards his crutch. There they stopped, millimetres from touching him. He tensed further, more than he thought possible. His stomach was drawn in to his backbone. His buttocks squeezed and tightened. It was like busting to have a pee when the nearest loo was five minutes away and up three flights of stairs. He could feel, too, a rising sexual expression of pleasure at the proximity of a female body. Damn those body parts that seem to have a mind of their own. Perversity thy name is penis.

'I think you could start applying some pressure, Sonia,' said Nuyen.

He smiled at Bromo: 'Unless, of course, Mr Perkins feels like answering my questions.'

Her hands hovered and moved slightly closer. They were just touching the fabric of his underpants. Thankfully, he still adhered to his mother's demands, given in childhood and remembered ever since: *always wear clean underwear*, she'd ordered - *you never know when you might be run over by a bus.*

He had often mused that clean underdaks would be the least of your worries if hit by a double-decker. But, to the women of his mother's generation, embarrassment hurt more than broken bones. Right now he would take embarrassment over anything the hand-clenching Sonia might have in mind.

He wriggled against the strap binding his arms. The muscles in his thighs tightened. One hand was touching his balls, encircling and closing. She raised her head and coal black eyes highlighted by a turquoise eye shadow stared at him. Bromo had long believed there was more to be read in a woman's eyes than in what came from her lips. Today's message was clear: I can and I will – with pleasure. Her hand closed slightly. The pain began.

'Well, Mr Perkins?'

Bromo squirmed, knees pressing hard against her thighs. The pain shot through his pelvis, up and outwards towards his stomach. Her grip tightened and the pain increased. Bromo felt his eyes squeezing tight shut and his mouth opening as another agonising spasm racked his lower body.

'Ah, his lips are moving, Sonia,' commented Nuyen. 'Your magic seems to be working. Perhaps just a little bit more.'

'No,' yelled Bromo. 'Enough. Let's talk. That's torture, not magic.'

'Cut the comments. Where's Rasheed?'

'Mack's.'

Nuyen pushed down hard on the desk, jerking upright and backwards into his chair. His surprise was obvious. Small word, big effect, noted Bromo.

'What d'you mean, Mack's? It's a deserted bloody factory. No one lives in a factory.'

'Rasheed does. All mod cons. Lots of room to expand.'

Sonia stood up and moved from her full frontal position. She eased past his knees to somewhere behind him. To turn and look would betray his anxiety. A waft of perfume was enough to assure him she remained close. Nuyen was still digesting the information. Time to test the waters.

'He's making himself comfortable,' said Bromo. 'Could be he sees it as a desirable inner-city apartment. Perhaps even a whole block of them.'

It was like firecracker night. The fuse had burnt right down. Nuyen exploded, slamming both palms down on the desk, propelling himself up out of his chair and leaning his face close into Bromo's, centimetres away.

'Don't mess with me Mr Perkins. You're obviously well aware that Rasheed wants to build apartments. We've seen you nosing around City Hall, asking questions, trying to get alongside the staff.'

Bromo judged the playing field was levelling out. He feigned innocence.

'So what's the problem? It's just another development. Surely you haven't suddenly gone all soft and joined the Greenies.'

Nuyen subsided into his chair.

'We had a deal. Rasheed's broken it.'

The rage had evaporated. In its place was cold, calculating calm. No one spoke or moved. The clattering of pans rose up the stairwell from the kitchens below. Cooks were shouting orders. The muffled rumble of a tram came and went. Nuyen flicked his hand at Sonia.

'Untie him.'

Bromo felt the strap being unbuckled. His arms came free and he zipped up his trousers. He took a look over his shoulder. She was still there, rock-still and alert, arms folded across her chest and ready for action. Nuyen spoke.

'I need your help.'

His mood had undergone yet another change. The tone was almost pleading. Bromo was wary. The perfumed persuader remained too close.

'You've got the wrong man. There's nothing I can do. Send in your heavy brigade.'

'They're not the ones playing around with my wife.'

Crunch! They'd got there at last. Bromo swallowed, did his deep-breathing routine, tried to show no reaction. He said nothing. There were times when silence was the only answer. Nuyen raised his eyes, looking beyond Bromo. He gave a slight nod of the head.

'Okay Sonia. Wait outside. I'm sure Mr Perkins won't be any trouble.'

She made hardly a sound. There was the slightest click of the door closing. They were alone. The blanket of silence was suffocating. Bromo had nothing to offer. It was Nuyen who would have to lift it.

'What has Aurelia told you about me?'

The question took Bromo by surprise. He'd expected accusations, threats, demands - anything but this almost gentle supplication.

'Nothing.'

They faced off across the desk, both hesitant, ill at ease, Bromo sensing a strange lack of animosity from the man he was cuckolding.

'Nothing?'

'God's truth.' Bromo paused. 'She's very loyal. I'm under no illusions. You're the main man.'

He couldn't have done better if he'd fed him a couple of uppers. Nuyen perked up, sat straight and gave the glimmer of a smile. He took a moment to digest Bromo's comments then leaned forward, speaking softly, confidentially.

'Thank you, Mr Perkins. That is good to know.' He paused. 'I will tell you something that is just between us.'

He picked up his cup, took a sip of the tea, hesitating, considering his words. He placed the cup gently and precisely on the table top, looking into it as if searching for guidance among the leaves. When he spoke, his voice was quiet, gentle, confiding.

'I am impotent, Mr Perkins. As you say in Australia, I cannot get it up. Many years ago, back in Vietnam, something happened. They were terrible times. Nothing can be done. We live with it. We have a convenient marriage but there are some things I cannot provide. So I am not angry with you, or with my wife over this. I can pretend to be angry, but it would be wrong.'

Nuyen sat back. Bromo read relief in his face. It couldn't have been easy. Not for any man, but especially not for one with his tough guy reputation. Men don't admit things like that, not even to their best mate; and often not to their doctor until things get beyond unbearable. They'd rather pop a couple of Horny Goat Weed tablets and hope they lived up to the flamboyant promises and pictures on the packet.

One thing he wouldn't do was gloat, despite the assumption Nuyen seemed to be giving tacit approval to his relationship with Aurelia. It certainly put her flirtatious nature in an entirely new light and explained why warnings of violence from Nuyen's protectors had never come true. Fiona's threats now meant nothing, eradicated by Nuyen's confession.

'Of course, that's not to say I will not let my staff practise on you if you do not help me.'

Once more a glimmer of a smile, hands open and upturned in an expression of reason.

'Now that we have talked like this you will understand it will be nothing personal. I think you see what I mean. It's a matter of business, not revenge. I'm a businessman, you are ... well, a sort of businessman. So, we do business.'

Bromo ignored this slur on his efforts to earn an income. Experience had taught him big didn't necessarily mean better, certainly not in the areas of ethics and efficiency. He played dumb.

'So, that's what this is all about: you want me to look after your company's travel arrangements? You don't need Sonia to squeeze my balls for that. It might be more than I want to take on at present, but ...'

'Stop.'

Another short fuse had blown.

'In case you had forgotten we are talking about me, you, and Peter Rasheed. Not some stupid travel arrangements.'

Okay, so playing dumb didn't work. Back to the main game.

'Why me? You and Rasheed are the ones doing business. And the way I see it, your business is not my business.'

'It is now,' barked Nuyen.

Neither spoke. It was if each was pausing to reflect on this new phase in their relationship. Bromo saw no overlap between his world and Nuyen's. Aurelia was their only link, and that was centred on quick fucks rather than fast bucks. Nuyen resumed his friendly pose, elbows tabled, chin resting on steepled hands, lips upturned with a smile of reasonableness.

'Let me explain. We are both migrants, but you are Anglo-Saxon; I am Asian. You were assisted, welcomed. My family had to plead and fight. They came with nothing. They were innocent victims. On the other hand, Mr Perkins, you have a dubious past. Yet it is you who is accepted.'

Bromo stiffened. Christ, word about his previous existence on the other side of the world was getting round far more than he'd realised. He tried to show no reaction, holding himself erect and still. He needn't have worried. Nuyen flowed on, his focus internal.

'I have worked hard and honestly but people still suspect me. I have learnt that if you are an Asian, a slopehead, you can buy influence but not acceptance. You, Mr Perkins, no one questions. I like that. It is useful. So, we do business?'

He uttered it as a question, but Bromo heard it as the statement Nuyen intended it to be. He also noted the underlying message: it was a job offer he was not meant to refuse. Just like the demands from the forceful Fiona Leoncavallo. He tugged at his earlobe. It seemed he'd suddenly become Mr Popularity. Everyone wanted a piece of him, or at least wanted him to do some of their dirty work.

'What sort of business?'

'Quiet business,' said Nuyen. 'Information. Finding documents. Asking questions. I believe it is something you used to do very well.'

Again there was that hint of people digging into ground that Bromo believed would never be disturbed. He took a long, slow breath, stilling the unease.

'Nothing illegal,' he said.

'Of course not,' smiled Nuyen. 'We are both honest businessmen, are we not? It's just that you are more familiar with the local ways. You understand the officials and their language. They will take you seriously. People will tell you what Peter Rasheed is doing. You will be able to find documents and files.' He paused. 'And computer disks.'

Bromo got the message but showed no acknowledgement. They stared at each other across the desk.

'You say nothing, Mr Perkins. Perhaps you would like another visit from Sonia.'

Bromo relented: 'Okay, you win. I'll see what I can find out. Just lay off the heavy stuff.'

'And the computer disks?'

Bromo shrugged: 'There's nothing on them. Just a lot of porno stuff. Tits and arse.'

'Ah.'

Nuyen smiled the smile that Bromo decided was nothing of the sort. It threatened rather than cheered; an early warning system of violence to come. Minnows would see the same expression as they swam in the path of a shark.

'Sonia.'

She must have had one hand on the door's handle, the other against its surface, ready to turn and push the moment he called. Her right hand came down heavily on Bromo's right shoulder as her left arm wrapped around his neck, jerking him backwards.

Her two sidekicks slid into the room behind her as Nuyen pushed himself up out of his chair.

'No, Sonia, no. That's not needed.'

She slackened her grip in response to Nuyen's command. Bromo spluttered, gasping for air.

'It's all right,' said Nuyen. 'Mr Perkins has agreed to help us. He's just leaving. Go with him. He has some computer disks he'll give you to bring back.'

The two heavyweights moved in on either side of Bromo, easing him towards the door. Sonia fell in behind him. The clatter from the kitchen got louder. Much louder. It seemed to be overflowing into the dining area. Voices were being raised.

'Another unhappy diner,' muttered Bromo.

His words were lost in the frantic screaming of a waiter

who'd suddenly appeared at the foot of the stairs, yelling and waving his arms in the direction of the restaurant.

'Come, come,' he screeched. 'Men smash tables.'

His English was limited, staccato. The message was clear and urgent. The three bodyguards hurtled down the stairs, following the waiter into the restaurant. Nuyen tumbled rapidly behind, elbowing Bromo to one side and stepping through into the restaurant. Bromo suddenly found himself alone. He paused, stock still, assessing the situation. Was he as free as he assumed? The wall between the staircase and the restaurant was plywood thin. The noise coming through the green painted sheets of board told of mayhem. Most of the yelling was in a foreign tongue; the thumps, yells and crashing of furniture and crockery were universal. It was on for young and old. He hoped Cheap Eats hadn't chosen today to do a review.

Bromo inched forward, a step at a time, prepared at any moment to have Sonia embracing him in a headlock. Two stairs further down and he decided everyone was too busy with the fracas in the restaurant. He ran the last half-dozen steps.

At the foot of the stairs there was a door on his right leading into the restaurant. Ahead was the street. He stumbled out on to the pavement, colliding with an elderly Chinese woman shuffling forward with a clutch of plastic bags in both hands. He held his arms up in surrender pose.

'Sorry, sorry,' he said.

'Don't worry, mate. She'll be awright.'

It was Gus Thompson. His bulky mass loomed over the fragile Chinese woman. He reached out an arm, pincering Bromo's elbow in a painful grip. He nodded towards the restaurant.

'Must be something they ate.'

Bromo followed his nod and glimpsed a melee of bodies and arms lacking any sense or pattern. There was no idea of who was fighting who. He saw one of Nuyen's bodyguards flailing away at a hooded figure. Sonia was weaving between upturned tables, sticking close to Nuyen. He grimaced as he watched her administer a quick karate chop on some unfortunate who stood in her way and keep moving towards the back of the room. Bromo winced at an added squeeze on his arm. Gus Thompson smiled at hi.

'Not a good place to be. Mr Perkins. You'd better come with me.'

'Do I have a choice?'

He knew the answer: there wasn't one. Thompson simply kept smiling - and tightened his already painful grip on Bromo's arm, guiding him towards a car that was double-parked, engine turning, a short fat man with dark glasses behind the wheel. Bromo felt Gus Thompson's hand on his head, pushing him down and into the car - a technique Bromo knew all too well.

'You've been watching too many cop movies,' he said.

'Good way to learn,' confirmed Thompson as he plumped in beside him. 'Lotsa good tricks.'

'Is trashing a restaurant one of them? Bit of a coincidence you being here.'

Thompson smiled: 'Don't know nothing about that. Lotsa bad people out there. Seems you just got lucky. Mr Delgado told me to look after you. Remember?'

The car purred away from the chaos. No one seemed to notice their departure. Least of all the occupants of the two police divvy vans now pulling up outside the restaurant.

'They'll sort it,' said Thompson.

The roads were greasily wet after another heavy shower, blown in with the cool change. Newspapers, wrappings and fast food packs that had been blown along the footpaths were now sitting soggily in the gutters, blocking drains and creating mini lakes of grimy water. A cyclist skidded across the tram tracks in front of them. The driver braked, held his line and cursed.

'Bloody two-wheelers.'

'We pay our taxes, too,' said Bromo.

'Christ, you're not one of them, are you?' said the driver.

'Fraid so. It beats driving ... most of the time.'

He'd had suffered crushed cartilage and a broken wrist from a couple of falls and got used to being abused by louts leering out of car windows, beer cans in hand. But it still remained his preferred mode of inner city travel.

'Cyclists travel a different world: they ride another route,' he muttered.

'Crap,' replied the diver, slowing the car to a gentle stop outside the supermarket where Bromo spent most of his house-keeping budget. 'This okay?'

'It'll do,' said Thompson. 'He can walk from here.'

Bromo raised an eyebrow: 'Aren't you escorting me to my door?'

'You'll manage. I'll be watching. You're as good as home.'

He leaned across and opened the door. Bromo ignored the suggestion he should get out.

'Tell me, you and Delgado, whose side are you on? What's your interest? Why that raid on Nuyen's place? Is Rasheed paying you?'

Gus Thompson listened without reaction. His broad, flat boxer's face showed no emotion.

'No go, mate. Too many questions. I just do as I'm told. Look after you; deliver you safely home. And here we are.'

He gestured towards the car door, opening it wider.

'You'll be right. Gunner's looking after you.'

He grinned. But it was the grin of menace and control, lacking any humour or warmth. He pushed the door open wider, almost skittling a man, frail and bent, toting two plastic bags of shopping.

'Go home, Mr Perkins,' said Gunner. 'You'll be safe there.'

Bromo eased himself out on to the footpath alongside a cafe's tables. Go with the flow, he told himself. Walking free on the street was better than being tied to a chair with Sonia squeezing your balls.

He gave a weak smile at a woman nursing her customary red wine, a thin cigar at her lips. Under the table, eyes flicking warily open, dozed her ancient blue heeler. Bromo and the woman had never met, never spoken, but each gave the other their due as a local, as a face on the street, as one who belonged and was part of the suburb's social fabric. Street talk was that the woman owned a block of the nearby shops and drifted from cafe to cafe keeping an eye on her properties and their tenants. Some even claimed her interests went much deeper, that she not only owned the building where porno books and movies were sold, but also the business.

Bromo nodded an acknowledgment in the woman's direction and kept walking. He couldn't get to the sanctuary of home quick enough.

TWENTY-TWO

He let the front door slam shut and dropped into the depths of his old armchair.

'Stuffed,' he said to no one but himself. 'Absolutely stuffed.'

He had a feeling things weren't going to improve until Nuyen and Rasheed stopped playing their deviously violent version of kick-to-kick that used Bromo Perkins as the ball.

He fumbled with his CD player. Mahler was in the slot. Too deep, too mournful and meaningful. He didn't need musical psychoanalysis right now. He thumbed through the racks of disks and opted for calm; for the soothing chants of Hildegard von Bingen. Better than a Panadol any day.

The music washed over him as he sank back into the chair trying to ignore the beeping of his answering machine. He'd been aware of its insistent noise for several minutes. It was hard to ignore; but he'd done his best.

There were two messages. The first he cut off as soon as the Indian voice began its preamble: 'Mr Perkins, we would like to offer you …'

He was a call-centre magnet. Every day, right on three o'clock, they began. Most times they rang off as soon as they connected to the answering machine. This one must have been more desperate to get her quota up. He relaxed. Message two was probably more of the same.

It wasn't.

'Bromo, Liz Shapcott here. Pick up if you're there.'

She sounded agitated.

'Didn't you listen? I told you to be careful. You could get hurt. Remember, I advised you to stick to what you do.' She paused. 'You do it well.'

Another pause, her voice calmer, softer.

'And thanks for the bookings.'

He played it again, trying to fathom the tone, weigh the voice, judge the message. What was its true purpose - to thank him, or to warn him? The thankyou seemed like an afterthought. He detected an anxiety, even a concern and, again, that underlying warning, which had so surprised him the first time she'd uttered similar words when he'd visited her at home.

Okay, so Liz Shapcott had some connection with whatever was intended for Mack's. Twice he'd seen her name on plans for the development at the site. As one of the area's leading architects, that was hardly surprising. She'd shown anxiety at his involvement with Rasheed, who was squatting at Mack's. But he sensed this latest message wasn't a simple concern for his wellbeing. She'd already told him to stay clear and stop asking questions. This time it sounded more like an order than friendly advice.

Bromo fingered his ear and rubbed at the lobe. He was beginning to feel like a ball in a lotto barrel, being tumbled around by forces he couldn't control. Some were unearthing his past, coercing him into involvements he didn't seek. Others were applying physical pressure to get him either deeply enmeshed or to quit while he was still in one piece. Everyone seemed to have persuasive muscle men, and women on call for their dirty work.

There was a two-day-old packet of bread in the fridge. He pulled out two slices and put them in the toaster. While they were tanning he flicked through the RAGE and RAID folders. It was more a distraction than with any hope of unearthing any answers. There were lists of council meetings, cuttings from the local papers, print-outs of emails to councillors expressing everything from undying support to extreme fury and a couple of simple flyers.

'Enough is Enough' proclaimed a black on yellow leaflet in the RAID folder. It opposed a multi-storey tower proposed for a riverside site but nevertheless favoured a massive building block going where there were now only trees and shrubs. An each-way bet.

'Green is Not the Only Colour' stated a foolscap sheet in the RAGE file. This pushed the case for transforming a block of shops into modern apartments.

Both were familiar arguments. They were the lifeblood of local politics in the inner suburbs. Somewhere in between their extremes was the only way forward if the demands of modern life were to be met. Yet compromise was hard to find. Although workers' timber cottages with outside dunnies belonged in the distant past, there were those who refused to accept the modern alternative.

The well-browned bread popped up from the toaster. He smeared on a thin veneer of butter and a hefty coating of honey.

As he closed the RAID folder, the contents fell back into place and bold lines on the back of the flyer caught his eye. It looked like the doodlings of someone as they drowsed through another boring meeting. Or was it? He looked closer. It was several roughly-drawn shapes - circles, squirls, plaits, entwined lines. A child-like attempt at an animal's head was encircled by some wavy lines. There were efforts at drawing a flower. And some lettering.

It was a sketch of the brooch he'd seen worn by Aurelia Nuyen and Liz Shapcott and spray-painted on the wall at Mack's.

The lettering indicated frustration: words, whole lines, crossed through and rewritten above and below. Always variations on the same few words, over and over. The scribbler seemed to have been playing with slogans and acronyms, seeking a snappy catch-cry.

Bromo noted 'Tiger' was part of every attempt. Allegiance to the suburb and its footy club was apparently as important as any other message being shouted. Tiger fans were like that - diehard and dogged, never admitting defeat no matter how many times their team lost its way to goal. The season had got off to one of the worst ever starts – four games and no wins. Still the masochistic fans returned for their weekly dose of dashed hopes and loss of face.

The other words were variations on a floral theme - Poppy, Poppies, Pops and even a detour into Rose, Roses and Rosie. All of which made sense of the tiger's head brooch with its red flower. Harder to understand were the slogans the doodler was trying build from these words. Poppy was being used as a base for something to do with pornography. Rose was being built into a protest over sexual exploitation. Judging by the graffiti Bromo had seen at Mack's, Tiger Poppies must have got the vote. What they stood for was anyone's guess. Perhaps he should ask for a membership form and see what response he got.

He reached for his phone and dialled. She answered on the second ring. He assumed a light, slightly effeminate, mincing voice,

'Tiger Poppies? How do I join? Is there a membership fee?'

Silence. He sensed tension and caution at the other end of the line.

'I didn't catch your name. Where did you hear about us?'

He struggled to keep in voice.

'Someone mentioned you down at the pub.'

He fumbled for a name.

'It's Marion.'

He hoped it fitted the voice. A convincing unisex tag. Again there was that doubting silence. He could almost grab the wave of suspicion flowing down the line. The response was guarded and diplomatic.

'We're always interested in new members, Marion, but we like to get to know them first,' she said.

There was another long pause. Bromo could sense her hesitating, evaluating her caller, choosing her responses.

'Perhaps you could give me your number,' she eventually said. 'I'll call you back when I'm free and we can arrange to meet.'

She'd trapped him. But he'd got the confirmation he wanted: Liz Shapcott was involved in Tiger Poppies. It was time to cut and run. His false voice was wavering. He couldn't sustain it. He tried for a convincing finale.

'Sorry, my mobile's out of action and I don't know where I'll be over the next few days. Perhaps I should ring you.'

She cut in: 'Don't worry, Bromo. I know where to find you . . . with or without the funny voice.'

The line went dead.

Shit, was everyone on Bromo-watch? Too many people seemed to be taking an uncomfortable interest in his whereabouts. Even worse, most of them didn't seem to have too much trouble tracking him down whenever they wanted to make his life uncomfortable. Knock at the door, ring the bell, send in the hoons. As easy as that. It was like being a billiard ball at the mercy of a tyro player – being bounced from cushion to cushion and never falling into the right slot.

Fiona contacted him at will, her tame gorillas hovering nearby. Nuyen used his heavy squad as a calling card. Delgado relied on the muscle power of an old bruiser. No doubt Gunner Thompson was lurking somewhere outside his apartment right now, ready to track any movement he made. It was an obstacle he didn't need if he was to keep his looming appointment at Pistons with Goth-girl Delia. A quick solution was needed.

Bromo glanced at his watch and stuffed the remaining triangle of toast in his mouth. There was time for a quick shower.

He refreshed his body with a stream of hot water followed by a rinse with a full-force blast from the cold tap.

He opted for an open-neck denim shirt, grey slacks and loafers, fluffed up his hair and fired a squirt of some so-called fragrance from the $2 Shop around his neck.

He checked Pistons' location in the Melway, picked up his mobile and tapped a number on the speed dial. His call was brief, terse and precise. He made another call, a bit longer, more explanation needed. Problem solved - he hoped.

TWENTY-THREE

HE HAD PASSED THE building many times, but always in daylight and not paying it any great attention. It was just another whitewashed brick wall with a couple of barred windows and a narrow metal roller door padlocked to the footpath. Its neighbours were a car-detailer's workshop advertising its presence with noxious and pungent fumes and an electrical appliance store which plastered its windows with offers of interest-free terms and washing machines at less than cost price.

Tonight the roller door was raised almost to the roofline where a narrow hand-painted strip of wood gave the name of the licensee. For the first time Bromo noticed a small brass plaque on the side wall confirming this was Pistons and it was open until late four nights a week.

Beyond the roller door was another – a leadlighted upper half over a panelled timber lower section. It led to a long, narrow room, dimly lit with a bar down the right-hand wall. Soft music – a tune he recognised from much earlier times but could not name – mingled with conversation from two couples and a foursome scattered among lounges and armchairs. It looked and felt like someone's lounge room and hardly the haunt of a Goth.

A lone woman was perched on a stool in the darkness at the far end of the bar. She waved a hand in Bromo's direction.

No one he recognised. Probably a case of mistaken identity. Mark her down as a possible for chatting up if Delia failed to appear. The barman leaned towards him with an unspoken but obvious question.

'A scotch,' said Bromo. 'A malt.'

The barman waved his hand at a line of bottles behind him.

'Any preference?'

'Any chance of a Laphroaig?'

'Of course,' said the barman.

His voice wavered between suggesting the question was a trip into the bleeding obvious and pride at the extent of his range.

'And I'll have a G & T.'

The voice startled him. For a moment he strained to recognise her. The hair was a close crop and she seemed far taller and slimmer. The woman from the far end of the bar had moved in alongside him – Delia the Goth, minus nose ring and lip bolt, inches higher on strappy high heels.

Bromo stifled his surprise.

'Didn't recognise you in civvies. Where's the witch's cloak?'

'In the wardrobe.'

'With the lion?'

She picked up on the reference and acknowledged it with a grin.

'Even witches and Goths take a night off."

'So it seems.'

He ran his eyes over her crisp white shirt, short bolero-like turquoise jacket and calf-length skirt, split to high up her thigh: 'I think I prefer this version. Can't imagine them letting you through the door in the other outfit.'

'That's for the office. It gets up their noses. Keeps 'em guessing.'

'They're not the only ones. You've got me puzzled, too. City Hall flunky, whistleblower, Goth, uni student . . . what else?'

She sipped her drink and gave him a sidelong glance, weighing him up.

'That's about it. Not much more to tell. At least for now.'

She was friendly, but guarded. Bromo was well aware she was still judging him, probably deciding the level of trust she could place in him. He wanted to keep the conversation flowing, waiting for that moment when he could steer it from the personal and into the real reason for them sitting on stools in a neighbourhood bar.

He took a gulp of his drink and set another course.

'So, city hall is where you're at now. What went before? What's the history? The background? Family? Is the Delia of today descended from a long line of Goths?'

For a few seconds, she went rigid. The smile lines around her mouth and eyes disappeared. Both hands gripped the stem of her glass. Bromo felt he'd touched a nerve - and she was trying not to let it show. He knew all too well the past was often unpleasant territory, a place well off the emotional tourist track. He'd made a bad step She took a hand off the glass and swept long strands of black hair back from her face.

'Too many questions.'

She gave him another assessing stare.

'You're a nosey bugger, aren't you?'

He shrugged, halfway between an apology and a withdrawal. He sipped his drink.

'Sorry, just interested, making conversation. Didn't mean to intrude.'

But he knew he had and felt contrite. He'd done enough trampling over people's emotions to know at long last when to draw back. It had been a hard-learnt and very costly lesson with many pitfalls along the way. He wasn't about to regress.

'You don't have to say a thing,' he said. 'We've got other matters to discuss.'

'Fair enough. I guess you've a right to know who you're dealing with. Perhaps I do have a story to tell.'

She caught the barman's eye and pointed to their glasses for refills. Bromo twisted in his seat to try to tug his wallet from a rear pocket but she trumped him with a banknote produced with a flourish from somewhere inside her jacket.

'My shout,' she said.

Her smile had returned. She swivelled on her bar stool to face him and put a hand on his knee. The familiarity surprised him.

'I'd like to talk,' she said. 'There's no one else I can do that with. Certainly not that lot at work. And I don't have a network of girlfriends.'

She gave a short laugh: 'Or boyfriends.'

Bromo was warming to her. This wasn't the same brooding, surly woman who'd crawled out from behind a desk at the town hall. He thought of telling her she looked much better minus the nose ring and lip-bolt and wanted to confirm her working hairstyle was really a wig but an inner voice urged caution. She seemed to operate on several levels and he wasn't sure he'd found her locator map. A bit like wandering into the Myer store and taking the escalator into women's underwear when you were looking for electrical appliances.

'I'm listening,' he said.

It was the only cue she needed.

'Mum was a cot case because dad was a bastard. An alcoholic bastard. It's the usual story, nothing new. Too much booze feeding too few brains. Only way to resolve an argument was to lash out. Didn't even need an argument. Just something he didn't agree with.'

'Nice guy,' Bromo commented.

'Then I got myself up the duff. Pregnant at 15. It was the turning point. Mum kicked him out and took care of the kid. Turned into the greatest grandma you've ever seen. And she got me back on track. Through high school and then studying urban planning and design.'

'And the goths?' asked Bromo.

'It's fun. A relief from work and study. It's not all for show. It's a genuine interest' she said. 'The serious stuff is kept for weekends. Sort of consenting adults in private but really all very respectable. Mostly involves a lot of very loud music in dark rooms. Goths are totally non-violent and we leave the rough sex and foul language to others.'

Bromo twitched as a trio of chattering twentysomething females, all with bulbous bare midriffs, burst through the door and gave high fives to the barman. He relaxed. Regulars.

Two men followed, and he tensed again. He watched the men unwind their ties to lessen the formality of their dark business suits. They, too, knew the barman.

'Hi Marco.'

'Hi Russ. Hi Tim.'

More regulars. Bromo relaxed.

'Cosy little place,' he remarked. 'The name had me fooled. So did you. I thought it was a hangout for the dark side, bikies, hoons, all that lot, leathers and Harleys. So, what's with the name Pistons?'

Delia laughed again: 'Simple. We're pissed on Wednesday, we're pissed on Thursday . . . '

'Enough. I get it.'

He felt the time was right to test the waters: 'So, what can you tell me about city hall – and the lovely Mr Delgado?'

Her head jerked up at the mention of the name, suddenly, surprised: 'You've met him?'

He played it down: 'We've had a chat.' He tried to hose down her obvious concern: 'We're both gym junkies. Seen him lifting weights.'

'Oh.'

She seemed satisfied, fingered her glass, studying its contents. Bromo knew better than to rush her. Her personal story appeared well rehearsed, one she'd probably told many times before, editing it over the years to suit her audience. Revealing what she knew about council business was different. She could well be putting her job on the line. He stole another glance at the entrance; twitchy, anxious. He felt himself slipping back into a mode he thought he had long shuffled off.

Delia looked down at the floor, shoulders hunched forward, one hand still resting on his knee, a touch of familiarity he sensed was entirely for her own support. There was no intention to give him any encouragement, physical or emotional.

'I'm not sure where to begin,' she said.

Her voice was soft and uncertain.

'There's just so much that's not right, not making sense. Too many people seem scared, or afraid to question things.'

'What sort of things?'

'Decisions, plans, accounts … so much. Papers disappear. Actions are approved but it's hard to find who actually approved them. Committee meetings are often closed affairs. A rubber stamp. Steve Delgado seems involved but doesn't put his name to anything. And so are Peter Rasheed and perhaps Gerry Nuyen. If you push too hard for answers you get told it's not your department, not your problem. It's like dealing with the three wise monkeys, seeing nothing, hearing nothing, saying nothing. Only there's so many of them, all too scared to do anything.'

She paused and took a sip of her drink.

'Is it corruption or incompetence?' asked Bromo as he stole another glance at the door.

An older couple had made a tentative entrance. They swapped looks, silent messages born of years of togetherness, reached agreement without a word being said and moved in towards the bar.

'That's what I'm not sure about,' said Delia, picking up the conversation. 'There's just so much that's not right.'

Bromo stiffened. There was noise outside, voices raised, but whether in anger or jollity he wasn't sure. His focus shifted from Delia to the doorway. Three big men burst through, jostling each other, voices loud with laughter, their torsos straining out of jumpers emblazoned with the Wallabies rugby emblem. There was no glancing around to decide where to sit. They seemed oblivious of anyone else as they made straight to the bar. Their priorities were inbuilt.

'Three beers, long necks, Cascade,' said one after a brief joust to be the first to place an order.

'What else,' commented Bromo softly as he turned back to Delia, his body again relaxed and relieved. 'It's energy food.'

'Big boys,' offered Delia. 'They'd make a girl feel safe.'

'In your dreams,' said Bromo. 'Rugby, beer and their mates come well ahead of anything else. You'd be running a poor fourth. Perhaps fifth if they've got a car.'

'They friends of yours?' she asked.

The question took him by surprise and he felt a guilty reddening of his cheeks. He wriggled uneasily on the barstool: 'Why?'

'Body language. They came in and you relaxed. Before that you were all uptight, half listening to me, half watching the door, expecting someone.'

'Bullshit.'

Not the best answer. She'd rattled him. She was astute and observant. He must be losing his touch; too long out of the field. She mirrored his thoughts.

'That's no answer. What's going on?'

He paused and gave her a dismissive smile.

'Nothing. Everything's fine. Anyway, back to the town hall. I thought we were talking about corruption.'

'Maybe, although I can't be certain it's as bad as that. There's certainly a lot of dead ends and blind alleys, things not matching up, people evading questions.'

Bromo sniffed and made light of her assertions: 'Sounds like every local government body I've come across and this was one of the worst in the country until it was cleaned up a couple of decades ago. State and federal governments are no better. They're all like that. I thought you had something more specific.'

She leaned forward, her back to the door, one hand again placed on his thigh as she glanced around the room, ensuring they were in their own private cocoon of conversation. No eavesdroppers. Her voice dropped to a whisper.

'I do. It's all to do with Mack's and Steve Delgado and demolition contracts and the redevelopment. There's a .... '

She got no further. Bromo's attention was diverted by another noise from the entrance as the door was pushed open. Delia brought herself upright with a push down on Bromo's thigh and looked over her shoulder. Steve Delgado had come striding into the room, still in his business suit, taking no notice of anyone else and heading straight for them. Delia reached for her drink. Bromo noted the taut neck muscles, lips pressed tight together, a glower darkening her face.

'Stay calm,' he whispered. 'Everything's under control.'

Delgado stormed up to them.

Delia rallied: 'Steve!. What a surprise. I haven't seen you here before.'

He ignored her greeting. Bromo showed little reaction, other than to flick a glance along the bar towards the trio of rugby men before turning to look at Delgado.

'Drink?' he asked.

'Stuff your drink,' said Delgado, standing within millimetres of them. 'Gunner Johnson's been keeping an eye on you. I thought I told you to stay away from her.'

The words were spuming out of his mouth.

'And I thought I told you that how she and I spend our private time has nothing to do with you or anyone else at city hall,' replied Bromo.

He switched to what he hoped was a placatory tone: 'You can either join us for a drink or push off. And as for Gunner .... '

Delgado wasn't listening. He turned towards Delia and inched closer, standing over her, menacing, arms at his side but slightly bent, fists clenched. His voice was raised, angry, stilling the conversation of other patrons and drawing their attention. The barman had moved closer, alert for trouble. Delia cowered back against the bar for support as Delgado moved even closer.

'Keep your nose out of what doesn't concern you,' he spat. 'Stick to the job you're paid to do or I'll make sure you're looking for another one.'

She recovered: 'Is that a threat?'

'Take it how you like. A warning.'

'From you or from your shady mates?'

It was a barb that struck home, stirring his anger. His right hand flew up, flicking towards her face but not landing as she ducked back. His other hand grabbed her wrist. Suddenly the space around them was filled with a rushing mass of fast-moving bodies, thrashing, eerily silent, as they gathered Delgado to them and powered him, helpless, to the far end of the room, his feet lifted clear of the ground. They carried him, legs flailing, through a door marked Private. It was as if he'd never been there.

'Never mess with front-row forwards,' said Bromo by way of explanation. 'They just love a rolling scrum.'

Delia shook her head and blew out her cheeks: 'Phew.'

One hand went up and raked through her hair. She looked more surprised than injured.

'So, I guessed right, you do know them. Were you expecting trouble to organise that?'

He sniffed: 'It's an old boy scout habit - be prepared. Delgado got up my nose. I asked some mates of a mate if they'd like a drink. Speaking of which ....'

Jason Conquest ambled through the door, ducking his head slightly for fear of hitting the jamb. He nodded an acknowledgment to Bromo.

'All fixed.'

He was not one for wasting breath on unnecessary words. Bromo knew what he meant. He eased himself off his stool and held a hand out to Delia.

'Come, let's go see what Mr Delgado has to say for himself.'

She took his hand and stretched her leg out towards the floor. He eyed the expanse of flesh revealed by the parting of her skirt and scored it a nine out of ten. She caught his admiring glance and smiled up at him, their eyes almost level, thanks to her precariously thin high heels.

'It's okay to look.'

He side-stepped her comment, flustered at being sprung: 'Seems they've gone down the back somewhere,' he said. 'This way.'

Bromo led them along the length of the bar, Delia close behind, Jason bringing up the rear. They navigated a small lounge area with its scattering of armchairs and low tables. Bromo headed towards the door in the far corner and slowly turned its handle, cautious and tentative.

'It's okay. Come in.'

One of the rugby trio greeted them. Steve Delgado was seated on an upright chair, his arms pulled tight and tied by cord behind the frame, a strip of gaffer tape across his mouth. The two other rugby types stood either side of him, watchful but relaxed.

'He got a bit noisy,' explained the man who'd greeted them. 'Had to quieten him. He kept calling for someone called Gunner.'

'Fat chance. He won't be coming,' said Jason.

'Fixed?' said Bromo. It was a statement rather than a question.

'Yeah,' said Jason. 'Tracked him all the way from your place. Nabbed him outside. He's in the ute. Tied up. Not going anywhere.'

'Thanks, mate. I owe you one.'

'I've heard that before. I'll add it to the rest of them. Might be cheaper if you bought a pub.'

Bromo shrugged. His debt was growing. Now there were Jason's three rugby-playing colleagues to add to the bill. He looked at them - big, looming chunks that personified the label of gentle giants, their muscle power mostly confined to destroying opponents on the field and doing helpful tasks off it.

'I think you lads can get back to the bar. The tab's on me. I'll yell if I need you.'

He gestured towards Delgado: 'I can't see our friend here causing too much trouble.'

Jason and his mates stomped out and the room felt considerably less crowded. Delgado was turned towards Delia, glaring at her. Bromo moved to face him, gripping him firmly.by the chin.

'Eyes front,' he said, twisting Delgado's head.

He applied pressure and watched his captive wince. He found a pressure point and squeezed harder. Delgado squirmed, his face creased in pain.

'Had enough?'

Delgado shook his head up and down. Bromo turned to Delia.

'Reckon I should stop?'

She adopted a pensive pose, hand up to her chin, hair falling forward, playing at thinking, considering.

'Hmmm, maybe. On the other hand ....'

She paused, then: 'Perhaps give it another minute. Make sure he gets the message.'

She turned away, leaving Bromo to make the decision. He gave a final squeeze then loosened his grip.

'That's what happens to bullies,' he told Delgado. 'They eventually come up against someone bigger and uglier than themselves. Their victim turns the tables. The bully discovers what it's like to be bossed and humiliated. If they've got half a brain they realise respect is earned, not beaten out of people. So shut the fuck up and get off Delia's back.'

Bromo took a couple of steps backwards, surprised at his own vehemence, at the way his voice had hardened and risen almost to a shout. He hadn't gotten this steamed up for ages. His cage was being rattled and he didn't like it. Too many people were having a piece of him, making life uncomfortable and uncertain, intruding where they weren't wanted, peeling back the protective layers he'd wrapped around himself. The anger still simmered within.

He moved back to confront Delgado, legs astride, hands on hip, noticing the beads of sweat wetting the man's brow. Again he gripped Delgado's chin, pushing his face up so he was unable to avert his gaze. The buffed and muscly body he'd seen in the gym was trembling under his grip. There was something close to fear in his eyes. Bromo pressed home his advantage.

'You're going to talk and there are two ways of doing it. We can leave that tape over your mouth and you can simply nod yes or no, or I can take it off and you answer in a normal voice. No screaming, no shouting. What's it to be, tape on ...

Already Delgado was shaking his head left and right.

'Good move,' said Bromo, peeling off the tape with one quick tug that produced a short, sharp gasp from Delgado.

'I hope it hurt,' said Delia.

He glared at her: 'You ...'

Bromo raised a finger in warning and Delgado stopped in mid outburst.

'Good man,' said Bromo.

He pulled over a bar stool that had seen better days, its plastic seat cracked and torn to show compressed wads of stuffing within.

'Right, it's obvious your boxer pal followed me here. As Jason said, he's been taken care of. What puzzles me is how you knew to come here. Gunner didn't get time to call you. Jason made sure of that. Surely you're not a grubby little stalker on top of everything else. You haven't been following Delia have you?'

Delgado gave a sheepish grin. 'No need for that. She left her mobile on her desk. Just a simple matter of checking her text messages.'

'Bastard.' She turned to Bromo: 'I told you he was a sneaky devil.'

Bromo put a cap on his fury and kept his voice low and level, but firm.

'Another black mark, Steve. And we haven't even begun to find out what you're really up to. What strings are you pulling at city hall - and who are you pulling them for?'

Delgado let his head droop. He studied the toecaps of his shoes and said nothing.

'Do we take that as a no comment?'

Still no response.

'What's your connection with Peter Rasheed?'

Silence.

'With Gerry Nuyen?'

He continued staring at the floor, motionless and silent.

'Where does Liz Shapcott fit in?'

Delia pushed in front of Bromo and moved behind Delgado's chair.

'I've had enough of this,' she said.

She leaned over Delgado's left shoulder and began running her hands over his jacket, patting the pockets.

'What are you doing?'

'Frisking him. Probably giving him a cheap thrill, too.'

Delgado's reaction was swift and raucous. Still lashed to the chair, he jerked his whole body sideways catching Delia unawares, toppling them both to the floor and letting out a scream as they fell: 'Someone get me out of here.'

He wasn't going anywhere. Jason and his mates burst through the door but their help was unneeded. Delia had clamped her hand across Delgado's mouth and was pushing down heavily.

'Here, take this.'

Someone pushed a roll of gaffer tape into her hands and she stripped it quickly across Delgado's mouth.

'Fixed,' she said, pushing herself up off Delgado.

She smoothed her skirt down; hunched her shoulders to settle her jacket back into place. Brushed her hands together. Bromo had hardly moved. He stood gawping at Delia. From council clerk to Goth, to slick chick and now action woman. This lady was one surprise packet. Delia moved back behind Delgado.

'Right, where were we?'

She resumed running her hands over Delgado's jacket then down past his waist and on to his hips, patting and prodding as she went. She flapped the jacket open and delved into an inside pocket.

'Got it.' She looked triumphant as she thrust a thick plastic card towards Bromo. 'His key-pass.'

She leant over Delgado again and pushed a hand deep into a trouser pocket. Bromo watched him squirm as she fumbled for a few seconds and then withdrew, clutching a bunch of keys.

'Right, let's go.'

She was already walking towards the door. Without thinking, Bromo started to follow. Then stopped, sensing things were getting out of hand. They'd trussed Gunner Thompson and dumped him in the ute, Steve Delgado was taped and tied to a chair and now Delia was about to walk out with his ID and keys.

'Where the hell are you going? What about him?'

'Too many questions, Bromo. That's all you seem to do. First it was me, then Delgado. It's time we began getting some answers. Where's the man of action people have been telling me about? If you want to know what's going on you'd better come with me. We should hit city hall just as security knocks off for supper. This is the chance we've all been waiting for.'

She'd stunned him again. What chance? Who'd been waiting? What was this woman on about?

Halfway to the door, Delia turned: 'My car's outside,' she said. 'And bring big boy Jason with you. We might need some muscle.'

TWENTY-FOUR

They angle-parked in the side street, away from the lights
and in the shadow of a high brick wall. As she drove Delia
somehow managed to slip off her high heels and slide her feet
into a pair of running shoes pulled from under the driver's
seat.

'Keep them there for my lunchtime power walk,' she
explained.

'I was more interested in how you drive and change your
shoes at the same time,' said Bromo. 'And without running
us off the road.'

'Multi-tasking. I'm a woman.'

True to form; it was the response he'd heard so many other
times as he risked life and limb while being driven by some
lipstick-applying female with one eye on the street directory
and the other on her sun visor mirror.

Jason's ute sidled into the space alongside.

'What next?' asked Bromo.

He realised he'd relinquished any leadership role he may
have been playing back at Pistons. He tugged at his ear lobe.
Why waste energy arguing with a Goth with attitude?

'We go and find some answers,' said Delia. 'That's if you're
still up to it.'

There was a teasing undercurrent to the hard stare she gave him. Again he was being challenged and tested by someone who seemed to know more about him than he thought was possible. Not only was the word out about that other life far removed from his present cosy existence, but people wanted a share of it. Delia opened her door and stepped out into the lamplit street.

'Coming? Or do you want stay here and play cockatoo? An empty car looks less suspicious than one with someone sitting in it at this time of night.'

She was right. Besides, the adrenalin was rising. The sense of being a piece of flotsam at the centre of a whirling eddy was getting to him. He'd had enough of the buffeting. It was time to cut loose. Bromo walked over to the ute where Jason sat placidly with.an arm resting on the open window while his left hand beat time to a rap song throbbing away on his tape deck.

'Feel like joining us?' asked Bromo.

'Maybe. Where're you going?'

He nodded towards the town hall: 'In there.'

'Your idea or Action Woman's?'

'Hers.'

'Thought so. Can't say no to them, can you?'

'It's happened.'

'Yeah, and they've made gold bars from dog shit.'

'Is this boys' talk or can anyone join in?'

Delia had moved quietly alongside Bromo.

Jason's fingers stopping tapping. He turned to her, an almost sheepish look showing his surprise at her sudden appearance.

'Sorry, luv. Just a bit of risk management. Guess we'd better get moving.'

He levered himself out of his seat.

'Do we need any tools?'

'Might be useful,' said Delia. 'Nothing too heavy though. A torch if you've got one.'

He was left buckling on a tradie's belt of screwdrivers, pliers and other small implements as the other two ducked under the boom gates to an office car park. He caught up as Delia led the way to the rear walls of the town hall, looming dark and shadowy above them. She took keys from her pocket and opened a gate in a high iron fence. Beyond was a narrow walkway leading left to the main front entrance and, to the right, to a rear yard with wheelie bins, bike racks and what looked like an old bus shelter.

'For the smokers,' said Delia, noticing Jason's wary glance in that direction. 'Can't have their fags getting wet.'

'Point the way - and no more talk,' said Bromo in what he hoped was an authoritative whisper.

The old urge to be in charge of his own destiny hadn't left him. Trusting the judgment of others had proved deadly costly on two occasions locked away in the deepest vaults of his memory. They shuffled quietly towards a heavy wooden door indicated by Delia. Set into the wall was a keypad of numbers and letters. Bromo nodded towards her, eyebrow raised. She raised a thumb in reply and moved ahead of him. Her fingers flitted over the keypad and swiped Delgado's ID card in the slot. She pushed on the door, gently easing it open.

They were in a corridor running between the outside wall and a partition made of chest-high timber panelling and a glass upper section. Beyond they could see a large open space that had once been a grand hall where balls and community festivities were held. Now it was a work area of desks and computers separated by filing cabinets and pot plants. Everything was dimly lit by the glow of street lights and a moon-filled night sky coming through windows high up in the wall. Delia pointed to their right and upwards. Bromo hesitated, and then motioned for her to go ahead. It was better to be led by someone who knew the way than have him stumbling along unknown passages and risking discovery just to cosset his ego.

Ten paces along, the partitions met to form a corner and a left hand turn. Cautiously they turned the corner. On their right was an inner wall housing offices hidden behind name-plated doors and frosted glass windows. Halfway along, the wall paused to make way for a wide stairway, its darkly stained and highly polished treads showing the indentations of decades of footsteps. A large church-like leadlight window at the head of the first flight of stairs bathed everything in a dulled multi-hued glow of reds, greens, blues and gold.

Delia stopped at the foot of the stairs. Bromo looked at her, then at the stairs and back at her. She nodded. It was as he feared: upwards and onwards. Not a good move. Escape would be harder if trouble came.

They went in single file, keeping close to the left-hand banister, a huge carved beam of polished timber rubbed even smoother by thousands of ratepayers and bureaucrats than its original craftsmen ever imagined. The top of the second flight ended in a balustraded gallery looking down into the workspace they had just skirted.

Poor bastards, thought Bromo. It reminded him of one of his junior schools where no one in the main hall and gymnasium could escape the critical eyes of teachers lurking in the upper gallery. The most innocent act or gesture could be misconstrued or seized on by those uncharitable guardians of his education. Too often he was singled out for a caning in front of the class for some minor misdeed. A repressed recollection of those days surfaced. The fingertips of his right hand rubbed soothingly at the palm of his left. The pain had gone but the memory lingered on.

A sharp dig in the ribs from Delia brought him back to the present. She pointed to an office door bearing the sign S. Delgado. There was no keypad this time, just a slot for the ID card. The door clicked and yielded to her touch. A window that still had the wooden slats of its blind twisted open let in a pale yellow light from the street. It illuminated an office setting like thousands of others - a scene straight out of an Officeworks catalogue. A large desk with drawers centre and right and a two-drawer filing cabinet return was topped by a computer workstation with a flat-screen monitor and compact printer. Behind the desk was a well-padded swivel chair with armrests. Two more visitor chairs were on the other side. A tall filing cabinet stood at an angle in one corner. A table covered in files, bulky ring-binders and rolled-up architectural plans took up most of the remaining wall. Bromo extended his arms towards Delia, palms upward in supplication.

'What now?' he mouthed.

She pointed to the desk and moved behind it. Bromo and Jason followed. She slid open the top drawer and started rifling through the contents. The two men watched over her shoulders, not sure what they were supposed to be looking for among the jumble of pens, pencils, stapler, boxes of paper clips, a couple of takeaway food shop leaflets and an assortment of teabags.

To Bromo it was obviously the junk drawer. Every desk had one. But Delia kept turning things over. Briefly she paused to touch Bromo on his wrist and point at the drawers in the return. He got the message and pulled on the handles. The top one budged; the bottom one didn't. Anything worth hiding would be locked away but he turned over the top drawer's contents just in case - mostly folders with circulation lists attached; the endless round of paperwork of minimal interest to all but a few on the roster yet needing to be glanced at, ticked off and passed on as if it had been thoroughly perused. Jason hovered, watching them go through the drawers.

'Need a light?' he offered in a whisper, waving his unlit torch.

'Not yet. Nothing to see,' replied Bromo. He turned to Delia.

'What are we looking for?'

She bent over a desk drawer, fossicking through its contents. She swept the hair out of her eyes.

'Not sure. I'll know it when I see it.'

Bromo picked up a hard-backed notebook and flicked over the pages. Several contained pairs of letters followed by numbers - AM 1500, ST 2000, LR 800 and others just as cryptic. He flicked his fingers at Delia.

'Here. This mean anything?'

She took only seconds to glance at the pages. Her reaction was immediate: 'Bingo. You're a gem.'

She pushed herself up on her toes and kissed him on the cheek. 'We've got him.'

Bromo and Jason exchanged puzzled glances.

'Look at this,' said Delia. She had opened the notebook and was running her fingers down a list of letters and numbers.

'DT 1000, AF 1500, TC 1200,' she read out.

'So what?' said Bromo. 'You'd better translate.'

'DT is Dan Tran, AF is Angela Fittipaldi, and TC is Trevor Cartwright. They're all councillors and I'll bet the numbers mean dollars. He's been bribing them. No wonder they keep making excuses about not turning up for meetings.'

'What meetings?'

'Planning committee, sub-committee, even full council, anything where there are decisions to be made and votes cast. These are the regular absentees.'

Bromo took the book from her. He pointed at another row of numbers.

'I suppose they're dates. Any idea if they relate to when meetings were being held?'

'It's easy to check.'

'Perhaps you should before jumping to conclusions.'

She gave him a look, one stop down from a hostile glare: 'You're the one who wanted evidence. Here it is.'

Bromo ran a hand through his hair: 'Yeah. Right. Thanks for the reminder. Anything else?'

Any reply was cut short. There was a heavy metallic clunk behind them, amplified by the quiet of the deserted building. Delia spun round, clutching Bromo by the arm. He pushed her behind him and twisted to face the door, one arm extended as if to ward off whatever was there.

'Sorry, mate.' said Jason, unfolding himself from where he'd been crouched over the desk drawer, a long hafted screwdriver in hand.

'Just thought I'd ease it open.'

He looked sheepish and apologetic.

'Something slipped. Sorry about the noise.'

He pointed to the open drawer: 'I found this.'

Delia let loose her grip on Bromo's arm and they sidled across to the desk. Jason flicked on his torch, shining the beam down on to a small handgun.

'It was underneath this.'

He held up a t-shirt decorated with the logo of a local fun run and the symbols of its sponsors.

'It's his gym gear,' said Bromo. 'He wears it all the time. Probably the only fun run he's ever been in. Most likely bought the shirt and didn't even bother running. Prestige without the effort.'

Bromo picked up the weapon: 'At least he's never waved this around at aerobics classes.'

He weighed the pistol in his palm – solid and stubby with a polished gunmetal blue barrel and wooden grip.

'Hmm. A Browning. An old model but still lethal. Semi-automatic. Good grip.'

His fingers fondled the stock. He felt a surge of tension mingled with excitement ripple through him. It had been a long time.

'I wonder if Mr Delgado has a licence for this.'

'More to the point, what's it doing hidden away in his office drawer?' said Delia.

'Probably putting the frighteners on someone,' offered Jason. 'Is it loaded?'

Bromo fiddled with a catch behind the trigger and released the magazine. 'Full,' he reported. He took a closer look: 'But nothing up the spout.'

'You sure?' asked Delia. 'It's designed to have one ready to go.'

Bromo and Jason exchanged surprised glances. Delia caught them. She looked flustered and shook her hands, palms up and facing them, motioning them to say no more.

'Just something I picked up,' she said. 'Been watching too many cop shows.'

Bromo turned the gun over: 'Chamber indicator says not. Better believe it. Want to check?'

She nodded her head, negative, calmer now, and resumed turning the pages of the notebook. Bromo replaced the loaded magazine, checked the safety slide and put the pistol in his jacket pocket..

'Can't have Delgado running amok among the ratepayers,' he said. 'Isn't it time we got out of here?'

As he spoke, a light came on somewhere outside the room. Its diffused gleam showed through the frosted glass of the office wall and seemed to be coming from the floor below.

'Security,' whispered Delia.

Bromo raised a finger towards her, then another and then a third, silently mouthing the numbers as he counted them off. How many? Delia raised two fingers, her lips forming an unuttered reply. Jason shuffled to the door and eased it open. He peered out and came back into the room. He, too, resorted to sign language – two fingers raised then one pointing downwards, indicating the lower level.

Delia motioned for them to gather by the desk. She tore a piece of paper off a pad and picked a pen out of a cluster in a coffee mug bearing the legend *There's Always Room at the Top*. Bromo and Jason watched her scrawl terse instructions.

Bromo's fingertips tapped nervously on the desk top as he read her note. He was losing control. Somehow Delia had taken charge, naturally, effortlessly. This was no ordinary front office clerk. There was an agenda at work and he hadn't received a copy. Jason stretched and rubbed one hand round the back of his neck, slowly turning his head, easing the tension. Delia wrote again.

'Possible? Can do?'

They didn't rush to answer. Eyes were averted as they assessed the risks.

Delia broke the silence as she picked up two folders from the pile on the table.

'Okay, let's do it. I'll use these as an excuse,' she whispered. 'And I'll hold on to this.'

She wedged Delgado's notebook down the back of her skirt: 'We might need it later.'

She moved to the door and slid out into the corridor. Jason followed, then Bromo. The click of the door behind him seemed to ricochet off the walls and they froze in mid-step, waiting for a reaction from the lighted room downstairs. Bromo counted off a minute but it felt like five before he tapped Delia on the shoulder and pointed forward. She led them back the way they'd come half-an-hour earlier, heading to the stairs. They descended the first flight and stood beneath the leadlight window. From here they could see the lighted room with its walls of frosted glass. A shadowy seated figure stretched their arms high above their head and coughed. Another person came into blurry focus, upright and moving towards the door. The first one stood and joined them.

Delia turned and looked at Bromo. He nodded and motioned with raised thumb over a clenched fist. Good luck. She stepped purposefully down the centre of the final flight, the light from the window catching glints of sheen in her black tresses. Jason, crouched close to the shadowy side of the wall, followed closely a few steps behind.

Bromo waited for a gap to open up before following them. As he reached the foot of the stairs he heard voices off to his right but didn't stop to look. More lights were coming on as he lengthened stride and pace towards the rear entrance. There was a shuffling behind him, heavy breathing, someone moving stealthily and gaining on him. He could still hear the voices in the distance, male and female, but the tone was impossible to judge. He reached the door where they'd come in and sensed his pursuer looming over him.

'Shit, mate, ease up. I'm coming with you.'

Jason's big paw of a hand pushed on the door above Bromo's head and they spilled out into the yard together.

Jason leaned up against a wheelie bin.

'Thought for a moment you were going without me.'

'Sorry, Jase. Didn't expect you so soon. Thought you might get held up back there.'

'Nah. Worked like a charm. Two boofheads up against one sassy chick. It's no match. She kept them occupied by schmoozing them with some yarn about working back late and needing to check a couple of files. They didn't want trouble, she's legit, got an ID, and even that couple of drongos could see the files weren't exactly top secret.'

Bromo tried the deep breathing. The tension was ebbing. They had to assume Delia had finished her performance and made her way through to the front of the building and out into the street. Possibly complete with an official escort. He gave Jason a light punch in the ribs.

'Come on, let's get out of here. With any luck she'll be waiting in her car.'

They stepped through the gate in the high metal fence and into the car park. Night turned suddenly into day. Two beams of light hit them full on from the direction of the boom gates.

'Police,' a voice called out. 'Put your hands up where we can see them and walk slowly towards us.'

'Shit, I feel like a roo in a spotlight,' said Jason. 'Can't see a bloody thing.'

'Turn the light down,' Bromo called out. 'We're not going anywhere.'

'Dead right you're not.'

The voice came from behind them.

'You can bring your hands down now, slowly, and put them behind you.'

Bromo felt handcuffs snapped shut around his wrists. The beams of light moved down off their faces. Three men and one woman clad in a mix of running shoes, jeans, sweat-shirts and hoods moved alongside, one holding each arm and propelling them forward. A firm downward push on the top of their heads guided them under the boom gates. A police divvy van was stopped in the street alongside Jason's ute. Gunner Johnson, released from where Jason had dumped him, was leaning against the vehicle, a smug smirk on his face.

'Fink I might lay charges,' he said. 'False imprisonment.'

Bromo noted a vacant space where Delia's car had been parked. The woman herself was as absent as her car. Perhaps she hadn't made it out of the city hall's front doors. But who had removed her car?

'Over here,' one of the men ordered.

He reached into the back pocket of his jeans and flashed a police badge at them. Detectives. A slim woman with long blond hair gathered in a ponytail gripped Bromo's arm and steered him to the divvy van, pushing him face forward against its side. She took a step back as her companion, a short and swarthy man with two days of stubble over his face and a nose showing signs of violent collisions, ran latex-gloved hands down Bromo's arms, legs and body. Bromo tensed and waited for the inevitable. These guys were good – hard, fast and efficient. For a few moments he thought he'd got lucky as his captor's hands skimmed over him from top to toe and missed the bulge in his jacket. No such luck: on their return journey they took a slightly different course, finding the hidden weapon.

'You have a licence for this, sir?'

The policeman dangled the pistol by its trigger guard: 'And a reason for carrying it with you?'

Bromo twisted his hand round and looked at him. They stared at each other and said nothing. Both knew the answer. Bromo stuck to the script.

'I can explain, officer. It's not mine.'

The pony-tailed detective joined in.

'They all say that. What's your excuse?'

'Whatever it is, I'm sure it'll be a good one.'

The uniformed presence of Senior Sergeant Grant Mayfield had emerged from the shadows.

'Mr Perkins has an interesting tale to tell,' he said. 'You'll find he'll be very useful with your enquiries. Put him and his mate in the van and we'll have a chat down at the station. Gunner can bring the ute.'

Bromo lifted his head off the van and turned to look at Mayfield.

The sergeant gave him a wink: 'I'll open the rear doors for you. We're all on your side.'

TWENTY-FIVE

The police station was metallic bright, shiny and new. Fanfares and publicity had accompanied its opening only a few months earlier. The government had trumpeted the event to thwart criticism that it was doing little to combat rising crime and that it was ignoring police force pleas to provide the resources and manpower needed to maintain law and order.

'Nice place you've got,' said Bromo as they were marched into the foyer. 'Great improvement on the old one. Hope the crims appreciate it.'

'It's not for the crims,' replied the man still gripping Bromo's right elbow as he steered him towards a steel-rimmed door leading beyond the well-lit reception area.

They went down a long corridor with doors opening off into offices and locker rooms. Bromo could hear the footsteps behind him of Jason and his escorts.

'In here. Sit.'

Bromo could see no point in disobeying. To sit would be a relief. He could do some deep breathing, gather his thoughts, guess their questions and work out some answers. The door clicked shut and they left him alone. He assumed Jason was in a similar room nearby. Poor bastard; he'd done nothing more than come along for the ride, to help a mate. He'd gone straight for years and didn't need hassles, which would inevitably have the cops digging into a record of misdemeanours that made an ill fit with the Jason of today.

The door opened. Sergeant Mayfield peered in, showing caution.

'I'm not dangerous. Not likely to lash out,' said Bromo.

He indicated the handcuffs still holding his arms behind him. He hunched his shoulders and rotated his wrists, trying to ease the stiffness.

'Any chance you've got the key?'

'You going to behave?'

'Come on, Grant. It's me, not some bloody serial killer or wife basher. Sober, too. Undo the cuffs.'

Mayfield moved into the room, closing the door and leaning against the wall.

'So, what's with the gun? I thought you'd given those toys away.'

Bromo felt the need to spread his hands, to plead, emphasise his case. All he could do was look hard at Mayfield, urging with his eyes.

'You know it's not mine. I was going to turn it in. Check if it was licensed. And in whose name.'

Mayfield grinned.

'Yeah, good one. I'll believe you, but you're going to have to do better than that when the heavy squad comes back. They're working on your mate right now. Seems he doesn't know too much. Says he went along for the ride – and to help you. Big mistake.'

'That's about it,' said Bromo. 'Poor sod. He's done nothing. He was just helping out. Heart of gold and all that. Surely, you know how it is.'

'Not really. Don't see too many saints around here. Mostly sinners. Anyhow, what was he helping with? Don't tell me you'd broken into the town hall to pay your rates.'

Bromo said nothing. Silence seemed the best option. So far there'd been no mention of charges, only the official cautions about him not being obliged to say anything but if he did it may be used in evidence whenever, whatever, da, da, da…… All the usual covering their backsides sort of stuff and no allegations or accusations. Perhaps they saw it as an open and shut case when three people – one of them with a loaded pistol in his pocket - crept out of the town hall well after closing hours.

Three people? It would have been if the instigator of their mission hadn't disappeared, along with her car. So, where the hell was Delia and what had prompted such a heavy police presence right on cue?. He looked at Mayfield, still lounging against the wall.

'What's going on? I'm beginning to smell something odd.'

'You probably need to change your jocks.'

Bromo stuck to the point; he didn't need smart-arse comments.

'You're not usually that quick off the mark. That's the second time this week. That young woman getting her gear off probably helped the first time.'

'Didn't do any harm,' smirked Mayfield. 'You under-estimate our efficiency.'

'You get a tip-off?'

The smirk broadened into a fleeting grin but he said nothing.

Bromo persisted: 'What's with the plain-clothes posse? What brought them along?'

Mayfield pushed himself off the wall and gave a couple of raps on the door.

'Too many questions, Bromo. You'll have to ask someone else. You're off my hands now.'

The door opened just wide enough for him to slide out into the corridor. Bromo slumped back in his chair, trying to ignore the irritating itch on his ear lobe. He hoped someone would come soon and unlock the handcuffs; the restraint was getting to him more than the actual arrest and what might lie ahead. He stood up and bent forward from the hips as far he could go, raising his cuffed hands up behind him. He breathed out, then in, as he returned to the upright pose. There were a couple of clicks and creaks from his hips and shoulders. He went through the same movement again and convinced himself he was doing good, easing his joints and settling them closer to where they should be.

'Once more with feeling,' he muttered as he bent towards the floor.

The door clicked and Bromo saw two pairs of running shoes enter the room. Before he could raise his eyes any higher, the female grabbed his wrists just as they reached their highest point and gave them a firm pull forward.

Bromo yelped: 'Bloody hell.'

'A helping hand,' said the woman.

Her nasally voice would make a buzz-saw sound sweet. 'It's always good to go the extra distance with your exercises,' she said. 'Or is this a new way to slip the cuffs?'

Bromo ignored her and the pain across his shoulders. As he sat down the man moved behind him and checked the handcuffs.

'Not too tight, I hope.'

'Got it,' said Bromo. 'You're the good cop, she's the bad cop.'

'We're both quite nice when you get to know us,' said the man, taking a seat next to his partner at a long steel table bolted to the floor.

'We're versatile; we'll play any part we feel is necessary.'

They flashed ID cards at him.

'Detective Sergeant Holmes,' said the man. 'Detective Constable Watson,' said the woman. 'And no funny remarks. There isn't one we haven't heard.'

'Perhaps I could be Dr Moriarty,' said Bromo.

Silence, accompanied by hard stares. Yep, they had heard them all. It was worth trying.. 'So, what are the charges?'

The detectives exchanged glances. Senior nodded to junior, giving her the go-ahead. Bromo wished it wasn't so: that voice was going to shred his brain.

'Charges depend on you, Mr Perkins. Unlawful restraint of a fellow citizen, break and entry, burglary, carrying a weapon, resisting arrest …'

'There was no resistance.'

'We thought there was, didn't we sarge?'

Holmes nodded.

'Very much so. Violent type. He had to be restrained. For his own good.'

So that's the way it was going. Nothing new; he'd seen it all before. Foolishly he'd assumed this new politically correct, bill of rights era of ombudsmen and complaints tribunals had stamped out such crude policing methods. The buzz-saw voice continued.

'The charges, Mr Perkins, largely depend on how much you can tell us about your recent activities, especially considering your background. You have become what we call a person of interest. You know the language.'

Bromo looked round the room. There was no sign of taping equipment or video cameras. Neither detective had papers or notebooks in front of them. It seemed nothing was being recorded.

'What's your interest?'

'We ask the questions,' said Holmes.

He leaned back in his chair, one hand clawing lightly at the waistband of his jeans, the other resting on the tables, fingertips tapping a regular soundless beat. The pose indicated patience and told Bromo 'we're waiting.'

'I've been helping out a few friends.'

Watson jumped in: 'Since when have Peter Rasheed and Gerry Nuyen been your friends?'

'Or Steve Delgado,' added Holmes.

Bromo shrugged.

'It's a tight community. More like a village. You get to know all sorts. Everyone's your friend.'

'Even when they're threatening you, or beating you up?'

'Takes all sorts. The rich tapestry of life in the suburbs.'

Watson curled back her upper lip and probed between her teeth with the nail of her little finger. She sniffed, curled her lip further back and dug deeper. Bromo caught a blast of garlic as she hunched into him across the table. He tried to shift his upper body out of range. Holmes frowned at the constable's molar manoeuvres but offered no comment. He didn't have to. His look said enough as he picked up the questioning.

'Stop stuffing us around, Mr Perkins. We'd like some real answers.'

Bromo nodded in Watson's direction: 'Flossing might help.'

She removed her finger and put both hands firmly palms down on the table. Bromo noted the fingertips turning white with the pressure. He was niggling her but she was curbing any impulse to bite back. Keep trying.

'Good meal, was it? Italian, I'd guess. Lots of garlic. Pity you missed out on the after-dinner mints.'

Still no outward reaction. She was good, but the downward pressure on the table was making the sinews in her hands and wrists stand out. It was a giveaway of which they were both aware; a tell-tale sign she couldn't hide. She slowly eased away from Bromo, pulling her hands back into her lap and gradually sitting upright.

'Deep breathing's good,' he offered as a victory blow.

'Enough.' Holmes barked. 'Cut the crap. We're not here to have a fight. Let's keep this on a friendly level.'

'I thought you were interrogating a dangerous criminal.'

'Call it a bit of byplay. Testing your reaction. We can still go down that track if you like.'

'So, what's this – a meeting of the friendly society for those who are armed and dangerous?'

Holmes stood up, hitched his jeans up to his waist and stepped round the table. Bromo tensed as the detective moved behind him. This was familiar territory: the heavy stuff was about to begin. There was a subtle waft of after-shave or body lotion from over his shoulder. Better than garlic-breath across the table. His brain did a random flash recollection of that woman on TV called the perfumed steamroller. Was Holmes the scented persuader?

There was a clink of metal and a tug at his lower arms. The handcuffs fell open. Bromo flexed his wrists and brought his arms round to the front, massaging where the cuffs had been. He rubbed his ear. Bloody thing was playing up again. Holmes moved off to the side, leaning against the wall, one leg bent and raised with the sole of his foot flat against the wall. Casual. At ease.

'You really are trying to be nice,' said Bromo. 'Doesn't quite go with the job. I can't see it catching on.'

He looked at Watson.

'Especially in some quarters.'

'We've got plenty to charge you with,' she rasped.

Bromo appealed to Holmes.

'See what I mean? Some people are simply not the friendly type. They chew garlic and spit nails.'

Holmes propelled himself off the wall and in two strides was grasping the edge of the table, leaning forward and thrusting his face into Bromo's.

'Last chance, Mr Perkins.'

His voice had gone up a decibel or two.

'Get this straight: we don't see you as a dangerous criminal but we're quite happy to treat you as one and throw the book at you. We do, however, see you as someone who's got himself involved in some messy local politics and who has contacts and information which could be very useful to us. Who could even work with us, instead of against us. Geddit? Is that clear enough?'

Bromo folded his arms across his chest. Time to reflect and consider. He'd detected tremors of impatience and frustration in the sergeant's voice. He saw them as warning signs, pointing to the endgame. He'd been handed the Get Out of Jail card – something not to be wasted. Perhaps one more roll of the dice was warranted.

'Sounds pretty good to me. First, though, who are you

lot? Which branch? What information do you think I've got that's of any use to anyone?'

The detectives exchanged looks. Bromo recognised a telepathy that hinted at a long-time working partnership. They would read thoughts before they were spoken. Out on the streets, they would know each other's moves before they'd been made. The secret of survival. Nothing was being said but they'd reached agreement. Homes eased himself back off the table and dug his hands into his jeans pockets.

'We're anti-corruption squad,' he revealed. 'A unit within a unit. Mostly undercover.'

'Federal,' added Watson.

'Looking at local government,' said Holmes.

'Inside and out,' Watson chimed in.

'Councillors and officials,' Holmes continued.

'Bribery, slush funds,' Watson embroidered.

It was verbal tennis. Bromo listened to them bat the words back and forth across the table. A smooth and flowing stroke player against a gritty and edgy net fighter.

'And where do I fit in?'

'Help us get close to the main players. Working undercover takes us only so far. There are places you've been going where we can't gain easy access without warning them we're on to them.'

'Such as?'

'Gerry Nuyen and that hideaway Peter Rasheed's got over at Mack's. We can get search warrants and bust the doors down but we need more to go on before that happens. Our whole case could be blown away if we don't get the right inside information.'

Bromo tried to still his reaction. It didn't work. He

twitched, eyebrows flickered upward, upper body tilted forward. Signs of interest.

'Surprised?'

Garlic-breath hurled the words at him.

'Didn't you know we've been watching you? You're slipping.'

It stung to think he'd been under observation and hadn't detected it. He shouldn't care. He wasn't in the game anymore. That was all long ago. Even so, a man had his pride. Watson was getting even, niggling him, and enjoying it.

Holmes let Watson enjoy her moment. She was playing Partners. Being part of The Team. One for all and all for one. Bromo knew all the mantras, the philosophies. He hated every one of them. He had squirmed through all the pep talks and team-building routines and graduated as a renegade, although that wasn't the label they'd attached. He was special ops - one who melded into the landscape and trod his own precarious path, unaided and unanswerable to any partners or team. Now he was being coerced into someone else's team and there seemed no way out. Join, or find your comfort zone permanently invaded.

'What's your answer?'

Holmes' voice was tinged with impatience.

'We need to know.'

'Do I have a choice?'

'Everyone has a choice. Yes or no, right or left, up or down, tea or coffee. It's their decision, as long as they accept the consequences are of their own choosing.'

'Very philosophical,' said Bromo. 'Touch of the Rubaiyat. Almost existentialist.'

'I prefer realist.'

Bromo held Holmes' gaze. For a few seconds they seemed frozen in time. No one moved; nothing was said. Bromo ran his fingers around the inside of his collar. The room was airless, oppressive. Watson had resumed digging her dinner from between her teeth.

'Okay, you win. I'll see what I can do to help.'

He noted the smidgen of a smile that flickered across the sergeant's face.

'So, no charges arising from tonight's episode?'

'What episode?' asked Holmes, presenting a mock look of surprise in Watson's direction. She shrugged, feigning puzzlement.

'At City Hall,' prompted Bromo.

'Oh that. The local uniforms tell me it was a false alarm. Fidgety security staff. No charges. Just between us, we got all the information we needed. Very productive, thank you.'

They'd caught him off guard again. He mulled over Holmes' words. A loaded pistol in a bureaucrat's drawer was far from legal but it hardly added up to evidence of corruption. He had to know.

'What information? I've told you nothing. Is there something I've missed? A loaded gun's not good but you've no proof Delgado was going to use it.'

Again there was that unspoken communication between them. An exchange of looks, an almost imperceptible nod of the head or a raising of the eyebrow.

'Okay, agreed. The gun is a side issue,' said Holmes.

He paused, weighing his words.

'What we needed and what we got was Delgado's notebook.'

Alarm bells rang. Bromo had handed the notebook to Delia. She'd flicked through it and stuffed it down her skirt when she went to soft-talk the security guards.

'Are you holding her, too?'

He didn't need to give a name. The reference was obvious.

'Can't you let her go if you've got the notebook? She's risking her job.'

His questions went through to the keeper. Holmes ploughed on.

'It was very careless of Mr Delgado to leave it in an unlocked drawer.'

Bromo caught the flicker of a smile. Jason's handiwork with his screwdriver had been acknowledged and passed over. Delia's presence was attracting No Comment. It was as if they'd never existed.

'So we're all in the clear?'

'If you help.'

Hobson's choice. They were back to the Henry Ford solution: any colour as long as it's black. Our way or no way. He was being drawn into that place he never wanted to visit again. He took a deep steadying breath. The deal was done.

'You win. Tell me what you want.'

Holmes and Watson stood up, languidly and almost as one. Bromo searched unsuccessfully for a smart riposte to wipe the smug smiles off their faces. Nothing came. Game over.

'One of our colleagues more familiar with the details will brief you,' said Holmes.

He rapped on the door to be let out.

'Please, come with us.'

An order, but at least it was a polite one. They marched in ragged single file to the far end of a long corridor of offices. The last door on the left was slightly ajar. Holmes leaned his head in.

'He's all yours, boss. Can I send him in?'

Bromo heard no response. There must have been a nod or sign. Holmes stood back and pushed the door wider open and ushered Bromo past him. He gave a wink.

'Have fun.'

Bromo stood stock still, stunned: 'Jesus.'

'Hardly,' she said. 'But I understand your surprise.'

Behind a desk cluttered with files and papers sat Delia – Delia the city hall clerk, Delia the black-garbed Goth, Delia the sparky night-clubber and now Delia the detective inspector, as was clearly embossed on a visiting card she offered him. A high-neck skivvy and jeans had replaced the party clothes. He stood clutching her business card, not noticing her gesture towards a cracked and scarred plastic chair.

'Sorry we've nothing more comfortable. Borrowed space. It's all that funds will allow. Bit hard on the bum but it helps keep conversations brief.'

'What?'

He looked up from the card, half listening to what she said, vague and puzzled.

'The chair. Won't you sit.'

She smiled and brushed strands of hair off her forehead. 'Might help ease the shock.'

Bromo took another look at the card: the police logo in the top left-hand corner, a couple of phone numbers centred at the bottom and Det. Insp. Delia Dunstan printed clear and bold in the centre. There was no address, location or affiliation to squad or section. A unit without a name.

'Sorry about tonight,' she said. She almost looked slightly guilty.

He shrugged: 'It's becoming par for the course. I'm just the bunny everyone's playing with.'

'I guess I owe you an apology … and an explanation.'

He fiddled with the card, flicking it, turning it over as if it might provide more information.

'No need to explain. This says it all. I'm pissed off that I didn't pick it. Definitely losing my touch.'

'And I would have been losing mine if you'd rumbled me. A lot of effort went into that role. It's bloody hard work'

'Keeping up appearances, you might say. You spun a good tale. How much of it was true?'

She flashed him an appraising look, making decisions. For the first time he noticed how deeply dark her eyes were now they were not rimmed by kohl and mascara.

The decision was made: 'We'll leave that for another time. Let's just say a good cover is essential in this job. A total new identity that doesn't let you down. As I said, I worked hard on that one. Now, about you.'

She opened a dark blue plastic folder pulled from under a small pile of manuals and binders. Her hair fell forward over her face as she studied it.

'I suppose it's been a while,' she said, not looking up, turning the pages in the folder. 'Years rather than months.' Bromo studied the streaks of colour in her hair, wondering how they could be so neatly contrived. He said nothing

'Some holiday.'

He refused to bite.

'Too young to retire. Got years left in you. Quite virile, I gather.'

It was a goading, throwaway line delivered with a slight smile and a toss of the head to settle her mane back in its place. It hit its mark. Bromo pushed forward, one hand on the desk the other scratching at an itch on his leg.

'I didn't retire. I stuffed up and it was suggested it might be better for my health if I joined the rest of the convicts and sailed off to Australia. Now I'm here I don't intend going back or getting my hands dirty again.'

They held each other's look. God, those eyes – not only deep and dark but smiling, too. There was a softness around them he hadn't noticed before. It spread to her mouth, which tended to turn up rather than down, contrasting so strongly with the doom-laden Goth of their first meeting. Maybe this was a woman he could trust.

'Care to tell me about it?'

Tempting. He'd played the scene over and over – the lone viewer in the cinema of the soul. It was always the same, shattering and providing no room for excuses. Things went wrong in Sofia, on the golden cobblestones in front of the Alexander Nevsky Church. All the training, mentoring and fieldwork amounted to nothing. You can cover all angles, and still get it wrong; be alert and alarmed and not detect the danger. Intelligence can be checked and double-checked and still prove false. When the enemy senses your hunger for information, they feed you tasty morsels and it's too late for an antidote by the time you discover they've been poisoned. That's how it had been.in Sofia, but he didn't want to go there now. He snapped out of his reverie.

'Like you said, we'll leave that for some other time.'

He put his toe in the water: 'Perhaps over dinner. With the real Delia.'

She coloured, half-smiled, flicked through the folder, then closed it firmly. Composure regained. His proposition was ignored.

'As you've gathered, we'd like your help.'

'What's happened to Delgado?'

'We collected him from Pistons and he's being held overnight at least. The pistol was not only loaded but also unregistered. He doesn't have a gun licence.'

'And the notebook?'

She slid open a desk drawer and brought out the notebook. She flicked the edges of its pages as if preparing to shuffle a deck of cards.

'We'll confront him with this tomorrow after we've had a closer look. First sight suggests it's a loosely coded record of dubious financial transactions. Simple stuff – initials, numbers, fairly easy to match with names known to us and we're getting a look at his bank accounts.'

Bromo stood up, rolled his shoulders and tugged his trousers up to his waist.

'Well, that's it, then. All wrapped up. You don't need me after all.'

She rested her elbows on the desk, hands clasped in front of her, looking up at him. Very appealing.

'Yes we do. So far, we only have half a case. With your help, we can close this whole corrupt thing right down once and for all. Please stay and hear me out, Mr Perkins. Or can I call you Bromo?'

They let the silence hang between them – she not pushing him any harder; he gradually losing the battle to preserve his life of solitude and non-involvement. He did a quick rewind. As a Goth, she had been quirky and diverting. In Pistons, she'd made attractive and enjoyable company. This intensely appealing and obviously competent policewoman, however, was something else altogether. Several rungs up the ladder. Slowly he set himself back in the rickety chair: 'Okay, Bromo it is – but only if you say yes to dinner.'

The answer never came. Three quick raps on the door were followed by Sergeant Holmes pushing it open and almost falling into the room in his haste.

'I need a word. Sorry to burst in, but this can't wait.'

Bromo tried to interpret the exchange of looks between Holmes and Delia. His presence stopped any further explanation from Holmes.

'Could you wait outside,' she said. 'I'll try not to keep you too long.'

Even before he'd closed the door behind him, Bromo heard a torrent of words from Holmes, his voice low and urgent. Within seconds Delia and Holmes rushed from the room. She had her arms half into a denim jacket she was struggling to put on. For the first time, he noticed a holstered gun at her waist.

'You'd better come with us. No time to argue,' she said. 'This is strictly unofficial. But like it or not, you're involved. And it's not very pleasant.'

TWENTY-SIX

Bromo was swept along in the rush, reluctant and bewildered, but recognising the urgency; anxious to know what new drama he'd been caught up in. In the yard, a divvy van was moving through the steel mesh security gates and out into the road, lights flashing. Holmes and Delia ran to an unmarked car.

'Get in,' she yelled to Bromo, pointing to the rear door.

Before he could close it, Watson plonked herself down beside him but said nothing. The car skidded out of the yard, close behind the van. The security gates slid shut behind them. The streets were quiet, almost deserted except for a steady procession of cars coming out of the city, their occupants heading home to the suburbs after a night on the town. Three youths were hunched over a pizza carton at the tram stop. A couple of shift workers pushed a shopping trolley out of the all-night supermarket. A group of women in flimsy dresses, tottering on over-high heels, arms crossed over their chests against the breeze, stood on the corner outside The Vine trying to hail a cab. Bromo broke the grim silence that had settled inside the car.

'Any chance of telling me what's going on?'

Holmes and Delia exchanged glances – to tell or not to tell?

'We'll know soon enough,' Delia said, speaking at the windscreen. 'It doesn't look good.'

The cars sped up Bridge Road towards the city, pausing briefly at the Lennox Street intersection then gathering speed down the slope past the hospital. Bromo heard the wail of a paramedic's wagon behind them. The divvy van weaved through the six lanes of traffic on Punt Road and led the way to a street of mansions facing the parklands surrounding the Melbourne Cricket Ground. The vast stadium loomed in the distance, an eerie blue glow illuminating its upper deck, making it look more like a space station than a sports arena. The cars squealed to a jolting stop at the far end of the street, hard up against the low railing separating road from grass and behind an already parked police car, unoccupied and with its radio chattering away unheard and unanswered. Across the grass, Bromo could see flashlights, the shape of people bent over, huddled together.

'This way.'

Holmes was out of the car and heading quickly towards the lights. They stumbled behind him across the uneven turf, Bromo and Delia keeping pace, Watson puffing several metres behind. A tall, grey-haired man stood off to the left, fondling two lean, sleek dogs.

'It's over there,' he said, pointing towards a 20-metre high tree.

Only the trunk remained, its branches and leaves long taken by storm, age and disease. Holmes stopped suddenly. His hands went deep into his jeans pockets. He slowly walked the last few paces to where two uniformed policemen were waving their flashlights over the scene. Bromo felt himself drawn trance-like, hypnotically and fearfully, alongside Holmes.

The tree was surrounded by a rusting, waist-high iron fence. Bent backwards over the railings, harpooned on their blunt tip, was the body of Aurelia Nuyen. Her head hung down inside the fence, a stream of dried-up blood caked her body and pooled on to a memorial stone labelling this as the Scarred Tree, a memorial to past centuries when this was an Aboriginal meeting place. Aurelia's already short skirt had ridden higher up her thighs. One flimsy high-heeled sandal had fallen into the dirt; the other was dangling off her foot.

They edged closer. Torchlight beamed on to her torso, strained taut over the fence. Her ribcage was clearly contoured beneath a white T-shirt, ripped in several ragged slashes and stained crimson with blood. Bromo gagged and looked away. His eyes watered and he felt tears on his cheeks. Shock turned to anger. Nothing justified this. Holmes lifted an edge of the T-shirt.

'Bloody madman. He must've gone crazy.'

The police shifted their beams away.

'We haven't touched her,' said one. 'Waited for you. It was all over when we got here.'

He gestured to the man with the dogs.

'He saw it happening. Called it in on his mobile.'

Watson was on her phone and casting around over the grass close to the tree. Delia was busy on her mobile, too, as she looked inside another car parked metres away up on the road, its door hanging open. Headlights still on. Aurelia's car. Bromo felt the anger rising in him. No one should get away with this. He took his chance and walked briskly over to the man with the dogs. Huddled up inside a grubby old anorak, he looked too dazed to bother asking Bromo for ID.

'Nice dogs. You okay?'

The man nodded, staring blankly ahead. He kept patting the dogs, probably comforting himself more than them.

'What happened?'

'They had a row. Up there. In the car. Screaming at each other.'

He turned slightly, indicating the road.

'She got out, tried to run. He chased her, shouting. Caught her by the tree. Stabbed her. Shocking. Stab, stab, stab. Awful. It spooked the dogs.'

Paramedics walked quickly, purposefully, towards them across the grass. They'd be sedating him. Taking him away for observation.

'He didn't move for a long time,' said the man, staring off into the gloom. 'He kept staring at her. That's when I phoned. I didn't know what to do. The dogs were growling. He sat there for a while but ran off as you lot came.'

'Where did he go?'

The man perked up, like a quiz show contestant offered his favourite topic. It was the question he'd been waiting for. He pointed to one of the many broad footpaths criss-crossing the park.

'There. It's the only way. Away from the road.'

Obvious. On match days, this was a massive car park. The rest of the time, locked posts prevented vehicles entering. Even the paramedics now only a few steps away had been unable to get their ambulance close to their patient. Gerry Nuyen had a head start to freedom and had to make it on his own. This had been a private fight between him and Aurelia and there were no hoons to protect him.

Bromo began moving away as the paramedics neared. He pointed to the man.

'He's in shock. Needs a bit of TLC. Dogs seem okay now.'

He saw Delia and Holmes coming towards him, converging on the dog-walker. It was time to go. Anger was the spur. He turned away, lengthened his stride and headed in the direction of the stadium.

'Perkins. Stop.'

It was Holmes. Bromo heard someone running behind him and broke into a trot. He looked over his shoulder. Delia was 20 metres away. He heard her yell.

'Bromo, come back. What do you think you're doing? Leave it to us.'

He hesitated and turned. She was stopped, hands on hips, one of them frighteningly close to her holstered pistol. He gambled she wouldn't give chase and leave the crime scene.

'You wanted my help,' he shouted. 'Now you've got it. He went this way and your cars can't follow.'

'The motor-cycles on are their way.'

'Too bloody late.'

He turned and began running up a slight rise. He couldn't imagine the squat and rotund Gerry Nuyen being all that far ahead. He crested the rise. Sparse trees dotted the parkland. A long incline led down to the wide paving of the main concourse encircling the stadium. Over to his right, a small fluffy white dog was scampering back to a couple embracing in the shadow of a tree. The flickering headlight of a commuting cyclist came towards him.

Bromo called out.

'You seen a man … running?'

The cyclist hardly paused, pushing down hard on his pedals: 'Down there. Near the Members.'

He added something else but his words were carried away on the breeze. Bromo looked towards the stadium and the entrance set aside for the exclusive use of members of one of the world's most popular clubs. Parents put their offspring on its waiting list at birth and hoped they might be enrolled before they were too old to flash their membership badges and enjoy their ringside seats. A lone figure was crossing the grass verge facing the Members, making a stumbling run from tree shadow to tree shadow but clearly visible in the gaps between.

Bromo took a deep breath, lengthened his stride and attempted the closest thing to a sprint that he could muster. All those hours at the gym were being summoned up for one struggling all-out run. A sign pointed to Olympic Way. It provided the impetus he needed.

'Going for gold,' he muttered, eyes focused on the zig-zagging figure now clearly visible as Nuyen broke cover from the parkland and began crossing the concourse.

Nuyen's huge start was a small advantage to someone not built for running. He may have been lean and hardened in his youth but the years had taken their toll. Bromo saw him stagger past a bright orange and green merchandising kiosk where punters paid good money on match days to buy hats, t-shirts and other paraphernalia promoting their favourite teams. For a while he lost sight of him behind four immense slate-grey obelisks bearing plaques honouring the city's sporting heroes. Then he saw him, running desperately on towards another merchandising kiosk, a twin of the first.

The gap between them was narrowing rapidly. Bromo could see Nuyen clearly as he skirted the kiosk and headed towards the broad, rising curve of the William Barak Bridge, linking the sports arena to the city. It was Nuyen's only hope of disappearing into the city's night-time confusion and perhaps finding a train or taxi to make good his escape.

Bromo remembered the breathing regimen taught to him by a French paratrooper during his basic training – count two in, three out. Old habits die hard. He was into a rhythm, sustained by his anger. Almost feeling good. The body was working, coming alive, responding. Nuyen was a hundred metres ahead, struggling hard towards the summit of the bridge

Bromo sprinted down the dip leading on to the bridge and shortened his stride as he hit the upward slope, lit by a soft yellow glow from lights on the underside of the guard rails. Distant sirens were getting louder as vehicles rushed to the scene. Police motorcycles had responded to Delia's call. He could call off his chase and leave them to do their job. Or he could corner the little bastard and find out what drove him to do it. Hate and fury drove him rapidly on.

Voices boomed out around him. He faltered, startled, seeing no one. It took several seconds to realise the voices came from the endless loop of a soundscape woven into the bridge's parapet – the stories and songs of the Aboriginal tribes which once owned this land. The great sweep of the bridge was designed as a tribute to the native peoples of the world. Their songs and stories accompanied everyone who took this route, although few paused to listen.

The incline was too much for Nuyen. Bromo saw him stop and bend over, hands on thighs. Nuyen heard Bromo's footsteps, looked around, and tried to move on. There was nothing left in his tank. Overweight middle-aged men don't run up hills. He was stuffed. He leaned against the parapet, gasping for breath. Voices were chanting, talking, singing from the speakers. Bromo ran up, lunging at him, screaming.

'Why, why, why? You fucking little bastard. She didn't deserve that.'

Nuyen drew breath, delved deep into his exhausted body's reserve tank, finding energy he didn't know existed. The last gasps of the desperate. He summoned up several stumbling strides, taking him out of Bromo's reach, closer to the summit and the downhill track to the city.

Bromo picked up pace, legs aching but still carrying him forward, determined to catch Nuyen. The gap between them was narrowing. Nuyen was slowing, faltering. The siren sound grew louder. Bromo glanced behind him, over his right shoulder, and saw two sets of headlights weaving through the parkland.

The two seconds of distraction were enough for Nuyen. His chest heaved with two huge intakes of breath, a renewal of energy, trying to draw more air into ailing lungs. He stopped suddenly, turned and faced the onrushing Bromo. He reached into the waistband of his trousers and drew out a short-bladed knife. His arm thrust towards Bromo, blade extended, catching a gleam from the bridge lights, making him come to a sudden awkward stop.

Bromo took a step back, widening the gap between them slightly. He focused on the blade. One sudden unseen lunge could easily rip into him. Nuyen wouldn't hesitate if given an opening. Bromo breathed deep, trying to keep the tremors out of his voice, staying calm, doing nothing to excite the man with the weapon.

'Give up, Gerry,' he pleaded. 'You're not going anywhere.'

Nuyen made a short, darting jab with the knife, not extending his arm but doing enough to make Bromo shuffle back another pace. Bromo raised bent arms in a surrender pose, open palms facing towards Nuyen.

'Drop the knife, Gerry. You've done enough damage.'

The beams of headlights from the police motor-cycles shone full on to Nuyen. His head twitched slightly right and left, nervous, on his guard, close to panic. He hadn't the breath or pace to run. Bromo breathed easy. It was a stand-off which would last as long as he stayed out of thrusting distance of Nuyen's blade. Time was on his side.

Bromo heard the two police motor-cycles roaring up the bridge behind him. There was the wail of sirens and the incessant blink of blue lights from patrol cars stopping on Brunton Avenue below. The strident sounds shattered the silence of their tense stand-off. Nuyen was spooked by the bright beams, a rabbit in a hunter's spotlights. The twitch of his head became a violent spasm. His whole body contorted and turned. He made a desperate lunge at Bromo with the blade and twisted away.

Bromo dodged to one side and hurled himself at Nuyen to gather him in. Nuyen lurched violently, backwards and away, striking the rail of the parapet just above waist level. The force of the impact drove his body upwards and outwards in a reverse roll, his arms flung wide. His head hit the tubular metal rail on the outside of the parapet, bouncing him further out over the maze of railway lines below. For one agonising moment he was frozen in time, going neither backwards nor forward. Bromo lunged towards him, seeking a hold on jacket, body, anything. It was too late. Nuyen spiralled backwards over the parapet, in free fall on to the rail tracks.

Bromo hardly noticed the police motor cycles whining to a halt alongside him. He stared off into the distance where the marble-white tower of Government House glowed in its floodlights. Seagulls flocked above the floodlit latticed steel dome roof of the Vodafone arena. The river snaked darkly beyond the rail tracks and tennis courts. Two helmeted, leathered patrolmen dismounted and walked to the parapet.

'You're too late,' said Bromo. 'He's caught the 10.20 from Sandringham, or the 11.05 to Glen Waverley. Or they caught him. He's gone. Kaput. Kerplunk. Rail kill.'

He was rambling, becoming incoherent. His heart was pumping frantically. He lowered his head into his hands and felt the firm hand of a patrolman grip his elbow. Sirens screamed beneath the bridge. More lights appeared at the foot of the incline from the stadium. Barriers had been lifted and patrol cars had driven through. He saw Delia running up the ramp, Holmes close behind. Delia stopped in front of him and spoke to the patrolman.

'It's okay. I'll take over.'

She reached up and grasped Bromo's hands, easing them away from his face. He shuddered at her touch. Holmes hovered, looking uneasy. Uniformed police emerged from more patrol cars. They unwound crime scene tape along the parapet to seal off a section of the bridge. Other police were placing portable floodlights on the rail tracks. Trains had stopped. Another unexplained for the city's frustrated travellers.

'We'll need a statement,' said Delia. 'You shouldn't have done that.'

It was a rebuke, but said softly, without bite. Bromo nodded. He knew the score. A blow-by-blow description would be needed. Only there were no blows. Simply a sudden movement, a flash of blade, a defensive rush, a stumble, a push, a fall . . . an unthinking reaction made in anger. Try explaining that one away.

Holmes moved away and began talking to the uniformed police. Delia let go of one hand and held on to the other. Bromo sensed her trembling, her body revealing a reaction her voice and face tried to hide; the personal within undermining the professional on the outside. Bromo felt a slight squeeze from her hand.

'He's not worth worrying about,' she said. 'Forget it.'

The anger welled up inside him.

'And Aurelia?'

She drew a deep breath, released her grip and looked away.

'Yeah, well. What can I say?'

They were isolated in a cone of silence, separated from the glare of lights, shouted commands and whine of sirens surrounding them.

'I'll get you home,' she said. 'Holmes can deal with this.'

He looked at her, bemused, uncertain. Her touch had been warm and comforting. He felt his anger subsiding. The shock of Nuyen's fall was already fading. He rested the tips of his fingers on his neck, feeling for a pulse. It seemed even and somewhere around normal; not racing. Delia had not moved, nor shifted her gaze.

'Who are you now?' he asked. 'Clerk? Goth? Copper? Or have you found a new disguise?'

She smiled. Her voice softened to little more than a whisper: 'I'm me. I'll take you home. You need looking after.'

She reached out and took him by the arm, leading him towards an unmarked car. She called back over her shoulder to Holmes. 'You can take over. Mr Perkins is going to file a report. We'll debrief tomorrow.'

They drove sedately and in silence along the same streets they had raced through an hour ago. Bromo gazed out at the couples in the cars around them, making their way home after shows and concerts or an evening of wining and dining. He and Delia looked no different from those other commuters. What was there to show they hadn't been laughing their heads off at a movie or tucking into a risotto and a glass of red instead of witnessing the bloodied body of a woman slashed to death and her attacker's fatal plunge on to the rail tracks? Such public faces with such private lives.

He directed her into the parking lot alongside his apartment. She stilled the engine, stepped out and slammed the door shut. It was done in one smooth unhesitating movement. Bromo, still in the passenger seat, gathered his wits. Her movements had taken him by surprise. They had removed the need for him to ponder the niceties of whether to ask her in for a drink. She'd already extended her own invitation. It was every lad's dream: come in for a drink, a coffee – the hidden message, the suggestion of something beyond a glass of rough red or a cup of Milo.

She'd already walked to the entrance door. He sensed he was being led - as if she was the host and he the visitor. He eased himself slowly out of the car and closed the door gently, but firmly.

'Where's your place?' she asked. 'On the top floor?'

Her questions came with a directness he found hard to counter. They removed the need for the usual 'will she, won't she' sparring that so often defined a first date. She moved in close beside him as he fumbled with his keys. He sensed impatience, a haste. It was as if she were on a high, still powered by the adrenalin that had seen her through the past few hours. It contrasted sharply with his own need to relax and shuffle off the horrors they'd seen.

She took his arm and powered him up the stairs. At the top, he offered her the key.

'Here, you do it. You seem to have more energy than me.'

Inside, she stood briefly, hands on hips, appraising the room.

'Hmm. Cosy.'

'That's one word for it. Suits me.'

'I can imagine. Where's the bedroom?'

He pointed, hoping it was somewhat tidier than usual.

'Can I get you a drink?'

'Later. We've got more urgent business.'

She took his hand and pushed through the half-open bedroom door, dragging him along, her haste now palpable. He shivered, but not from any chill or draught. The night remained warm and muggy. This was a shudder of excitement and arousal. She released his hand as she tripped over a shoe discarded on the floor and stumbled towards the bed.

'Shit. Untidy bugger.'

He was dazed by the pace and suddenness of her movements. Surely, this wasn't what it looked like. It couldn't be happening. There'd been no small talk; no batting of innuendoes back and forth, no furtive touches and glances.

She sat on the edge of the bed, her body bent forward, hands reaching for her runners, tugging them off her feet. She stood, slipped her jeans to the floor and there was the clunk of her gun hitting the carpet. With one continuous movement she pulled the t-shirt over her head, ribs clearly defined, stomach flat and smooth, as she stretched upwards, hair now tousled and falling over one shoulder. As her hands reached backwards to unclip her bra, she threw him a commanding glance.

'What are you waiting for? Don't just stand there. Get your gear off.'

Her words jolted Bromo out of his daze. Briefly he imagined her ordering a strip search in the holding cells. Then he caught the beginnings of a smile and registered the softness of her voice. This was something else. He kicked off his shoes and fumbled frantically with zips and buttons, feverishly shedding clothes as if every item was searing his skin. She slid a flimsy, lacy pair of pale blue boy pants down her legs and stood stock still in front of him. He made a silent appraisal: buck naked and beautiful. He was given only a fleeting look. There was a whirl of bodies and limbs as she extended an arm, grabbed his wrist, thrust a foot behind his lower leg and pushed firmly with her other hand against his shoulder.

Bromo felt himself spinning around, tumbling backwards, bouncing down on to the bed with Delia sprawled on top of him. She moved rapidly, sitting astride him and pinioning his arms wide, like a roo skin pegged out to dry. He made a token struggle before deciding to save his energy. Savour the moment. To lose was better than to win. Unarmed combat had never been more deliciously enjoyable.

She rose above him, wriggled and opened herself wide, taking him deep into her. Every muscle and sinew in her arms stood out as she pressed down on his wrists. Her lower limbs were thrusting with a manic frenzy. Her eyes were open, staring down at him, but he sensed they were not seeing. She was elsewhere, breathing rapidly, noisily, in shorter and shorter gasps. Bromo felt an exquisite agony coursing through his body. He tried to raise his hips and match her frantic rhythm.

'Don't,' she yelped through her gasps. 'Stay still.'

'Can't,' he grunted. 'Gotta move.'

The pressure on his wrists increased. Her hips thrust faster and deeper.

'This isn't about you, Bromo. It's about me.'

He was beginning to hurt. Ecstasy was turning to pain. She gave a massive downward lunge and let loose a long, agonised yell. The pressure on his wrists relaxed as she collapsed forward on to him, her body suddenly slowing to a gentle pulsating quiver. He felt rivulets of sweat flowing between them.

She nuzzled into his neck and planted a soft, lingering kiss.

'Thanks,' she whispered. 'The next one's for you.'

They slid under the doona and dozed, entwined together. They enjoyed small snatches of talk punctuated by long silences.

Bromo was still perplexed. He had to know.

'What was that all about? You jumped me. It was incredible. But why?'

'Need,' she whispered. 'Relief. Therapy, if you like. It's been too long.'

'Why me?'

'You were there.'

He tensed, feeling hurt. She sensed the barb and drew him close to her.

'Sorry. That was badly put. I wouldn't have done it with just anyone. I'm starting to see you as someone special. This is the real me.'

One of the long silences descended before she stirred.

'You were in the right place at the right time. The last few months have been hell. No let-up. Playing a role, pretending to be someone else, always on my guard. A double life. Surely you know all about that.'

He said nothing and closed his eyes. He remembered. Now was not the time to talk about it.

Sometime later he found himself responding to the gentle movement of her hands. He stirred. They took time to caress and explore each other's body, discovering the curves and crevices, easing away all remaining tensions. The hard-edged fire and frenzy of their earlier coupling had evaporated. She was now sensuous and glowing. She moved slowly and languidly as she gently guided him into her. She was as good as her word. This time was for him.

TWENTY-SEVEN

The thump of the heating system as the shower came on dragged him up out of a deep sleep. The doona was curled back where Delia had slid from the bed. He'd heard and felt nothing. Bromo rubbed his eyes and stretched out. A spasm of cramp grabbed his right foot. He tensed, waited for it to ease, and slowly sat up.

The horrors of the night before came rushing back – the sight of Aurelia's mutilated body, Nuyen plunging to his death – and he closed his eyes. It did no good; the vision remained on his inner screen.

There was daylight coming through chinks in the blinds. He sensed the day was already warm. There'd been only a slight cooling change overnight. He glanced at the bedside clock – 6.18. Far too early – a subhuman hour made only for garbage collectors and newspaper boys.

The pounding of the shower stopped and Delia shuffled into the room, one towel draped around her, another being used to dry her tousled hair. She leant over him and planted a kiss lightly on his brow.

'Didn't mean to wake you, but I'll have to go soon. Too much to do.'

Bromo understood, but didn't want to. She'd wrapped the

towel around her sarong-style, but too loosely. He tugged at the towel and it fell away. His eyes took a slow and admiring tour of her body. He reached out to draw her to him, but she pulled away.

'Stay,' he pleaded.

'I can't. You know that.'

He did know it, but had no wish to see it happen.

'We've both work to do,' she said. 'Unfortunately, last night's business was only part of it. It's even more urgent that we wrap this up and we're going to need your help.'

He clasped his hands between his knees, watching her ruffle her wet hair with the towel.

'Be an angel and make me a coffee while I get dressed,' she said.

He rolled back on the bed, disgruntled and letting his body language show it.

'What was this - a one-night stand?'

She stepped sharply away, turning from him and gathered her clothes.

'Who knows? I hope not. Time will tell. It was something we both needed.'

He had to accept the verdict. Be grateful and go with the flow. She was right. This was the way it had to be, at least for now.

'How do you take it?'

She misunderstood his question.

'Hard, like you.'

He grinned, spirits rising.

'I meant the coffee.'

She chuckled at her error.

'Little milk, no sugar. Any chance of a slice of toast?'

He took a robe off its hook and drew it tight round him.
'Can do: Cooking skills 101.'

By the time the coffee was brewed and the toast tanned she'd reverted to the trim, neat plain-clothed policewoman of the night before, brisk and efficient as she spread a lavish layer of honey over the browned bread. They sat close together on high stools ranged along the kitchen counter-top. He rested one hand on her knee.

'So, what do you want from me?'

'Access – to Mack's and to Rasheed. We'll do the rest.'

'When?'

'Later. After I've spoken to the rest of the troops. I've got to debrief first.'

He squeezed her knee.

'Can't see that being too much of a problem. You do it so well.'

This time she caught his wordplay.

'When the occasion's right.'

Another peck on his cheek, an adjustment of her belt and an official sounding reminder that 'you'll be hearing from us' and she was gone – back to that other world where women had their bodies slashed by unbalanced husbands who leapt to their deaths rather than face the consequences.

TWENTY-EIGHT

DECISIONS. SHOULD HE OPEN the windows and balcony doors and let the north wind blow through, or close everything tight to stem the hot and dust-laden gusts for a few more hours? It was an annual dilemma. It divided the city's residents who lacked air-conditioning into two schools of thought, and neither had ever been proved conclusively correct.

Bromo decided to open everything up. A hot breeze was better than no breeze and if things got really bad a quick cold shower worked wonders. It was shaping up as a day when inactivity became the enforced order of things. At least it wasn't going to be as hot as first forecast. The bureau had revised its predictions and brought the expected top temperature down to a mere 36 degrees.

Delia had said they'd be in touch. No time had been mentioned and he couldn't see himself sitting around all day waiting for a call that might not come until tomorrow. If he was going to do anything, earlier was better than later.

The radio flowed from talk-back into the morning news. It launched into a brief report of last night's events. Few details, no names – a police media liaison summary that sated the appetites of news editors and filled the gap between stories of endless conflicts in the Middle East and an update on a footballer's broken leg.

Bromo resorted to old technology and used his landline to dial a number. She picked up on the second ring. She was home; that's all he wanted to know.

He drew on a pair of tattered and stained shorts, stuck his arms and head through a T-shirt long past its prime and laced his feet into a pair of reliable old runners. He set a gentle pace as he jogged through back streets, eyes stung by swirling eddies of dust and patches of sweat already dampening his top.

Liz Shapcott showed no surprise when she answered his push on the entry buzzer. She came halfway across the courtyard to greet him, wrapped in a billowing green and turquoise cotton smock, her feet bare, toenails painted a bright scarlet.

'Heard the news?' he asked.

'Couldn't miss it,' she replied, brisk and alert. 'Phone hasn't stopped ringing. When did you find out?'

The anger stirred in him. The words started out slowly, measured, in monotone.

'I was there, Liz.' He felt himself losing control. She had to understand. He raised his voice, now almost screaming. 'I was there. I was there. I was there.'

Liz stopped and gripped his forearm. Her voice lost its hard edge and softened.

'Oh, Bromo. I didn't realise. I didn't know. It must have been terrible.'

The bile rose. The scene at the Scarred Tree replayed without him pressing the start button. He choked, coughed and swallowed.

'Yes, it was. Bloody awful. Perhaps you'd like a blow by blow description.'

The bitterness was undisguised. He pulled away from her grasp and pushed angrily past her into the factory she'd made a home, still ranting.

'After all, it's all because of some stupid petty dispute over a development site you were helping design.'

He made for the Apple Mac in the far corner and started rifling through the sheaf of papers still rolled up alongside it. Liz held back, watching and wary.

'This is what it's all about,' Bromo shouted at her. 'Development, protests, high rise, low rise, greenies, profits, open space, parking, how many units you can squeeze on to one site, minimum standards, maximum profits.'

Liz padded softly across the floor in his wake and stood, arms folded, patiently listening, holding back, resenting his intrusion into her private papers but tolerant, recognising his need, fearing his anger. This was the release he had to have – going full throttle, valves fully open. Soon, he ran out of steam, couldn't sustain it, sounding off but not fully believing his own words. He set the rolls of plans back in their place and collapsed into the chair facing the computer.

'You done?'

Only two words, but said with so much meaning. Liz spoke them softly yet firmly. Bromo detected a medley of messages – concern, comfort, annoyance and denial. Too much to handle. Pick one; leave the rest to later.

'Sorry,' he said. 'I was out of order. Shouldn't have done that. You're not really to blame. You're only a bit player. A walk-on role.'

She moved behind him and put her hands on his shoulders, pressing down, kneading firmly and rhythmically, thumbs finding pressure points, fingers probing deep and easing out strands of tension.

'Relax. You've got to unwind, get rid of the demons.'

Her fingers dug deeper, feeling the knots in his shoulders and neck, the ball of her hand rocking back and forth in support. She leaned over his shoulder, the mass of tightly curled tresses tumbling down his front. The pressure of her fingers was easing back, becoming more caress than massage.

'Let me help you relax.'

Her words had the opposite effect. He tensed. It was another offer almost too good to refuse. This must be his lucky day: every woman on his radar was offering to bring him comfort through personal therapy. It would be all too easy to accept Liz's unmistakable offer – to see if the reality of their coupling matched his occasional fantasy of the past.

Her mobile rang. Dilemma solved. She stood up and reached for the phone. He breathed deeply and relaxed. Perhaps the massage had helped.

'Yes?' she snapped, clearly annoyed by the interruption.

She moved over towards the kitchen area, a hand brushing back her curls, feet kicking at the folds of her wrap as it trailed on the floor. Bromo noted she was doing more listening than talking. He caught an occasional 'Yes', 'I see' and then a louder, more demanding 'Why?'

She kept moving, restless, flowing around the room, stealing an occasional glance in his direction.

Bromo rolled the bundle of plans back and forth, playing the nonchalant role. Me? I'm not prying, not eavesdropping on your conversation, even if I do sense I'm involved. She raised her voice and looked pointedly at him.

'Okay, half an hour. I'll be here.'

'And I won't.'

To Bromo, the message was clear. He stood up.

'What was that all about?' he asked.

'The police. Some detective called Watson. Says they want to talk to me, but won't say why. The usual thing, a few a questions they want to ask me. Why do they always try to pretend it's so bloody simple and innocent?'

'Isn't it?'

She busied herself at the kitchen sink, running the tap, rinsing cups, her face turned from him.

'How would I know? They refuse to discuss anything until they get here. Probably a lot of fuss over a parking fine.'

'Yeah, sure. Just the sort of thing the fraud squad would get involved in.'

'Fraud?'

Her movements slowed, shoulders tensed. Still she faced the wall. Bromo guessed her reactions, sensed a tightening of her face. The body language spoke loud and clear.

'Yes, fraud. Watson was there last night. She probably helped scrape Gerry Nuyen off the Glen Waverley line. Or she lifted Aurelia off the railing impaling her. A shit job.'

Her scream echoed around the room, bouncing off the scrubbed brick walls.

'Stop it, Bromo.'

She spun round from the sink, her gown swirling and spiralling, briefly clinging to breasts, hips and thighs, defining the contours of her body, then falling loose and shapeless.

'Stop it,' she screeched again. 'I'm sorry for you, Bromo. Terribly sorry. And about Aurelia, too. It's awful. But it's got nothing to do with me.'

'Hasn't it? You and your bloody Tiger Poppies or whatever they're called - what about them? Strange that their slogan should be emblazoned on a wall inside Mack's while you're drawing up plans for its development.'

She stuttered and stammered.

'That was nothing. Something to keep a street kid occupied. It hardly exists.'

'Enough to get special brooches made. I found one in Rasheed's house. You've got one, given to you by Aurelia. She was involved. A brooch-carrying member. And now she's dead.'

He ran out of steam. Liz grabbed his wrists and tried to draw him to her, shaking and stuttering, shocked at the implications of his words

'We've done nothing to justify this,' she sobbed.

He detected hurt among her surprise. Maybe he was on the wrong track. Change direction. He picked up a roll of drawings and brandished it at her.

'Okay, if not the Poppies, what about these? The poor sods around here endured years of corruption and nepotism from the people who were supposed to be looking after their interests. Rigged votes, bribes, kickbacks, jobs going to incompetent mates.'

Each point was hammered home by a downward beat with the roll of papers; a conductor stressing every note of a concerto.

'The crooks got caught, weeded out. Those days are supposed to be well behind us. Surely you're not going to help them return.'

He thumped the papers down on to the table. Liz stared at them, transfixed. Bromo accepted her look as one of genuine surprise. She'd failed to make the connection. Pieces were missing from her jigsaw. He could provide them now or leave it to the police to fill the gaps. There was no debate: she was too good a friend and client and there could well come a time when those healing hands might be just the remedy for singledom and celibacy.

'What about them?'

'Who's paying you?'

Again, that look of puzzlement.

'What? My clients, of course. The usual professional fees.'

'And Steve Delgado?'

Bull's-eye! Her face said it all: he'd scored a direct hit. Enough to sink her into a deep soft leather armchair, where she sat, expressionless and still, silently inviting him to explain.

'That's why Watson and her mates are calling on you,' he said, finding a seat on the lounge, less intimidating, no longer standing over her.

'They've got Delgado's diary,' he said. 'It contains a list of initials and figures. LS is among them. They've jumped to conclusions that it's shorthand for people, Liz Shapcott possibly, and the bribes Delgado has been paying.'

'And receiving,' she said, her voice a soft, dulled monotone.

Life was full of surprises, forever sticking out its foot and tripping you up right when you were sprinting for the tape. Bromo felt himself stumble. He paused, adjusted his thoughts. They were heading in a new direction.

'You – paying him?'

She nodded, head bowed. Confessions were never easy, especially for good Catholic girls.

'I needed the work. There was too much to lose and he could take it all away. He's a standover man. Sometimes it's harder to fight than give in.'

She seemed to have shrunk, sinking deeper into the chair. A cartoonist would have depicted her with a black cloud of depression looming overhead. Bromo felt the roles of comforter and comforted had been reversed. It was his turn to provide the solace.

'Game's over, Liz.'

She sat up, eyebrows raised in query.

'Delgado's in custody, along with his little black book and a loaded gun.'

'And me?'

He stood up and moved alongside her.

'Come clean. Tell them all you know. You can't bring Aurelia back but we can stop any more bloody mayhem. They need your help.'

She looked up, showing the slightest of smiles.

'Okay.'

He put a hand on her shoulder.

'I'm going before they get here.'

He gave a gentle squeeze.

'Be strong. Next time it's my turn to give the massage.'

TWENTY-NINE

HE PUFFED AND SWEATED his way back home. The temperature had soared in just an hour. The footpaths were a mess of litter, the hot north wind vandalising the streets as it blew newspapers, wrappers, cartons and the detritus of overflowing rubbish bins anywhere it wanted. Empty pizza boxes chased Big Mac wrappers along the gutters. Giveaway newspapers chronicling the council's strategies and misdeeds wrapped themselves around chair legs at pavement cafes deserted on a day when air-con comfort was a no-contest winner over outdoor dining.

Delia's car was in the parking slot. He stopped, bent over, puffing and slightly woozy. The heat had got to him. She stepped out and put a hand on his back.

'You're hot.'

'Thanks for the compliment,' he gasped. 'You're not too bad yourself.'

She chuckled.

'It's not what I meant, but thanks all the same.'

He stretched up. The dizziness had passed.

'Where were you?. I've been waiting.'

She'd reverted to official mode. There was an admonition in her tone.

'You were supposed to wait here.'

He gave her the innocent look.

'Out for a run. Clearing the cobwebs. Secret men's business.'

'Bullshit.'

'Take it or leave it.'

'You don't need exercise and no one in their right mind runs in this weather.'

'So, I'm crazy.'

She grasped his arm, firmly, and began guiding him towards the entrance.

'Stop playing silly buggers. Let's go upstairs, have a cup of coffee and talk things through like a couple of good friends.'

He heard the undertones of pleading in her voice and knew she was right. So difficult. He recognised the divide between the official and the personal. It was a double game as complex and stressful as that played by any secret agent. Never get involved, they'd told him. It was a universal rule.

Delia stopped, let her arm drop to her side, and moved to face him. Her brow was more creased than he had noticed before, lines radiated from the side of her eyes, a cluster of crow's feet at the edges. The stress and anxiety showed. Her grip tightened.

'Don't spoil it, Bromo.'

But he did. He always did. So many relationships, so many disasters. There was no reason it should be that way. Others managed. Worked through their problems. They not only survived, but blossomed and bloomed. Why not him? He attempted a smile.

'This time, you make the coffee while I take a shower.'

He felt her take his arm again, this time gently, not pushing or guiding. The policewoman as lover.

'You talk, I'll listen,' he promised as he turned the key in the lock.

His promise held good. Fresh from the shower, he sat and listened with just a towel gathered round his waist, relishing the breeze blowing in, as she outlined developments. He made no comments, asked no questions. She was on auto pilot, her facts well-ordered as she ran through what had happened since last night. He accepted it as a carefully edited version, omitting the heavy stuff and pushing the positives. The councillors identified by initials in Delgado's book had crumpled when confronted by investigators. They'd admitted accepting cash and other inducements to miss crucial meetings or to vote as Delgado had told them to. They had no excuse other than greed. The principle of doing the right thing by the ratepayers who had elected them seemed a foreign concept.

'Sadly, they're not unique,' said Delia, twirling a spoon through her coffee. 'Corruption in local government is far worse than anything you'll find further up the tree. Hiawatha he say 'Big fish in small pond makes nasty stink.''

Bromo laughed. The light relief was welcome. It showed she could switch off, or at least ease the tension. He took his coffee mug over to the sink.

'And what does Hiawatha have to say about Liz Shapcott?'

'Who cares?'

There was a sharp edge to her response.

'I do,' he said.

A Katusha rocket fired into the room wouldn't have been more devastating. He'd pressed the wrong button – again. He tightened the towel around his waist and fumbled for words.

'She's a client.'

The image of Liz's hands massaging his neck intruded on his thoughts. An interlude. He rushed to dispel them.

'She's a friend. Nothing more.'

'Sure?'

'Positive.'

'And Fiona?'

His head spun to look at her. Which role was she playing now – cop or lover? The questions were ambiguous, the official tinted with the personal. Guilt was welling up inside him – the guilt of erotic thinking, of fantasies, rather than any reality. Every contact with Fiona had been tinged with innuendo, with hints of what might be. And there it had ended.

'She's nothing,' he said.

It was the truth in terms of actions but a lie where thoughts were concerned.

'You were nice and cosy in the gallery.'

'She needed help.'

'Nice one, Bromo. From what I hear she wasn't in a hurry to get dressed.'

'Blame her, not me. Sounds as if Sergeant Mayfield has been adding some facts of his own making.'

He was on the defensive and didn't know why. What was it with women? They were so unforgiving. Made you so angry. Goaded you into saying things you didn't really mean and would regret as soon as you'd said them. Like now. He thumped his hands down on the kitchen bench and leaned towards her, glaring.

'Instead of making false accusations about my dealings with other women wouldn't you be better employed finding out why Aurelia was killed.'

He might as well have dropped a tray of best Bohemian crystal. The effect was devastating. Implosive. A cushion of silence formed an impenetrable barrier between them. They glared across the benchtop, frozen in the moment.

Bromo was the first to move – a slight shuffling of his bare feet on the tiled floor, guilt and embarrassment welling up inside. His arms hung loosely at his side, hands turning slowly to palms upwards in a gesture of helplessness. Where was the rewind button? Go back. Delete the past few ghastly moments. Pick up the pieces.

Her hand went up, brushing fallen fronds of hair off her forehead. She fixed her eyes on him, stern and unblinking. It was a stare designed to make criminals think twice before pitching her a false story. She broke the silence.

'Right, let's get a few things straight. One – never, ever, try to tell me how to do my job. Two – like it or not, you are still involved in this case and I'm not quite sure which side you're on. Some of your actions have been dubious to say the least.'

She paused, lowering her gaze, studying the smears on the benchtop. Bromo said nothing, digesting her reprimand, sensing there was more to come. There was.

'One more thing…'

Her voice had dropped a tone and softened. He crossed his fingers, hoping.

'…I do understand your concern and we are moving quickly over the Aurelia business. One of Gerry Nuyen's protectors has decided to talk. She saw what led up to it.'

'Not the lovely Sonia.'

Delia smiled.

'Yeah.'

She paused, raising her eyebrows, smiling slightly.

'Not another one of your women?'

This time it was a gentle jibe, not a barb. Bromo felt the tension ebbing.

'You could say we once were very close,' he said.

'This time I'll say nothing.'

'So far as Sonia is concerned, intimacy can be a pain.'

'I get the message. She's a tough young woman. It must've hurt.'

He shrugged. It was a blip that had faded from his radar. Time to move on, if only he knew which route to take. He needed guidance, but Delia had the map. He gave it a go.

'And us?'

'Now's not the time, Bromo. Let's wait and see until after we've put the lid on this. All things are possible.'

He uncrossed his fingers.

'Thanks.'

It was the best he could hope for. He hitched up the towel and eased his backside on to a bar stool facing her.

'What do you want me to do?'

Delia told him, concisely and efficiently. It was a briefing just like old times, except that now the threat was on his own doorstep, not in some alien territory which could be as difficult to combat as the people lined up against him.

After a couple of minutes he held up his hand.

'Hang on. The brain's not what it used to be. I need to make notes.'

He fetched a spiral-backed pad and ballpoint. The pen scratched, didn't write. As he walked to the back room to retrieve a replacement, the towel loosened and fell to the floor.

'Nice arse,' she called out.

He wiggled his backside in response, rewound the towel and completed his errand. It took another five minutes for Delia to complete her briefing, Bromo diligently jotting down salient points, places and times.

'All clear? Any questions?' she asked.

'Yeah. Back to where we were - why Aurelia?'

He sensed her tussling with her conscience: to tell or not to tell. Too many police operational secrets had been leaking into the public domain. Delia was making a risk assessment, judging him. Surely she could see it was too late for that. They'd come too far. Trust was no longer an issue. Delia walked round to the sink, cup in hand, and ran the tap, rinsing out the coffee dregs, taking her time. Bromo remained hunched over the bench, back turned, willing her to open up. He heard the cup being put down.

'Okay.'

She had made a decision.

'It seems that Aurelia had begun a personal crusade against porn sites on the net. She believed local women were being secretly photographed and their pictures misused to attract punters. She tried stirring up opposition and wanted to find the women and alert them.'

'So that's what the Tiger Poppies are all about,' said Bromo.

'You know about them?'

'They're around. I've seen signs of them.'

He thought of the brooches at Rasheed's home and on the scarf at Liz Shapcott's – given to her by Aurelia. And there was the graffiti on the wall at Mack's. 'The women asked him to do it,' the street kid had said of the artist.

'Aurelia apparently found some computer disks among Gerry's stuff,' continued Delia. 'She confronted him with them when she found her own picture on the site. They had a blazing row and she said she was going to get Liz Shapcott and the rest of the Poppies to help her expose him. He snapped, jumped in the car alongside her. And the rest we know.'

She moved towards the door.

'It's time I got going. We'll meet up later. You clear on everything?'

His hand went to his ear and started rubbing.

'Who's providing the Valium?'

She chuckled.

'You'll be right. There'll be plenty of support. It's a piece of cake for someone with your background.'

'That was in the past. I'm not the man I used to be.'

She looked back over her shoulder as she opened the door. 'Oh, I wouldn't say that.'

He noted she said it with a smile.

THIRTY

Delia's departure left Bromo with the best part of a day completely free. There were no clients demanding itineraries to be finalised; no last-minute bookings to be made. With a diary clear of appointments, the next few hours were his to fill and even enjoy.

Fat chance: that was for those who looked on the bright side. Any power of positive thinking lingering in his disillusioned soul had suffered a short-circuit. The shock and pace of the past twelve hours were starting to hit home. He felt drained, physically and emotionally. He drifted listlessly from room to room, tidying clothes, folding unread newspapers, rinsing cups, closing and opening windows. There was nothing to be done until well into the evening. Only one crucial phone call had to be made. First, he had to collect his shattered thoughts and start thinking of something other than Aurelia's bleeding body and Nuyen's look of horror as he spun out over the railway tracks.

'Confront your demons, mate,' he muttered as he used the bathroom mirror to assess the need to put a razor through his stubble. Hanging around the apartment was not the answer.

The forecast was for a cool change, the wind swinging around to the south and possibly bringing a few light cleansing showers. That meant shorts and T-shirt for now and stuffing a hooded top in his backpack for later.

Church Street was putting on its usual show of stop-start traffic caught up with the system's oldest trams clattering towards their Victoria Street turnaround. The litter bins overflowed, elderly Vietnamese women pushed laden shopping trolleys, dog-walkers paced round and round the perimeter of Citizens Park. Thin and wasted youths clustered in the grounds of the high-rise commission flats. Drug dealers lurked around the phone booths used by the tenants, waiting for calls. Catch their eye and they'd mutter 'You buying?' out of the corner of their mouth. Bromo looked elsewhere.

He slowed to a stroll as he neared the Hanoi Heaven Restaurant, eyes alert to anyone else taking an interest in Nuyen's establishment. He pretended interest in the racks of cheap household goods lining the pavement. Brooms, detergents, plastic buckets, mixed in with plastic sandals, gaudy ornaments and even a set of hula-hoops. Bulk wraps of a dozen toilet rolls for a couple of dollars seemed a bargain worth returning for but not something he could spend too long contemplating. He shifted his attention to a display of backpacks and thumbed through a tray of mock leather wallets, eyes shifting right and left to detect any other idlers.

He moved on and wasted moments comparing prices of the joints of pork and chicken neatly arrayed in the butcher's shop. A high turnover ensured it offered some of the city's best value.

Hanoi Heaven was next door. It was empty; the door shut. Bromo pressed his face against the window, one hand above his brow to shield against reflections. There was no movement inside. No signs of kitchen staff preparing for lunch trade. A handwritten note on the door consisted of several lines in Vietnamese and a single message in English: Closed.

Squeezed on to the doorstep was a fading bunch of flowers and a small red shrine with the remains of burnt incense sticks protruding from its crevices. Someone mourned Nuyen's passing, or at least pretended they did.

Bromo stepped next door, into his favourite fish shop, already busy with people clinically checking the produce for bright eyes, debating the merits of tiger prawn against king prawn, calamari versus octopus, taking tongs to turn over trays of pipis, clams and mussels. Luc was behind the counter. Bromo caught his eye and nodded towards next door and Hanoi Heaven.

'Lost a customer,' he said.

'No customer. Bad man.'

Like many of his countrymen, Luc had learnt the basic vocabulary of his new country, but little of its grammar.

'Didn't he buy his fish from you?'

'Not buy. He take.'

He lifted his hand from the fish he was cleaning and waved it to include the whole shop.

'This all Nuyen's.'

'What, he owns it?'

Luc used his other hand, the one holding the filleting knife, to describe a much larger circle.

'This shop. Six shops.'

Bromo reflected. He shouldn't be surprised. Many migrants built the security of their families on the rock of real estate. Taking his fish supplies in lieu of rent probably worked wonders for cash flow and in cutting taxes. Bartering was in their blood, a tradition of the marketplace.

'We pay big rent,' said Luc. 'He say he protect us.'

The bleeding obvious struck again. No wonder Gerry Nuyen had a team of hoods on his payroll. They were the collectors who would break a window, ruin a shop's stock or cut the power to freezers full of fish if the rent was as much as a day late. Luc's mention of big rent implied payment was well in excess of the usual commercial rates.

'So, it's good that he's gone,' suggested Bromo.

Luc shrugged as he ran a scoop through a mound of prawns, turning them over, bringing cubes of ice to the surface.

'Good news, bad news. It's nothing. New boss will come.'

It was an inescapable fact of their lives. You accepted it as inevitable and built the costs into your business plan. Put the unpaid-for trays of fish and seafood down as spoils. Write them off against profits. Show the excess rent paid for fake protection as levies and fees. Luc waved his scoop over the display cabinet. His eyes asked an unspoken question.

'I'm having the mussels,' answered Bromo and shovelled the gleaming black molluscs from a tall bubbling water tank into a plastic bag.

He jiggled the bag, assessing the weight. About a kilo. Already he was visualising a few chopped shallots, some segments of potato, a generous pour of white wine and a meal to slaver over. His spirits were lifting and the demons being held at bay. Soon he'd have them on the run. An assistant wrapped in a heavy rubber apron weighed his bag, a few coins changed hands and he gave a parting nod to Luc.

'Take care. Don't upset the locals.'

Outside, Bromo gave an involuntary shiver, his body briefly shocked by hot gusts of wind coming so suddenly after the refrigerated cool of the shop. He threaded his way through the traffic stream and away from the retail strip.

The Nuyens' house was only a short stroll away, nestled in a quiet backwater untouched by developers and where trees valiantly surviving amid traffic fumes and industrial grime lined the streets. The trees were English imports neatly planted in bluestone surrounds or in individual plots cut out of the road surface, their roots cracking the footpaths in their search for water. No matter where you came from, putting down roots was always a problem.

The houses were an architectural nightmare, everything from simple early Victorians built close to the footpath, through ornate double-storeys from the boom days and the solid L-shaped Californians that followed to ugly mid-50s redbrick. A terrace of five low cottages from the 1870s abutted a pair of gracious Edwardians set well back from the road. These were neighbours to a couple of cement rendered brick monstrosities with cracked windows and weed-filled gardens.

Even a hundred metres away the Nuyens' house, secreted behind a high white wall, stood out like a pacifist at a gun rally – pristine, clean and sparkling. All that could be seen above the front wall was the upper level of an ornate stucco façade showing a trim of white cast iron lacework. The house had all the signs of recent renovation and no doubt followed hundreds of others in boasting a modern extension and patio around the back. On the footpath outside Bromo could see two women, one short and stocky the other tall and lean, bent in towards each other. Their body language spoke of argument and confrontation, the taller, with hands on hips, trying to use her height advantage; the shorter standing firm, arms folded.

With a few more steps Bromo put names to faces – Fiona Leoncavallo on the right facing off against bodyguard Sonia standing firm on the left. One pushing, the other resisting. Fiona's stance indicated urgency and dispute. Sonia's was one of resistance and rejection.

Fiona saw him. She stopped in mid tirade and turned quickly away, stumbling briefly as a heel caught in a pavement crack. Bromo lengthened his stride. It was too hot to run and she was already opening the door of her car. Sonia hardly moved, only her head going from side to side, watching Bromo approach and Fiona depart. Her arms remained folded. The white T-shirt was stretched tight. He noticed the wire spiralling away from an earpiece. From the other ear dangled two thick intertwined gold hearts. A body mike was clipped to the neck of her top. He moved in close, standing alongside her, casual and conversational. She shifted her feet and turned her body to face him full-on, a determined block between him and the front gate. Bromo leaned into her.

'Whose balls are you squeezing today?'

She smiled. It was a face without malice. Open and pleasant, slightly tanned, gently touched by cosmetics.

'Just keeping watch,' she said.

Bromo indicated the earpiece and wire.

'Is that for show or is there someone on the other end?'

'Try me.'

It was tempting. Her boss was dead but she was still connected.

'So, who's paying your wages now?'

'The family.'

It hadn't occurred to him. They'd never talked about mothers and fathers, brothers and sisters and all the other twigs and branches of the family tree. Aurelia had existed in isolation. They fed each other's needs. There was no extension to their relationship beyond their interludes of lust and passion. Aurelia had never mentioned parents or siblings; and he'd never asked.

'Whose family? His or hers?'

'Hers. They're pretty cut up.'

'Bad choice of words.'

She blushed: 'Yes. Sorry. Not thinking.'

Bromo gestured in the direction of Fiona's car.

'What was she doing here?'

'Claimed to be a friend of the family.'

'Since when?'

'Can't say. That's the story she told me.'

'Nothing else?'

Sonia hesitated. Bromo sensed an internal debate. To speak or not to speak? And if she spoke, what to tell and how much? Her words tumbled out in a rush.

'She was going on about a business arrangement and some files she needed to pick up. Yeah, that was it.'

Sonia pointed back over her shoulder, indicating the house beyond the security gates.

'They didn't seem all that keen. Told me to tell her to come back later. That's what was going on when you turned up. Seems you frightened her away.'

'I tend to have that effect on women.'

She grinned. Perhaps she wasn't so hard after all. Simply doing a job. Or perhaps it was relief that they'd got off the topic of Fiona.

'You want to go in?'

Bromo stuck his hands in his pockets and shook his head. He didn't know them. What could he say? That he fucked their daughter and saw her die? That was it in a nutshell. Needy people, not even lovers, with nothing shared outside their secret cocoon of rushed passion. It took death to illuminate a life and by then it was too late to encompass the family and friends that surrounded it.

'Think I'll give it a miss. Tell 'em I called, if you like.'

'Okay.'

Bromo edged away, seeking the sparse shade of a silver birch; they were two immigrants enduring the heat of an alien land.

'What's next for you? I suppose you and your mates will have to find someone else who needs their rent collected.'

It was as if his question had never been. She reached down behind her, picked up a drink bottle, gulped a mouthful and took a dutiful look up and down the empty street. A slow day for the muscle trade. Bromo wasn't in a hurry. She'd ignored him but at least she hadn't told him to piss off. He persisted.

'Anyone else looking at your CV? Bouncer for hire, daylight kidnapping done discretely, ball-squeezing a specialty. Surely someone's going to want to fill Gerry's shoes.'

She sipped at the drink bottle, gazed back with an expression that said nothing, impassive, neutral.

He took a punt.

'What about Peter Rasheed?'

Bromo saw her tense, then cover it up with another swig of water. Another guess.

'So that was what you and Fiona were getting fired up about. Nothing to do with missing files.'

She inched towards him and put one hand up to the body mike, clicking a switch.

'That on or off?'

'Off,' she said.

Bromo had no way of being sure. He had to trust her.

'They don't need to know,' she explained. 'I'm doing them a favour by being here. It's for Gerry as much as anything. He wasn't all bad.'

'If you say so. Try telling that to the guys along Victoria Street. Can't see them lighting candles for him.'

'The boys looked after that side of things. Not me.'

'So that makes it right, does it?'

To her credit, she looked chastened. There was a slight lift to her shoulders and a sagging of her body. She made no reply.

'What's next then? Rasheed or something else?'

She offered him the drink bottle. Bromo took a sip while she tugged up her track pants. She was regaining composure, shifting back into duty mode. Her hand moved up to the mike. Bromo's arm flew out towards her neck and grabbed her round the wrist, forcing down and back towards the wall.

'Not so fast,' he hissed, keeping his voice low and urgent. 'I asked you a question. I'd like an answer.'

The speed of his reaction had startled her. She was off balance and angry.

'What's it matter to you? Gerry's not going to be bothering you anymore.'

Bromo pressed back harder on her wrist and moved in closer, their bodies almost touching. There was that waft of perfume he'd caught back in Nuyen's office. This time, roles were reversed. He put a foot on top of hers and pushed down hard. She grimaced.

'That hurts.'

'It's meant to. You should get a feeling for it. It's what happens to your victims.'

'What do you want?'

'I told you: an answer. I want to know where you intend working after this. Who's stepping into Gerry Nuyen's shoes, doing the heavy stuff?'

They were locked together. She glared up at him. A car drove by, its youthful occupants trailing their arms out of the open windows, holding on to cans of beer. The driver tooted the horn. His front seat companion leaned out and yelled.

'Go man, go. Get it on.'

The car roared on and Bromo eased the pressure on her hand. He stepped back off her foot.

'Well?'

She flexed her fingers and massaged her wrist.

'I'll probably go back to my nightclub work,' she said. 'A door bitch.'

'Could be difficult.'

She looked surprised.

'Why?'

'You need a licence for that.'

'I've got one.'

'For now.'

Her brow furrowed further. Bromo pressed home his advantage.

'A few words in the right direction and you could have problems. You're not the only one with contacts.'

He stretched a point.

'I've been making friends down at the cop shop. In police-speak, they tell me you're a person of interest.'

All confidence was fading. She processed his words, seeking a meaning.

'I know too much,' he said. 'Seen too much. We might even get Luc and his fellow shopkeepers to give you a reference. Could make interesting reading on the CV.'

It was sinking in. He'd scored a hit. He stepped back and allowed space between them. The sun disappeared behind a cloud but the heat remained. He looked up at the sky. One fluffy ball of cirrus was hiding the sun but bigger and darker rolls of cumulus were massing in the distance. The cool change was on its way. She brushed herself down as if he'd somehow dirtied her. She sipped at the water bottle then sprinkled a few drops over her head, brushing it back with one hand.

'So what do you want?'

'Information. And don't say "I only work here". That won't wash.'

'Okay. You win. But not here.'

She cocked her ear to one side and pointed to the earpiece. She covered it with one hand then used the other to switch on the mike. Several times she said 'Yes' Instructions were coming down the line. She gave a final 'Okay' and flicked off the mike.

'Seems that's it. They reckon they'll be all right. Another hour and I can go. They're paying me off.'

Bromo smiled.

'It seems you're going to need that bouncer's licence sooner than you thought.'

It was good to be on the winning side and kicking goals.

THIRTY-ONE

They arranged to meet over on Swan Street, at the Booklovers Café – convenient, on the far side of the suburb and well away from the paths trodden by Rasheed and Nuyen. Bromo used the time before their meeting to take the mussels home and get them into the fridge. He felt like joining them. Rivulets of sweat were trickling down his back. His hair looked lank and lifeless. Grit and dust whipped up by the hot wind stung his eyes. Lucky mussels – relaxed and cool in their icy domain.

He dunked himself under the cold shower, the tap open full blast. Reinvigorated and refreshed. A few light pats with the towel to dry off.

He needn't have bothered. He was halfway down the Gipps Street hill when the searing north wind suddenly gained in strength, did a rapid pirouette and transformed itself into a chilling southerly. Its twirling dance was accompanied by an immense downpour that sent streams of rain water racing down the gutters.

There was no shelter. By the time he reached the café he was drenched. He scurried inside and drifted slowly along the shelves of second-hand books on the far wall, all the while keeping an eye on the door, the water dripping to the floor.

He wandered from Philosophy to Self-help, bypassed Religion and slowed for a closer look at Food and Wine.

Sonia arrived five minutes later, removing a bike helmet as she entered and wiping a towel down bare legs clad in tight thigh-length bike shorts. She laughed at his sodden state and threw him the towel.

'Here, use this. You look like you need it. At least I was sort of dressed for the weather.'

He gave his hair a thorough rubbing, invigorating as well as drying.

'What's with the bike? I had you tagged as a VW Golf type.'

They pulled solid wooden chairs up to an equally solid timber table.

'Just shows how wrong you can be about people,' she said. 'Perhaps you should try getting to know them first.'

He'd been ticked off but with a disarmingly seductive smile. Flirting seemed to be the preferred sport of these bright and brittle women in their 20s and 30s. Fiona, Aurelia, even Liz Shapcott, and now Sonia all enjoyed played havoc with the emotions and the libido, teasing, ever-changing, casting lures, reeling them in, then letting their catch run free. They played more roles than an overworked extra in a soap opera.

Sonia had returned the tough little enforcer and the door bitch to central casting. No longer needed. They were characters from another time and place. Sitting opposite him now was a spunky and sporty young woman to whom a bike ride in a rainstorm was all part of the day's fun. She put her elbows on the table and rested her cheeks on her balled knuckles.

'So, Mr Perkins, you're going to make sure I keep my security guard's licence if I spill the beans on Gerry Nuyen.

What happens if I decide to chuck it in and go back to my other career?'

It was direct and to the point. She'd grabbed the initiative. Bromo wasn't ready for it. He thought he was the one with all the aces. He tried to take it in his stride.

'I'll order some coffee. How do you take it?'

'Soy milk cappuccino, thanks. No sugar. And one of those little friand things if there are any left.'

She oozed confidence.

Bromo joined the queue at the counter and spun out his time talking to the couple of book-loving fanatics who had transformed a gloomy old shoe store into a book exchange, café and reading room. On his way back to the table he paused to peruse a table laden with books. Thinking time. He placed a tall metal place marker holding the number 12 on the table.

'Your number's up,' he said. 'You got the last of the friands.'

Sonia looked up at him. There was that smile again. Enough to charm the pants off a priest. Full of confidence. A winner's smile.

Bromo waited while a waitress put their drinks and food down and removed the table marker. He leaned forward from the waist, chin almost touching his coffee cup, and spoke softly.

'Understand this. whether or not you want to keep your licence is not going to matter. You are going to face so many charges of assault and battery and threatening honest citizens that you won't be reading the job ads for quite some years.'

Her smile faded.

'Bluff. You've no evidence, no witnesses.'

'Haven't I? I seem to recall I was there when you lashed me to a chair in Gerry Nuyen's office.'

'But no witnesses.'

He studied the table top and breathed deeply. Sometimes the long way round was the quickest way. He ploughed on.

'There was no shortage of witnesses when you helped strip Fiona and turned her into a work of art.'

She gave a short gasp.

'That was the boys.'

His stab in the dark paid off. It was the admission he wanted. He put a clamp on showing any reaction.

'No one saw me there,' she hastily added.

Bromo tried to lock his eyes on hers but she shifted her attention to breaking off a piece of friand.

'Okay, we'll let that pass for now,' he said. 'But the proof is there.'

She gave him a quick glance at the mention of proof, uncertain, wondering, then switched back to studying the cake.

He continued, his voice low and measured.

'We also have the shopkeepers who have seen you doing your party tricks when their rent is due.'

'I wasn't there. The boys did that.'

'And when the police catch up with them do you think they're not going to share the blame around.'

Sonia sipped her coffee. A slight smile lit up her eyes. She raised her head, the overhead light catching the thick gold double loop earring in her left ear.

'You're still bluffing, Mr Perkins. Those studs won't say a thing because they don't want their wives to know what went on when things were quiet at Gerry's. They called it playtime. I was the playmate. I'm sure you can imagine the rest. That's one reason I'm getting out and don't need you or that bloody security licence.'

He'd had enough. He grabbed her wrist and the friand dropped to the plate.

'Get this straight, you know and I know you were at the gallery. What your role was, I'm not sure. But you were certainly there and assisting in an assault. That's enough for me, and the police. Unless, of course, you help us wrap this up.'

'I can't.'

He released her hand.

'Can't or won't?

As her fingers worked at breaking off a piece of cake her eyes looked quickly up, above Bromo's head. Within seconds he saw the look of fear cross her face, sensed a presence behind him and felt the heavy pressure on his shoulders. There was also something hard and unyielding boring into his ribcage.

Bromo cautiously looked left and right. To any of the café customers taking their heads out of their books and papers it would look as if he'd just been greeted by a couple of good mates – big and bald mates, clad in black and with misleadingly gentle smiles on their faces. He spoke to the one on his left.

'Didn't take you for a bookworm.'

The hard object dug deeper into his ribs.

'Sonia's coming with us,' came the grunted response.

Bromo saw the signs of panic striking Sonia – a hand picking the cake into crumbs, the other stirring a spoon in an empty cup, her eyes wide open and flicking rapidly left and right, looking for escape. He willed her not to run, fearing the outcome. These were men with serious intent. She leaned over, raised herself up out of her chair and reached for her bike helmet.

'You won't be needing that,' said a voice on Bromo's left. 'There's a car ....'

Sonia's movement was swift and accurate. Pure martial art. Her arm swung the bike helmet hard and fast, arcing it up and over Bromo's head and into his guardian's cheekbone. Fibreglass met bone with a crunch. The hard object stopped digging into Bromo's ribs. The man on his right had released his grip as he leaned away to avoid the helmet. Bromo helped him on his way with an extension of his elbow and a swing of his arm into the man's midriff. Scared customers jumped from their seats and scattered to the rear of the shop.

Sonia continued moving. In three long graceful steps she was around the table and reaching for the arm of the man hit by her helmet.

'That won't be necessary, miss. We'll take over now.'

It was Holmes. Watson was next to him. Two uniformed police were standing over the man Bromo had struck.

'Seems the cavalry's arrived,' said Bromo. 'What kept you?'

'We didn't expect this,' said Holmes. 'We've been keeping tabs on this pair of charmers most of the day, seeing who they're talking to, where they'd lead us. Maybe give us an excuse to pull them in.'

'Be my guest,' said Bromo.

He took Holmes' elbow and steered him over towards the counter. Watson and the uniformed police were escorting the two thugs out of the shop. Customers were slowly moving back to their tables.

'Those two are all yours,' said Bromo. 'But leave the girl with me.'

Holmes looked doubtful.

'I'll vouch for her,' Bromo assured him. 'You can get her statement later.'

Holmes was hesitant: 'What do I tell the boss?'

Bromo looked around the shop, at the shelves of books from floor to ceiling, latest releases to the front, a pile of remainders on a central table.

'Tell her we're choosing titles for the next Book Club meeting and discussing the role of the crime novel in modern literature.'

Holmes gave him a wary look and stepped towards the door.

'Yeah, right. That'll really please her.'

Back at their table, Sonia was sitting calmly, arms extended, palms flat down on the surface and her eyes closed. Her breathing was slow and controlled. Bromo sat. She sensed him arrive and opened her eyes.

'The cops wanted you to go with them.' he said. 'I've promised you'll talk later.'

She nodded.

'Thanks. It seems I've just changed sides.'

'It's called going straight.'

'I'm not a crim,' she snapped.

'You're walking a very fine line.'

She shrugged, chastened.

'I guess I was looking for a bit of excitement and got carried away.'

Bromo gestured towards the door.

'You nearly were. Those two didn't come bearing gifts.'

Sonia laid a hand gently on his forearm.

'So, what's the deal?'

'Information. Aurelia's dead. Nuyen's dead. Help me tidy up the loose ends. There are still some loose cannons out there who've been rattling my cage. Rasheed, Fiona, Delgado and a few heavy-hitters we probably don't even know about. That pisses me off. I want to know who and why so we can put a stop to it.'

She looked around the room, contemplating, considering.

'If I tell you what I know, you'll put in a good word?'

'So good you won't recognise yourself,' he said.

Bromo put a hand in his pocket and drew something out, his fist clenched around it, holding it towards her.

'Do the right thing and there's even a bonus,' he said.

She looked puzzled, trying to read his eyes; glancing down at his fist and back up to his face. It was a moment to savour. Ekeing out the suspense, like they did for birthdays and anniversaries in those heady early years of his first marriage. He unclenched his hand. In his palm were two entwined gold hearts attached to a stud for pierced ears. Sonia gasped. She raised a hand to her ear, feeling the earring, checking it was there.

'Yeah, that one's okay,' said Bromo. 'This is its twin. The one you dropped and left behind. In Aurelia's gallery. Remember?'

She feigned puzzlement, saying nothing.

Bromo closed his hand over the earring.

'I found it on the floor. Right behind the trestle where you'd put the naked Fiona on display.'

He put the earring back in his pocket.

'Start talking.'

THIRTY-TWO

THE DEEP BOWL OF mussels, the juices mopped up with chunks of crusty bread, proved every bit as lip-smacking as Bromo had anticipated. It was a simple dish that never failed to evoke fond memories of a long-ago holiday excursion into coastal France. The local specialty of moules marinieres had become almost a nightly staple. Viewed in hindsight, that trip marked the starting point of his ventures into foreign lands, few of them taken with the carefree approach of that first innocent meander along the Channel coast. Then, as now, he accompanied the soupy dish with a crisp white wine. Tonight, however, he limited his intake to a single glass rather than the more customary bottle of those far-off times. His brain needed to be alert and his body unhindered by alcohol.

His mobile trilled its operatic melody.

'Morningstar Home for Middle-Aged Misfits,' he said. 'How can we help you?'

Delia was on the other end. She chuckled at his greeting then quickly switched to official mode.

'You okay? Everything set?'

'Better than expected. Sonia proved more than useful.'

'From what Holmes told me she also packs a hefty punch.'

He spoke without thinking.

'Yes, she's quite a girl.'

Whoops, too late. He'd done it again. Put his foot right in it. He could almost see the snarl coming down the line. He heard the sharp intake of breath. An overlong silence.

'Anything else?'

Delia's voice had turned sharp and brittle.

There was little he could do. Pretend it hadn't happened. He made a rapid judgment and fell back on the old need-to-know argument.

'Not right now. It can wait.'

Delia was already testing boundaries by involving him in police business. He had little doubt of her reaction if she knew he was embroiling Sonia in the night's operation.

'We need darkness,' she said.

Bromo agreed. They set a time well after sunset.

'Have you made the call?'

Her voice maintained its firm, official edge. Bromo visualised her sitting at her desk, running her eyes down a checklist, ticking off every detail of their plans, leaving nothing to chance.

'Just about to,' he said. 'Can't foresee any problems.'

'I expect to hear if there are.'

'Take care, Bromo,' she said.

Her voice had softened and dropped a tone or two. She'd recovered, refusing to be needled by his reference to another woman.

'I really don't want you getting hurt,' she added. 'Leave the heroics to us this time.'

He smiled. Was that a warm and fuzzy feeling rippling through him? Funny how some women could affect you like that, get under your guard, while others left you stone motherless cold. Whatever, always tread with caution.

'Yes, ma'am,' he said, making light of her words and ring-ing off.

Bromo needed to make the promised call before Sonia arrived. He found Fiona's number in his list of contacts and pushed the dialling pad. She answered on the second ring and showed little surprise at hearing his voice..

'How's the invalid?' Bromo asked.

'Much better. Feeling quite cheerful.'

'Death does that to some people.'

Fiona rattled on.

'He's sitting up, walking around. Reckons it's safe to go home.'

'So, it's back to business, then. Scaring the locals, setting up porn sites. Bribing councillors.'

'That's not Peter.'

She was on the defensive.

'He's not like that. It was all Gerry Nuyen's doing.'

'And bin Laden's up for sainthood. Get real, Fiona. The man's a crook.'

'What's that make me?'

'Not much better. More of the same. Aiding and abetting. A person of interest, in police-speak'

Bromo detected a change in her breathing, a tensing as his point drove home. He settled deep down into his armchair, legs crossed at the ankles, head well back. Nice and relaxed. Feeling good and taking his time.

'There is, of course, a way out,' he said.

'Is there?'

Reluctant, but interested.

'We could clear the decks, start afresh. Save a lot of police time and all those hours in court, big fines and even prison.'

He dangled the bait and waited patiently for her to bite.

'What have you got in mind?' she said, her voice tinged with caution.

The first nibble. Start reeling her in.

'A merger. All these bashings and killings are because Rasheed and Nuyen fell out. Now Gerry's gone, perhaps we can put things together again. That's what consultants do, isn't it? Fee for service. All care and no responsibility. Play one side off against the other then take the money and run.'

Bromo slid further down in his chair, enjoying the moment, now letting her run with the line like a fighting trout. He could almost feel her digesting his bait. Then rejecting it.

'I don't think so, Mr Perkins. You may have done some work for us but there's no way you can fill Gerry Nuyen's shoes.'

He took the rejection calmly.

'Just the hired help, eh?'

'You said it.'

Time to stop the line running and reel her back in.

'Sorry, Fiona, but that cheap little blackmail trick with the photos was wide of the mark. Gerry told me he really didn't care. Aurelia and I had much more going for us than a couple of nights in the sack.'

He'd got her attention.

'What do you mean?'

He piled it on.

'Business secrets, files, disks, information. The bricks and mortar of shady deals.'

Fiona said nothing. There was no way of knowing whether she was accepting or rejecting his words. The quarry was lying doggo. He took the risk of throwing out an extra lure.

'Why do you think I was round at Aurelia's house today?'

She swallowed it.

'Okay, let's see what you've got.'

Within minutes he'd arranged to call on her and Rasheed that night at Mack's. They set a time and agreed a signal by which she'd let him in.

He had half an hour to wait for Sonia to arrive then they'd be on their way. He put a couple of fingers up to his neck resting them gently just under the jaw line, testing his pulse. It was beating slower than average but well above his normal level.

Just like old times.

THIRTY-THREE

THEY ARRIVED OUTSIDE THE looming mass of Mack's on schedule. The street was dimly lit and deserted. Bromo noted the cars parked across the road, nose-on to the footpath and with no signs of occupants. The terrace of single-storey houses was in darkness. No lights showing. Everyone was in bed or in their back rooms, watching TV. No one on the streets.

The area provided overnight parking for residents and became an expensive daytime hazard for visitors when its parking meters came into operation. One van was squeezed in between the line of family saloons and chunky four-wheel-drives. Delia's people were in place and ready.

Bromo took Sonia's arm as they walked along the street, close to the factory wall, a strip of litter-strewn grass separating them from the road.

'Keep walking and slow down,' he said. 'Remember, we're out for an evening stroll.'

They passed the door set back in a dark alcove where Bromo had left the building on his last visit.

'Don't look now, but that's the way in,' he said out of the corner of his mouth.

They walked on past the bent and graffiti tagged roller doors. Two solid looking joggers in dark blue Chesty Bond singlets and track pants came towards them, breathing hard. One winked at Bromo as they passed.

'Bit bleeding obvious,' Bromo muttered. 'Hope they don't wear themselves out before they're needed.'

They stopped at the corner beneath a huge real estate agent's board seeking offers for 'this incredibly located property with unlimited potential.'

Bromo looked along the side street. No traffic. No movement. The air was balmy after the earlier storms. It carried the sound of a television turned up to high volume and laughs from people enjoying a backyard barbecue. A dog barked. All innocent; everything normal.

Bromo took a quick look at his watch and looked at her: 'All set? Here we go.'

He squeezed Sonia's arm and began guiding her back the way they'd come. They took a quick look around as they reached the alcove then ducked inside, their rubber-soled feet scuffing against a mess of old newspapers, beer bottles and plastic food containers.

'Ready?' whispered Bromo.

Sonia nodded. He rapped hard three times on the door, counted to three, then knocked again, four times, counted to three and hit hard twice more. They heard metal grating against metal, a loud click and the scraping of the door on the concrete floor as it slowly opened.

'Go,' commanded Bromo.

Sonia rushed past him through the widening space between door and jamb. She spun on her feet back behind the door. Bromo heard a short, sharp female yell of 'What the fuck?' as he followed through the gap. He turned and pushed the door almost closed behind him, not quite snibbing the locks home. Sonia was holding Fiona around the wrist, pulling her arm to full stretch and pressing down with her other hand on her shoulder.

'What do you think you're doing?' gasped Fiona, bent over, her voice directed to the floor.

'Grabbing the initiative, applying a bit of gentle pressure, securing our ground, call it what you will,' said Bromo, casting his eyes around the factory. She'd kept her promise: the heavy brigade was off duty.

'Where's Rasheed?'

Fiona squirmed under Sonia's grip but said nothing. Sonia pushed down on her shoulder, producing a squeal of pain.

'Over there. In his room. Waiting.'

Bromo nodded to Sonia.

'Okay, ease off. Let's go and talk. You've already had your fun with her.'

He caught Fiona's puzzled look as Sonia released the grip on her shoulder and led her by the hand towards the desk against the far wall.

'What fun?' she said.

'In the gallery,' he explained. 'Masked people blindfolding you, removing your clothes and strapping you to a frame.'

A blush of embarrassment coloured Fiona's cheeks as she lowered herself meekly into her chair.

'I did wonder. I assumed they were all men. Very gentle men.'

She twisted her head to look at Sonia, standing behind her, a cautionary hand on each shoulder.

'Come to think of it, one did have a lovely soft touch. Rather special, gentle and feminine.'

The women smiled at each other. Communication without words. Silence hung in the air. Bromo shuffled his feet. This wasn't the script he'd been working on. It was like being lost in a multiplex and drifting into the wrong cinema – viewing the misty-eyed romance instead of the action-packed crime movie. Hard-edged deals were turning into a love fest and he was running out of time. Delia had given him a deadline to do things his way. It was rapidly approaching. He raised his voice.

'Rasheed. Out here.'

It echoed off the walls and iron roof, startling the two women. Fiona snapped back into business mode, hands firmly set on the desktop, her laptop, CDs and a memory stick on one side and a neat pile of folders on the other.

'I thought you were bringing files and disks,' she snapped.

'A furphy,' said Bromo.

'You mean a lie.'

Rasheed emerged from his cabin. He hobbled towards them, leaning on a walking stick.

'So, you have nothing.'

Bromo glanced at his watch. It was time to hurry things along.

'On the contrary, Mr Rasheed. I have knowledge, and so do the police. I believe knowledge is power.'

'Bullshit. Money is power.'

Bromo smiled.

'We'll debate that another day. Right now I can tell you that RAID and RAGE do not exist. They were the creations of this so-called consultant.'

He gestured towards Fiona. She showed no reaction.

'It was amateur stuff. A few flyers and letters and snappy slogans rushed out on her computer. It was all designed to create a rift between you and Gerry Nuyen and break up the partnership. Trouble was he believed it and that's why his thugs turned you and your house over. It's just lucky for you we chose the wrong spot to roll your car into the river.'

Rasheed shrugged, making a reasonable attempt at contrition.

'And me, what had I done to be strung up in the gallery like that?'

As Fiona asked the question, Sonia put a comforting hand on one shoulder. Fiona reached up and placed her hand on top. Bromo took it in. The sisterhood at work. He'd never understand.

'You upset Gerry by trying to muscle in on his dating site,' he said. 'That upset Aurelia when she thought it was Gerry, not you, who was using her and other women to attract porn customers. A touch of artistic revenge from the Poppies.'

He let the information sink in and drew a CD from his pocket.

'This is Gerry's master disc. It's a legit site, no porn and a pretty good money spinner from all the lonely hearts. signing up to seek their soulmate.'

He looked at his watch. Split-second timing was needed. He held the CD lightly between thumb and forefinger and waved it back and forth for a few seconds. Rasheed hobbled towards him. Bromo did a silent countdown in his head. Seconds to go. Bromo laid the disk on the desk.

'It's yours,' he said. 'In return for this.'

His hand came off the disc. He reached out and grabbed the laptop and swooped up the memory stick alongside it. Fiona flung out an arm, reaching to gain a grip, but missed. There was a loud crash as the door was flung open. Two helmeted special operations police burst through then stood stock still, braced, legs apart, weapons pointing forward.

'Police. Freeze. Do not move.'

Their yelled commands were superfluous. Everyone obeyed. Holmes and Watson walked in, hands on holstered weapons at their hips. They were followed by Delia and two uniformed police, a male and female.

Rasheed was the first to speak.

'What are you doing here? Why the police? The guns?'

Delia walked cautiously towards him.

'Mr Rasheed, you are occupying these premises unlawfully. You have barricaded yourself in and made entry impossible and dangerous. That's why Mr Perkins had to talk his way in and why we have armed police.'

Rasheed whipped his walking stick up and forward, waving it furiously at Delia.

'It's my place. My bloody place. People try to take it off me. I have plans to make it into beautiful buildings, good homes, shops, gardens and people try to stop me. Council, Nuyen, everyone against me.'

'That's true. It's all he wants to do.'

Fiona's voice was a soft call for reason against Rasheed's outburst. She leaned back in her chair, eyes half closed, Sonia's hands now gently massaging both shoulders.

Delia ignored Rasheed's pointing stick and moved alongside him. His fury had evaporated. She signalled to the special ops police to lower their weapons. An excessive show of force. It wasn't necessary.

'I think you'd better come with us and talk things over,' she said. 'It seems your old partner Gerry Nuyen was using Steve Delgado to get you offside with the council.'

'Forget the high-rise and keep your promise of a bit of beauty and greenery and you'll win them over,' advised Bromo.

'And give Liz Shapcott a call. Get her to draw up some fresh plans. She's on your wavelength.'

Holmes and Watson went through to Rasheed's rooms. The uniformed police moved either side of the desk. Delia began leading Rasheed to the exit, slowing her pace to match his hobbling gait. They were halfway across the vast open space, midway between desk and door, when a fearsome banshee yell ripped the orderly calm apart. It ricocheted off the bare walls, shocking everyone into stillness.

'Leave him alone.'

The screamed command rebounded around the factory, echoing and repeating. The lean, lanky youth who had bailed Bromo up on his last visit to Mack's stood in the gap leading through to the other half of the building. He was teetering on bare feet, hair falling over his face, the gun clutched in his hands pointing directly at Delia.

'Leave him be,' he screeched. 'This is his place, our place.'

No one moved. The two uniformed police stood erect and still. Sonia's hands had stopped their massaging. Bromo saw Holmes peer briefly round the corner of Rasheed's living quarters. And just as quickly withdraw. There was nothing he or Watson could do from there. Only the two special operations men were out of the youth's line of vision, away to his right and standing motionless back against the wall.

The explosions when they came were sudden, brief and decisive, reverberating around the space, piercing eardrums. The youth crumpled to the floor, his leg shattered by a bullet from the special operations men. His finger had squeezed his own weapon as he fell, sending a spray of shotgun pellets towards the roof and out of harm's way.

Bromo ran over to the youth. Holmes raced up and crouched down alongside him. Bromo wrapped his arms around the youth's frail body, feeling him shivering violently. Watson scampered alongside. 'Drugs more than fear,' Bromo informed them.

Holmes rolled up the leg of the youth's cargo pants, easing the cloth away from the bloody wound.

'Paramedics are on their way,' he said. 'We had them on standby.'

He turned to the two riflemen, standing off, visors lifted, looking at their victim, their faces showing concern.

'Good shooting lads. Couldn't stand the papers running another death by trigger-happy cops story.'

Two paramedics arrived as Rasheed joined the growing circle surrounding the writhing figure on the ground.

'He's not a bad kid,' he observed. 'Bit wild, but they're okay.'

He waved his stick towards the other side of the factory.

'Several of them live in there. They looked after me.'

Bromo moved out of the paramedics' way. Delia was in the gap leading to the other room, talking to Watson and Holmes. He sauntered over to them.

'We've got to clean this place out,' said Delia. 'Get Human Services in to take care of these kids. Change the locks. Hand it back to its proper owner.'

'Rasheed?' asked Bromo.

'Maybe. Looks like it. But he's got to go through the proper channels, do the paperwork, sort out the business with Nuyen. I think he's coming round to our way of thinking.'

She took Bromo to one side.

'Thanks for your help. You'd better make yourself scarce. You weren't here.'

'And later?'

She touched him gently on the arm and gave it a light squeeze.

'We'll see. I'll give you a call.'

He nodded. There was no debate. He walked slowly towards the door, hands plunged deep in his pockets. His fingers touched metal. He stopped and turned back. Delia moved to block his way. He raised his hand, palm upward and open.

'Give me one moment.'

She moved aside, watching as he approached Fiona and Sonia. They'd hung back from the activity around the shot youth. Fiona had distanced herself from Rasheed. No longer the loyal attendant.

Bromo drew his closed hand from his pocket and extended it towards Sonia. He uncurled his fingers to show the earring of two entwined hearts.

'As I promised. It's all yours,' he said.

'Perfect timing,' she said.

She lifted the bauble gently from his palm and reached up to insert it in Fiona's ear.

'Very symbolic,' said Bromo.

He studied them briefly – it was a queer world, indeed – and headed for the door.

A bottle of Lagavulin, an armchair and a Philip Glass CD were calling.

Or maybe he'd play something from many hundred years earlier. Hildegard von Bingen was a very understanding woman.

www.ingramcontent.com/pod-product-compliance
Lightning Source LLC
Chambersburg PA
CBHW051438050726
47593CB00005B/1827